Commitment

Commitment

by

Margaret Ethridge

For Diane -
Happy reading!
Margaret Ethridge

Turquoise Morning Press
Turquoise Morning, LLC
www.turquoisemorningpress.com

Turquoise Morning, LLC
P.O. Box 43958
Louisville, KY 40253-0958

Commitment

Trade Paperback ISBN: 9781937389864
Digital ISBN: 9781937389819

Editor, Jennifer Johnson
Cover Art Design by KJ Jacobs

Trade Paperback release, February 2012
Digital Release, January 2012

This edition is published by agreement with Turquoise Morning Press, a division of Turquoise Morning, LLC.

Dedication

Thank you to my publisher, Kim Jacobs, for her continued belief in me and my pursuit of this dream, and to my editor, Jennifer, for the one-liners that make me smile even when I think I'm losing my mind.

This book would not exist if it weren't for a bevy of beautiful critters who poked, prodded, and pummeled this story into shape. Their input is always welcomed, their support unflinching, and their friendship truly treasured. They are and always will be Super Cool.

I want to dedicate this book to those daring people who attempted a fling, and ended up with a spouse.

It can happen, you know….

Contentment

Tom Sullivan wants a woman who is willing to accept him as he is. The successful divorce attorney has seen enough of the flip side of love to know better than to promise forever. Women have tried to pin him down, but none have managed to make it stick.

Until Maggie McCann.

Maggie is only interested in one thing. Her fortieth birthday is looming and the *tick-tock-tick-tock* in her head means her biological clock is about to strike midnight on her dreams of finding Prince Charming. Armed with a new plan for her happily ever, she foregoes the Fairy Godmother routine and makes an appointment with a fertility clinic for a rendezvous with a sperm donor.

The last thing Maggie needs is to get mixed up with a player like Tom Sullivan.

A chance encounter and the opportunity to scratch a decade-long itch prove irresistible, and what starts as a one-night stand turns into a game of cat and mouse when Tom learns of Maggie's plan to start a family on her own.

To Maggie, messing with a player like Tom Sullivan is the single-girl equivalent of playing with fire, but she convinces herself to take what she can get for as long as she can and expect nothing more. But Tom falls hard and fast for Maggie, and now that they're planning to have a baby together he starts banking on his own a happily ever after.

If only he can get her to commit…

Chapter One

The kitchen gadget aisle of Bed Bath & Beyond isn't the place to make major life decisions, but there she was—there *it* was—staring her right in the face.

"No."

The word popped out of her mouth before it registered with her brain. Maggie McCann glared at the plastic tube then turned away, feigning interest in a set of matched measuring cups until she could gather her wits. The answer wasn't unreasonable. The thought was ridiculous, the location…highly inappropriate.

Inappropriate, but not unusual. A born nester, Maggie liked taking a spin through the housewares superstore. She found it relaxing. There was nothing in the world she wanted more than to have a real nest to feather. Not that the apartment above her shop wasn't real. The entire brick and mortar building was very real. She had the gigantic mortgage to prove it. But she wanted a house, no, a home.

Maggie didn't consider her forays into this Valhalla of domestic bliss a stop gap. These excursions were not a desperate attempt to fill an empty life with candleholders, no matter what Oprah implied. She just had an itch for Egyptian cotton, and the best way to scratch that itch was by indulging her yen for plush, thirsty bath sheets. Hell, the terry cloth tantalizers practically leapt from the shelves and into her arms, desperate to be the towel she wrapped around her bubble bath-scented body. Maggie clutched the latest volunteers to her bosom. How could she deny them their destiny?

Under normal circumstances, she didn't bother with the kitchen section of the store. Maggie shopped to satisfy her bed and bath jones. She considered anything that required her to spend time slaving over a hot stove definitely 'Beyond', but her ancient can opener was grinding to a slow and painful death.

Sadly, Fred was the only one around to witness her heroics when she called 'Clear!' and jolted the appliance back to life with a stout slap. Not that he cared about her histrionics. The only thing that ever concerned Fred was his next meal. The longer she took to serve him, the louder his complaints. Just that morning, in the midst of her appliance saving routine, the overstuffed tabby took his dissatisfaction out on her by stepping on her toes, butting her with his head, and nudging her with his bulky body before he resorted to violence.

The pebbled scratch on her ankle itched. She wanted to blame cat scratch fever for the heat coursing through her body, but she knew Ted Nugent didn't hold the answer. Panic clawed at her throat. Maggie focused on every piece but the one that called to her. She scanned the rows, desperately searching for the fancy hand-held can opener she'd seen advertised on TV—the one that guaranteed a soft silicone grip and safely rounded edges.

She spotted her quarry and stretched to yank the package from the wire hook. It clung for dear life, almost as if the damn thing sensed it was doomed to an existence filled with tomato soup and economy-sized cans of Gourmet de Gato.

"Join the club," she muttered.

Maggie gave the opener another yank and it surrendered, sending her stumbling into a display of mixing bowls. She gasped and flailed. The turquoise towels she'd taken hostage in the bath department fell to the floor in a heap. She caught the edge of a shelf and the can opener landed on the heap of terrycloth with a muffled *plop*.

Above her head, the rattle of plastic and cardboard warned of imminent disaster. Maggie groaned in surrender as bubble-packed kitchen gadgets began to rain down from over-stocked hooks. A torrent of teaspoons and tablespoons clattered against the flour sifters, colanders, and measuring cups lining the bottom shelf. Her jaw dropped, and her eyes popped. A melon baller teetered on the edge of its hook, telegraphing its intent.

"No, don't jump!"

It didn't heed her plea. On its descent, the thick silicon handle caught the top of the package on the rung below. Maggie winced as she made eye contact with the dastardly implement again. The cardboard backing swung wildly, rocking to the tip of the prong.

"Oh no…."

Maggie stared in horror as it let go. The bulbous rubber ball caught the edge of a mortar and pestle set and sent the plastic tube bouncing in her direction. Her grip on the shelf tightened as her knees buckled. She blinked in dismay when the taunting tool defied all laws of physics by landing face-up, its tapered tip pointing directly at her.

She stared down at the turkey baster, blinking back the hot rush of tears prickling her eyes. "No." Her whispered refusal lacked conviction, and she knew it.

"That's okay. It happens all the time." A woman in a blue polo shirt hurried over. "I'm so sorry. Are you okay?"

"No." Maggie shook her head to clear it. "I mean, yes. Yeah, I'm fine. Sorry about the mess."

"Sometimes the stockers get a little overzealous," the woman said, offering an apologetic smile. "I hope you weren't hurt."

"No, not at all."

Pulling a card from her pocket, the woman stepped over the forgotten towels. "I'm Jackie Dunforth, Store Manager. Take that up front and tell them I said to give you twenty percent off your purchase."

"Oh, that's not necessary—"

"You almost got sliced by a grater. It's the least I can do."

Maggie bent to scoop her selections from the floor, carefully avoiding the turkey baster as she groped for the can opener. "Thank you." She juggled her purse, towels, can opener, and business card.

She didn't bother shaking her hair back from her face when she straightened, hoping a curtain of hair might camouflage her flaming cheeks. "Sorry," she whispered again and slinked away.

"Oh! Ma'am?" The manager's voice rang out, echoing through the aisles. A grimace twisted Maggie's lips. She turned, eying the store associate warily. The woman held up the turkey baster, waving the damn thing in the air like a flag for all to see. "Did you forget this?"

Maggie shook her head a tad too vehemently. "No!" The woman took a quick step back, a puzzled frown creasing her brow. Dragging in a deep breath, she straightened her shoulders and tossed her hair. "I don't need it, and it's not my fault if the damn thing is suicidal."

With that, Maggie McCann, towel tramp and candle craver with an itch for Egyptian cotton, turned on her heel and fled from the beyond and the terrifying thoughts a taunting turkey baster implanted in her mind.

****

Maggie set her cell phone and a wine glass brimming with merlot on the edge of the tub. A tortoise shell hair clip clutched the shower curtain. She piled her mop of hair atop her head, ruthlessly twisting the tangled curls into a sloppy knot before plucking the clip from the curtain.

She hissed as she dipped her foot into the steaming froth of bathwater. The scratch Fred gave her that morning burned like a sonofabitch. Maggie glared at the fat orange tabby curled on the bathmat.

"Just wait 'til I get a real man," she muttered, sinking into the sea of bubbles.

Fred twitched his tail, dismissing her threat with practiced ease. The wretched beast could afford to be cocky. He knew the only tongue she'd scored in the last six months rasped like sandpaper against her skin, and the only moans of ecstasy she'd incited came when she opened a can of tuna.

Maggie curled her fingers around the stem of her wine glass. The deep burgundy liquid swirled against gossamer-thin glass. She took a tiny sip and groaned her appreciation. Cradling the glass between her palms, she met Fred's unwavering stare.

"You know I love you, even if you are a total shit." Maggie downed a bracing gulp of the wine. "Still makes you more fun than most of the men I've dated."

The cat lifted his ginger nose and sniffed, blithely disregarding the backhanded compliment. Maggie sighed and sank lower, bracing her feet beneath the faucet. The 'Do-Be-Do-Be-Do-Me' red polish on her toes winked at her through the haze of foam. One more hit of wine and she closed her eyes. Within minutes the tension ebbed from her shoulders, the knots in her neck unraveled, and the cool base of the wine glass came to rest on the generous pillow of her right breast.

Maggie refused to think about her packed appointment schedule, the attitude adjustment she needed to administer to her senior nail technician, or the fact that she managed to while away another rip-roaring Friday night cruising the Bed Bath & Beyond and seducing her cat into taking a bath with her. That was all too depressing. Instead, she drifted away on a cloud of gardenia-scented bubbles.

Running. She was running on a concrete treadmill, her feet pounding the pavement, and her breasts bouncing higher and higher with each step. She hooked an arm around her ribcage in an effort to stay the worst of the jiggle and glanced over her shoulder.

The cartoon turkey pursuing her gobbled, its wattle wagging like a Cocker Spaniel's tail. Her breath hitched. A stitch tore into her side. Her knees threatened to buckle. He was gaining on her. She sped up, tossing her breasts over her shoulder like a Continental soldier and broke into a sprint, determined to make the bird eat her dust.

Her gaze fixed on a shadowy bundle on the doorstep of her salon. The turkey gobbled a warning. She clutched her aching ribs, running as fast as she could. Daring a backward glance, she spotted the plastic turkey baster clasped in his feathered fist. She stumbled over the lump on her welcome mat, falling to her knees in front of the plate-glass door.

The squirming, squalling baby someone left on her doorstep stilled. He stared at Maggie with placid blue eyes. The infant giggled when the turkey gobbled again. She reached for the tiny bundle. The baby smiled, those indigo eyes locked on Maggie. Then his rosebud lips moved and the annoyingly smug voice they used in those disturbing E-trade commercials came out.

"Hey, Ma."

A bell rang and Maggie jumped, dropping her wine glass into the rapidly cooling water. "Wha?" Merlot swirled among the waning bubbles. Her cell phone hummed again, the short ring-ring burst of a British telephone-inspired tone jolting her back to reality.

"No more wine." The plastic casing slipped in her damp fingers. She fumbled with the buttons. "Hello?"

"Mags? It's Tracy."

She blinked, stunned to hear her old friend and former roommate's voice. "Tracy?"

Tracy Sullivan chuckled. "I know it's been a while, but surely you haven't forgotten me entirely."

Pink-tinged bubbles popped. Maggie fished the empty glass from the tub and drew her knees to her chest, wrapping a slippery arm around her legs and curling into a ball. She lunged for the plug. "Trace. Yeah. Hi. Hi! How are you?"

"I'm okay. How are you?"

She stared at the swirling eddy of water draining from the tub. "I'm, uh, wet. I was just getting out of the tub."

"Oh. Well, I won't keep you. Actually, I'm surprised to find you home. I thought maybe you'd be out, being Friday night and all."

"Saturdays are busy for me, so I like to stay in on Fridays." The fib rolled off her tongue so easily Maggie almost believed it herself.

"That makes sense. Listen, I'm sure you already have plans, but I'll ask anyway." Picking up the nervous edge in her old friend's voice, Maggie frowned. "I was wondering if you wanted to have dinner some Saturday night."

"Saturday night?"

"Any Saturday," Tracy said in a rush. "Sean goes out on Fridays to play poker, and I get Saturday nights to myself, and I was thinking it's been a while since I saw you—"

Maggie jumped at the chance. "Forever. How's tomorrow?"

"Tomorrow would be great for me."

"I have a three-thirty facial. I can hop the Metra and be out there by about six. Can you pick me up at the station?"

"Definitely."

"Great. I'll check the schedule and give you a call before I board."

"Great."

Tracy's stunned tone made Maggie smile. She stood, and pinkish rivulets of water streaked down her bare body. "I'll probably need a margarita by then."

"A margarita sounds perfect," Tracy answered with a wistful sigh.

Plucking the turquoise bath sheet from the towel bar, she wrapped her body in its plush cotton decadence. "You okay, Trace?"

"I'm great," her friend replied with a shade too much enthusiasm.

The Tracy Sullivan Maggie knew and loved wasn't a natural enthuse…enthusiast…whatever. "What's going on?"

"What? Oh, nothing. I just…It's been a while."

"A long while," Maggie confirmed. "Is everything okay?"

"Everything's just the same as it has been."

The obvious evasion tugged the corners of her mouth into a frown. Her friend wasn't normally an evader, either. Fred unfurled his portly frame, rose from his comfy spot on the bathmat with a languorous stretch, and sank his claws into the top of her foot.

"Ouch! Dammit, Fred!" She clutched the towel to her bosom and danced off of the mat, shooting a scornful glare at her abuser.

Tracy laughed. "You still have Fred?"

"The stupid cat's too mean to die," she grumbled. The man in question stretched his ample bulk then sat up, curling his ginger tail around his feet.

"He's got to be close to twelve now."

Giving her feral feline wide berth, she reached for her robe. "Yep. I got him when you were pregnant with Erin."

Tracy's smile carried through the phone. "Yeah, I remember. He was so cute."

"Yeah, well, he's old and fat and foul now." She cinched the belt on the bathrobe, sucking in her gut and glaring at the pumpkin colored tabby. Maggie spared the mirror a glance and winced. She ran her hand over the knot of auburn hair and narrowed her green eyes to slits. "Kinda like me."

If nothing else, her grumbling complaints scored a genuine laugh from her friend. "You aren't old or fat, and you could never pull off being foul."

Her hand fell, her fingers curling into a loose fist as the warmth of Tracy's laughter trickled through her. She sighed and closed her eyes. "I can't wait to see you, Trace."

"We'll catch up on everything tomorrow. Call me from the station."

"I will. See you tomorrow."

She dropped the phone into the deep pocket of the robe with a sigh. Fred wound his plump body around her legs then gazed up at her, his emerald eyes wide and innocent. Unable to resist, she bent and gave the beast a scratch behind his ears. He stretched to meet her caress, exposing his snowy white bib.

Maggie yanked the clip from her hair, shaking the tangled mass free as she straightened. Orangey-red curls tumbled around her shoulders. The deep vee of the ankle-length chenille robe revealed the pale skin of her chest. She searched her reflection in the mirror then spun away, stalking toward the kitchen in a quest for more merlot.

Pulling a clean glass from the shelf above the sink, she yanked the cork from the bottle on the counter. Ruby red relief swirled into the goblet. She tipped her head back and downed the glass in two long gulps.

Maggie caught her reflection in the polished chrome toaster. "Crap. I'm beginning to look like my damn cat." She set the glass on the counter and hung her head. "And I'm talking to my toaster."

She gave the toaster a shove. "You'd better not keel over too. I'm not going back to the kitchen side of the store. It's too damn dangerous."

Fred meowed piteously and hopped onto the counter. She shooed him down, snagged the bottle and trudged her way toward the cramped living room and her nightly date with Letterman. Fred claimed her lap the minute she flopped down, blocking the bottle on the coffee table. She threaded her fingers through soft ginger fur and smiled. "Saving me from myself again?" The cat blinked lazily and kicked his motor into high gear.

Maggie blew out a breath, let her head fall back against the cushion, and blinked at the ceiling. "I love you too, you fat lump."

Chapter Two

"Never in my life have I ever met a man more scared of commitment." Mehgan Barlow's glare cut through the gloomy ambiance of the trendy West Loop restaurant.

Tom Sullivan shook his head, a small smile tugging at the corners of his mouth. "I just don't think I need new blinds."

"I'm not talking about the damn blinds!"

He watched as angry color rose high in her cheeks. Angry, aroused, embarrassed, or agitated—he loved the way women wore their emotions like a second skin. Stifling a sigh, he glanced at the nearby tables attempting to gauge exactly how many people would witness the demise of his latest attempt at a relationship. The stunning blonde across the table from him refused to flinch. A part of him admired her for it. Actually, he admired a great number of things about Mehgan, but predictability wasn't one of them.

"Mehgan…" He leaned in closer, hoping the pale glow of a single votive candle would be enough to help convey his sincerity.

"Exactly where do you see this relationship going?"

He blew out a breath and closed his eyes. "At the moment? I'd say it's going down the toilet."

"What do you want from me?"

The ardent plea in her voice pinged his heart but failed to penetrate. "I want what I said I wanted all along."

"A *relationship.*" Somehow her tone imbued the word with more sinister portent than the poor thing deserved. "What does that mean to you?"

"It means *this*," he said, waving an impatient hand between them. "We enjoy each other's company—"

"In bed," she spat.

"And out, hopefully," he conceded. "We care about each other, listen when the other has a crappy day, laugh at each other's stupid jokes…."

"And that's it," she concluded in a flat tone.

"Isn't that all anyone wants, really?"

Her jaw tightened. Those perfectly glossed lips thinned into a hard line. "I want more than that."

His head began wagging before his tongue could catch up. The waiter appeared with their entrées. He stared at the paper-thin slices of beef tenderloin, mandatory dollop of couscous, and artful drizzle of unidentifiable sauce and wrinkled his nose. He eyed Mehgan's miniscule sliver of salmon. A Filet-o-fish could kick its ass, but if he got lucky she'd storm out without touching her food. It didn't look as if dessert would be happening, and Tom knew he'd be hungry again in an hour. Their waiter faded into the gloom, but Mehgan's angry glare shone like a beacon. The sooner he kicked it into gear, the sooner he could eat.

"This is all I have to give."

His standard answer tripped right off his tongue. Her corn silk hair slipped from her shoulder when she ducked her head, masking her expression. It was all he could do to refrain from brushing it back. He wanted her to see him clearly.

Angry tears brimmed in her big brown eyes when she glanced up, and a surge of relief coursed through him. Anger and disappointment were his expertise. He cleared his throat, the well-worn 'It's not you, it's me' speech running through his head.

Before he could open his mouth to utter the usual platitudes, his soon-to-be-ex pulled her napkin from her lap and balled it in one fist. "People are right about you," she hissed in a trembling voice. Tom opened his mouth to ask who, but she pushed her chair back from the table and rose to her feet. "You're arrogant, condescending, and completely…misogynistic."

Tom shook his head, a spurt of anger bubbling up in his throat. The first two he was willing to own, but the last was completely wrong. He hadn't lied to her or led her on. He made a point of being very careful with the women in his life.

"I never—"

The protest died on his lips when she spun on her stiletto and stalked from the restaurant. His gaze fell to the teeny, tiny portions on his plate. He swiped the pad of his forefinger through the saucy swirl and popped it into his mouth. Cognac instead of red wine. Not bad. When the waiter appeared, surreptitiously reaching for the abandoned salmon, Tom grunted, "Leave it."

The young man backed away, smoothing nervous palms over the long white apron tied at his waist. "Can I get you anything else?"

He speared a half-dollar-sized medallion of beef. "Just the check," he muttered before popping half of his dinner into his mouth.

"Very good, sir."

Both meals were history in six bites. The waiter placed the leather folder on the table and Tom pried a credit card from his wallet, slipping it inside without a glance. He knew there was no use in checking the total. He'd never be able to read it in the dim light, no matter how hard he squinted.

Twenty minutes later, the door of his Lincoln Park condo slammed behind him. Tom winced and tossed his keys into the chipped dish one former girlfriend or another had ordered from the Pottery Barn catalog and shipped directly to his door. The fact that he couldn't recall the dish's benefactor meant either his memory was slipping, or he really was everything Mehgan accused him of being.

He raised his chin, yanking at the noose around his neck until the knot of his tie unraveled. The watered silk slid from his collar with a soft *zzzhut* and trailed behind him as he stomped into the living room. He dropped onto the couch. The lining of his suit coat billowed like a parachute when the pliant leather caught him with a sigh.

"Sarah Ann Waverly," he blurted. A triumphant smile spread across his face. "She bought the bowl."

Twisting, he slid down until his head rested on the arm of the sofa. "Misogynist, my ass. I love women."

He toed off his shoes, let the tie fall to the floor, and unbuckled his belt. The hook on his suit pants gave way and he exhaled his relief. His fingers slid between the buttons on his crisp blue shirt. Absently he stroked his stomach, hoping to calm the twisting sensation in his gut.

The need to connect with someone who understood had him fumbling in the breast pocket of his coat for his cell. His thumb slid across the screen and he tapped a speed dial key. Pressing the phone to his ear, he shifted, trying to get comfortable on a couch built for looks and not comfort.

Once the call connected, he skipped the preamble. "Hey. Do you think I hate women?"

His little brother, Sean, laughed. "Yes. You're a raging queer. The shoes gave you away."

"No, seriously…"

"I think you've laid more women than I've ever laid eyes on. So no, I'd say you probably don't hate them. Why?"

"Mehgan says I'm a misogynist."

"Mehgan's the shrink?"

Tom pushed his fingers through his hair. "Family counselor."

"Yeah, shrinks aren't real high on my list right now."

"I didn't ask you to kiss her. I only asked if you think I'm a misogynist."

"I'm not sure a guy who's as clumsy as you are could qualify to be a massage artist."

"Don't play dumb," Tom growled.

Sean chuckled again. "Misogyny, no. Misogamy, yes."

"There's my brainy Bob the Builder," Tom said, his smile blossoming.

"If you married that pretty girl from Kenya you could also score on miscegeny."

"Okay, give it a rest, Mr. Webster. Christ, Sean, what do you do, stay up all night reading the dictionary and playing with yourself?" His brother's silence spoke volumes. Tom squeezed his eyes shut, pinching the bridge of his nose between his thumb and forefinger. "Sorry," he said in a gruff whisper.

"Nah, it's okay."

Tom's temper flared. His fingers curled into a fist. The leather sofa bore the brunt of his aggression. "I hate this. I hate that I can't even blow you shit! I hate that this is still going on! When are you going to end it?"

"I'm sorry my marriage falling apart is taking such a toll on you."

The ice in his brother's tone chilled him to the bone. Sean wasn't the cold one. Sean wasn't supposed to be bitter and sarcastic. That was *his* job. Tom's lips thinned into a tight line. His fingers squeezed the phone's plastic casing so hard it should have shattered, but his plea came out in a whisper. "Let me file the papers, Sean."

"No!"

"Let me shake her 'til her teeth rattle."

"Get in line."

"Let me do something!"

Sean's tired sigh blew like a gust of wind down Canal Street. "Tell me about your date," he said at last. "How come you're calling me and not making sure she's callin' your name?"

He tried to smooth the furrows cutting across his forehead. "Well, apparently the fact that I don't want her ordering new blinds for my bedroom means I can't commit, and the reason I can't commit to a woman as evolved and self-aware as Mehgan Barlow is that I am a misogynist," he explained with deliberate patience.

"Makes perfect sense to me."

"Figured it would."

"But she chose the wrong one. You're a *misogamist*."

"Which one's that?"

"Hatred of marriage."

"Ah, right. Well, maybe she just misspoke," Tom said with a rueful laugh.

"Probably. Heat of the moment and all that." The two men shared a good laugh at his expense. "So, why were you breaking up with her?"

"I told you, the blinds."

"No, what's the real reason?"

"That *is* the real reason," he insisted, leveraging himself into a sitting position. "First it's a bowl or some blinds, next they're picking our matching bands." Tom ran his hand over his face, dragging at the corners of his mouth. "We both know how well that works out."

Sean snorted then fell silent.

His gaze roamed the living room, searching for a place to light. It landed on the funky tribal mask Elinah Hart gave him. When he ended their relationship she claimed she gave him a priceless family heirloom. He made some snide comment about the 'Made in Indonesia' sticker pasted to the inside and she hurled it at him with surprising accuracy. He hadn't even cared enough to duck.

There were very few people he cared about enough that he'd dodge the blows. Sean was one of them. Sean's estranged wife, Tracy, another. "How are things?" he asked at last.

"Things are things."

Sean's cryptic answer spoke volumes. He and Tracy had been living in a virtual standoff for the better part of two years. "I hate hating her," Tom admitted.

A few seconds of silence ticked by before Sean cleared his throat. "Things are gettin' a little better."

His eyebrows etched the furrows in his forehead a little deeper. "They are?"

"Well, it's not all *War of the Roses* anymore."

"I have to admit, I kind of admire you for hanging in there. Most guys would have cut and run by now."

"I don't have a choice."

Tom shook his head at his little brother's stubborn streak. "Yes, you do."

"No, I don't. Listen, I don't expect you to understand. You can't possibly understand."

Heat prickled his cheeks, and he turned his head as if Sean was sitting right there—as if he was scared to face the truth shining in his little brother's eyes. "You're right. I can't possibly."

The silence stretched taut between them. As usual, Sean broke first. "So, you and Mehgan?"

"Done."

"Three weeks? Four?"

"Five, asshole."

"What's the record again?"

"You're like a broken record."

"Showing your age," Sean said with a chuckle. "Hell, people don't even buy CDs anymore."

"Feeling my age," Tom admitted with a tired sigh.

"Still dying your hair?"

Tom bristled. "I don't dye my hair." Switching to counter-offensive mode he asked, "Where's your beautiful bride tonight? Holed up in the basement avoiding your ugly ass?"

"Actually, she's out."

"Out?"

"Yep."

"Out where?"

The pregnant pause before Sean answered spoke volumes. "I didn't ask."

"Uh-huh. What did your spies tell you?"

"I don't have spies. I have kids."

Tom waved a dismissive hand and leveraged himself from the couch. "Po-ta-to, po-tah-to." His stomach growled so he padded to the kitchen. Two plates of play food were definitely not going to hold him to the morning, no matter how artfully arranged or how many ethnicities they fused into one. "I say you interrogate the littlest one. He always squeals."

"I didn't have to put the squeeze on Kevin. Erin gave up the goods," Sean admitted, referring to his middle child and only daughter.

"Oh?" He plucked a bottle of water from the fridge then rummaged through a cabinet until he unearthed a bag of potato chips. Scowling at the crumbs dusting the bottom of the bag, he plunged his hand inside. "And?"

"I don't know where she went, but she's out with Maggie."

Tom shoved a handful of broken chips into his mouth and brushed the crumbs from his chest. "Maggie?" he mumbled as he chewed.

"Maggie McCann. Her old roommate? The redhead," Sean prompted.

He licked potato chip crumbs from his lips, savoring the salty goodness melting on his tongue. Tom didn't need to jog his memory. Any man who'd ever sneaked a peek at Tracy's friend Maggie would never forget her.

The mere mention of the name conjured a Technicolor still shot in his brain. Redhead wasn't a good enough word. Her lustrous hair—cinnamon swirled with a hint of aged burgundy—tumbled to porcelain shoulders, tempting the saints the way it curled against the ivory column of her throat. The translucent skin of a milkmaid stretched over the lush curves of a courtesan. Her green eyes flashed and gleamed with wicked good humor when she smiled. And her smile…That wholesome toothpaste ad smile hit a guy straight in the gonads.

In other words Maggie McCann was the kind of woman he avoided like the clap. Her damn smile packed more punch than an atom bomb and was a thousand times more dangerous than anthrax. "Yeah, I think I remember her."

Sean snorted. "I'm sure you remember her tits. You practically dove into her cleavage at our rehearsal dinner."

"That was a long time ago."

"You've seen her dozens of times since then. Some things don't change."

Tom couldn't help it. He did what any good attorney would do when faced with a line of questioning he found untenable, he turned it around. "And some things *do* change. I seem to remember a couple of people who couldn't wait to get hitched. Now you're both just sitting around waiting to get divorced."

"Fuck you."

"You're not my type."

"I'm done," Sean growled.

The phone went dead. Tom checked the display, inhaling deeply through his nose. Tossing the phone onto the counter, he scowled at the potato crumbs once more. "Way to go, asshole."

Leaning against the counter, he tipped the bag to his lips and emptied the dregs into his big, fat mouth. Chips clung to his lips. He crumpled the bag as he chewed then stuffed it into the stainless steel trash can left behind by another woman hell-bent on redecorating his life.

"Sherry Hanson," he murmured to the empty room.

His shoulders slumped as he shuffled from the kitchen. He scrubbed a hand over his face, dislodging the last of his snack. Plodding his way toward the bedroom, Tom berated himself for his insensitivity. Then again, he and Sean rarely pulled punches, physical or verbal. He had the broken nose to prove it.

A beer and a mea culpa. That's all it would take. He might have to let his little brother get a few digs in, but everything would be okay. Everything had to be okay. Sean wouldn't stay mad at him. His little brother was the yin to his yang. Or yang to his yin. Whatever. Maybe he'd even let his baby brother flatten his nose again. Then they could call it even and have that beer.

Tom stripped off his suit coat and tossed it over the arm of the overstuffed chair Mary Sobinski picked out for the room. He unbuttoned his shirt and yanked it from his arms, chucking it toward the wicker hamper Jonelle Middling insisted he needed. The navy pinstripe pants Ann Chandler said cupped his ass perfectly dropped to the floor. He stepped out of them and dove for the bed, needing a few minutes to gather the strength to brush his teeth.

The dull throbbing behind his eyes matched the pulse strumming in his ears. He drew in a breath then expelled it carefully. His fingers slipped under the hem of his undershirt. The hair covering his knotted stomach tickled his palm. A montage of the women who'd drifted in and out of his life played behind closed eyelids, and his brain cataloged each corresponding bit of detritus they'd left behind—the single man's version of Concentration.

An image of the one woman among many he'd never touched, never tasted, never dared to even sniff, flashed before his eyes. Tom sighed and gave into the temptation. He hadn't laid eyes on the woman in years, yet he had no difficulty conjuring the memory of Maggie McCann in the wicked sundress she'd worn to some backyard barbeque at Sean and Tracy's house. White with red polka dots. Halter top. Gorgeous tits. Generous ass.

His hand slipped under the elastic waistband of his briefs and imagined he was untying the knot at the nape of her neck. He could almost feel those flame-red curls searing his fingers. The cool velvet of her skin would soothe the ache while his boiling blood pumped through his veins. He pictured the pulse in her throat throbbing, those full pink lips bare and swollen from his kisses, and her emerald eyes, hazy and lazy with desire.

Full, plump breasts spilling into his hands. Every inch of her soft, round curves molding to him. She'd whisper his name.

Tom yanked his hand from his shorts and flung himself from the bed. He stared at the mussed comforter accusingly, as if the midnight blue duvet cover Wendy Nelson picked out was the reason he was panting like a pug after a tussle with an ottoman. He spun on his heel and stalked to the bathroom.

Leaning on the vanity, he stared hard at his reflection. He didn't like what he saw. More gray in his hair. The lines around his eyes and mouth dug deeper. The stubble poking through at his jaw was tinged with red and white. He closed his eyes and pushed away from the mirror, rocking back on his heels.

Showing his age. Sean was right. He wasn't twenty anymore. Hell, he wasn't even thirty or forty. Forty-six was on the downhill side of fifty.

Tom met his gaze in the mirror, bared his teeth, and sucked in his stomach. He carefully ignored the slight bulge of flesh above his hips and patted his still-flat abs. The ceramic toothbrush holder Charlotte Lowenstien placed on his vanity wobbled when he yanked his brush free.

He glared at the three open holes on the cup, wondering what in the world he could have possibly said or done to give a woman as smart as Charlotte the impression he'd ever need more than one. Reaching for the toothpaste, he squirted a generous stripe onto the brush. Frankly, he wondered why any of them even tried. Like any reasonably sane divorce attorney he was virulently opposed to marriage. He'd seen enough of how determined and vengeful a woman can be once they're on the other side of the altar. The whole relationship thing was just a game of cat and mouse, and Tom was equally determined he would never be some feline female's prey.

But he liked women. Really, he did. In his twenties he tore through women like a starving man at a smorgasbord, and they all but leapt onto his plate. By the time he hit thirty, he'd honed his tastes, appreciating his women the way a foodie appreciates truffles, pate, or any of that other crap he wouldn't touch with a ten foot pole. And every woman he dated seemed to think she had the flavor he'd savor. Forty came and went, and he mellowed a bit. Tom wasn't opposed to a long-term relationship. The trouble was finding a woman who didn't think a relationship entailed redecorating his apartment or the third finger on his left hand.

He stared at the toothbrush holder then peeked through the door at the rumpled duvet. Tomorrow, he'd be back on the prowl again. Tomorrow, he'd start all over with the same old blinds and a ceramic toothbrush cup he never wanted. A long, tired sigh seeped from his throat and a smirk twisted his lips as he saluted his reflection with the dripping toothbrush.

"At least my gums aren't receding. Yet."

Chapter Three

Early Monday morning, Maggie unlocked the rear door of The Glass Slipper Day Spa & Salon and slipped inside. The alarm's beeps pierced her skull like ice picks. Maggie feared the size of her head would give the aliens from *Mars Attacks!* a run for their intergalactic money.

She punched in the security code, picked her way past the shampoo bowl and styling stations, and tried to avoid catching a glimpse of herself in a mirror. It wasn't easy. The spa's interior was a veritable funhouse. Scanning the glossy plank floor for unswept hair seemed a valid excuse to avert her gaze. The elastic holding her ponytail tugged the tiny hairs at the nape of her neck. Just a little more pain as punishment for her over-indulgence.

She skirted past the closed doors of the treatment rooms and ducked into the snug, cozy space at the very end of the narrow hallway. Her office. Her haven. This was the heart of the business. The business she never dreamed she ever wanted.

The overhead lights sprang to life and Maggie reeled back, shielding her eyes. Once she blinked away the dancing spots, she lit a candle and switched on the sound system. The soft strains of soothing strings built to a gentle soar. She hadn't a clue what the tune was or who composed it, but she hummed along, every lilting note long committed to memory. There would never be any of that twangy New Age crap in her spa, and certainly no Kenny G.

Lowering herself into the leather chair behind the open desk, she turned on the computer and pushed off with her feet. She closed her eyes as she rolled back to the wall and waited for the machine to boot. A low groan slithered from her lips. She tried to lose herself in the sweet, swirling music, wishing it could carry her away from the prospect of payroll and inventory. She wanted to escape her aching head, the worry making her stomach roil, and the constant trickle of fear tripping its way through her veins.

The marital troubles her friend Tracy confessed over margaritas and hot fudge sundaes Saturday night scared her. For far too long she'd held Tracy and Sean's marriage up as her ideal. Tracy had everything—the handsome, hard-working husband, the perfect suburban home, and three lovable ragamuffins. All that was missing was a damn Golden Retriever.

The morass of mixed emotions her friend's confession unleashed set Maggie back on her spiked heels. Sympathy, resentment, heartache, and jealousy battled for dominance, but lost by a mile. The fact that Tracy Sullivan had everything Maggie ever wanted and stood on the brink of throwing it all away made her unaccountably…happy.

And that made her horrible—a horrible, terrible excuse of a woman. Her good friend broke down and confessed the collapse of her marriage, and a tiny, ugly little part of her rejoiced. She couldn't help it. For some reason she found perverse pleasure in learning her perfect friend was royally screwing up her perfect life.

Of course, by the time Tracy dropped her in front of her Wicker Park building, Maggie was sufficiently wretched enough to polish off the rest of Friday night's merlot. She coaxed the sympathy and heartache she wanted to feel for her friend from the evil clutches of that happiness. By Sunday morning she was forced to admit another illusion lay shattered. That night, Maggie sat in her living room wearing Betty Boop pajamas and drenching Fred's fur with fat, salty tears. She amped the pity party up a notch by making mad, passionate love to a bottle of meritage and passing out on the rug.

The computer beeped and Maggie surged forward in the chair. Her stomach lurched and her giant head spun. She let it fall forward into her hands. Pressing the heels of her palms to her brow, she vowed to be better, to atone for her sins. She promised herself she'd order inventory, process the week's payroll, and make her twelve o'clock meeting at Haven House even if it killed her. A sharp, stabbing pain in her temple indicated that it damn well might.

The spa was closed. Mondays were the days she usually got things done, and she had a full agenda. Too full to nurse a case of Bordeaux brain. Desperate, she promised the hangover gods if they made it stop, she would call Tracy and repeat her offer of a spa night for just the two of them. She swore she'd stamp out that little spark of happiness, even if it scorched the soles of her beloved Louboutin slingbacks. Desperate times called for drastic measures.

Covering her stomach with one hand, Maggie also silently pledged to ban the grape from her apartment. Except on social occasions, of course. Starting now she'd be the friend she always thought she was and the strong, independent woman she wanted to be—not this clenched-up, wine-drenched, unholy mess of girl.

****

"You're so good with them, Maggie."

Maggie's head popped up and the tubes of mascara samples she was packing into a large black case spurted from her clenched fist. Sheila McKenzie, the diminutive founder and director of Haven House, stood just inside the doorway to the common room. The silver-haired woman chuckled as she scrambled to recover the wayward wands.

She shook her head, flashing a sheepish smile. "Sorry. I didn't know you were there."

Sheila patted her carefully coiffed hair and floated into the room. Maggie watched the woman's tiny feet, determined to figure out exactly how the spry septuagenarian pulled the whole floating thing off while wearing three-inch heels.

"Nothing gives a woman a shot of confidence like a swipe of lipstick," Sheila murmured, choosing one of the tubes arrayed on the table and twisting its base until a stick of bold vermillion appeared. A benevolent smile touched the corners of her more subtly shaded lips. "I haven't received your R.S.V.P. for the benefit yet, Maggie."

"You don't think it's a little perverse to hold a five-hundred-dollar-a-ticket fundraiser for women who are wearing other people's cast off coats?"

One perfect eyebrow arched. The older woman's warm brown eyes gleamed with an unidentifiable sparkle. "Not at all. Most of those people have forgotten how much they paid for last season's coat and you can bet they paid much more than five hundred dollars for this year's latest trend."

Maggie gathered the remaining tubes and pots of make-up and dumped them into the case. She nodded to the tube in Sheila's hand. "That one would suit you."

A smile quirked Sheila's lips. "Do you think so? It's been a long time since I tried to pull off a color so daring."

"Somehow I find that hard to believe."

The older woman threw her head back and laughed. The rich, bawdy guffaw contrasted sharply with her conservative knit suit. Silvery tresses glinted in the harsh florescent light. Her chocolate eyes flared. "Maybe in my day…."

The laugh gave Maggie permission to prop her hip against the low table and ask the question she always wanted to ask. "How did you end up doing this?"

Sheila's smile didn't slip as she capped the lipstick and dropped it into the pocket of her knit suit. "I used to be a social worker. I saw a lot of abuse—women, children…."

"You were?"

The smile turned a touch enigmatic. "Maggie, didn't your mother ever tell you that you can marry more money in five minutes than you can make your entire life?"

A startled laugh burbled from her lips. "No, but my Grandma told me if I wished on the evening star, my prince would come."

Sheila's brown eyes twinkled like the evening star. "Your grandmother sounds like a wise woman."

"She was."

The older woman tugged at the hem of her immaculate suit jacket. "Then I suppose she also told you those princes can be damn unreliable. Best not to wait on them."

"No, she didn't tell me that part, but I think I figured it out on my own."

"That's because you're a smart woman." Sheila sighed, her shrewd glance taking in the entire common room in the blink of an eye. "Besides, even if you snag one, you never know when you'll lose him. When Howard passed away, I found myself at loose ends."

"So, naturally…" Maggie prompted, gesturing to the cinderblock walls of the renovated building that now housed ten abused women and their offspring.

"I don't have children or grandchildren, and there's only so much bridge one can play. I started Haven House twenty years ago, but it wasn't until after Howard was gone that I mustered the nerve to stop being the woman who signed the checks and took the plunge. Getting involved, personally involved…" She flashed a brilliant smile. "Best decision I ever made."

"You're saving their lives."

"They saved mine," Sheila corrected.

Maggie shook her head, undeterred. "You take them in, feed them, clothe them, provide counseling, teach them job skills—"

"And beauty skills," Sheila added, nodding to the case. When Maggie rolled her eyes, she shook her head adamantly. "Do not discount what you do for them, Maggie. Their bruises are more than skin deep. On top of being frightened, they feel unworthy, inferior, and ugly. After an afternoon with you, they actually want to look in a mirror. That's a huge step."

"Sometimes it feels silly. Like I'm arming them with a tube of lip gloss and saying, 'Go get 'em, Tiger!'"

"You know it's so much more than that," Sheila chided. She pulled a rectangle of cream-colored card-stock from her pocket. "Here's your ticket. I'll expect to see you a week from Saturday."

"Does anyone ever tell you no?"

A smug smile tugged her lips. "It happens. Not very often, but it does."

Maggie reached for her purse. "Let me write you a check."

Sheila waved a dismissive hand. "Don't bother. I already invoiced ten tickets to Howard's old firm." A devilish smile curved her lips. "They really do need to pay closer attention to their bookkeeping."

Maggie laughed. "You're a shyster."

Sheila stole a quick glance at her watch and turned for the door. "I have to go. The attorney who handles the legal work for the ladies will be here shortly. I have a few notes I need to add to the files."

She waved the ticket. "I'll see you next week."

The older woman paused in the doorway. The calculating gleam in her eyes had Maggie taking an involuntary step back. "He's single, you know, and handsome as the devil himself."

"And I was just leaving," Maggie said pointedly.

Sheila rolled her eyes and chuckled. "You're right. Men are a terrible pain. Who needs one? Besides, from what I hear, he's something of a man slut."

"Sheila!"

"I just call them as I see them." She pulled the lipstick from her pocket. "Thank you for the little pick-me-up. It's just what I needed."

Biting her lip, Maggie slung the strap of the heavy make-up case over her shoulder. The angry wail of an unhappy infant drowned out the clip-clop heels. Plaintive cries echoed from the back of the building. Another shriek pierced her soul, knocking her legs out from under her.

Her teeth clacked when her rump hit the cool metal folding chair. The strap slid from her shoulder and the bag dropped to the floor at her feet. Maggie's gaze locked on the garland of crayon-colored pumpkins, pilgrims, and turkeys strung from one end of the room to the other. She avoided looking at it all afternoon, but even as the cries subsided into muffled sobs, she couldn't tear her gaze from her fine, feathered friends.

Maggie ducked her head and concentrated on pulling soft, deep breaths, but the truth smacked her in the face. Repeatedly. Fairy tales don't exist. Her prince may never come, and even if he did, no one could guarantee the happily ever after part. Tracy and Sean Sullivan were proof of that.

She didn't need a man to make her happy. There was only one thing missing from her life. The one thing she wanted the most. Even that one thing was still possible. All she had to do was take the plunge. Take a chance.

The turkeys stared her down, their beady black magic marker eyes double-dog-daring her to make the call. Never one to back down from a challenge, Maggie pulled her cell from her purse and scrolled through the address book until she found the number she needed. She pressed the phone to her ear and closed her eyes, concentrating on pulling each breath in then pushing it out.

"Hello. This is Maggie McCann." The steady calm of her voice shocked her from her stupor. Gripping the phone harder, she dove in head first, certain her hammering heart would follow. She raised her gaze to the festive garland once more, determined not to let the turkeys stare her down. "I have an appointment for my annual next Monday, but I was wondering if Dr. Stephens could manage a little extra time for a consultation."

Chapter Four

"You came!"

Tom passed his coat to the young woman stationed at the coat check stand and accepted the ticket she gave him with a flirtatious smile. He turned that smile on the silver-haired dynamo clutching his arm. "You threatened me," he said, dropping a kiss to Sheila McKenzie's cheek.

She slipped her tiny hand into the crook of his arm and beamed up at him. "Nonsense. I would never resort the threats."

He chuckled and shook his head. "Blackmail."

"Blackmail? That's an ugly implication."

"So is implying I bat for the other side."

"The Cubs? Certainly not." She gasped, but her eyes twinkled with mischief. "I know you're a South Side boy."

"You know what I mean."

"You must admit it is uncommon for a man as handsome and successful as you are to remain unfettered. Whatever the reason may be, I certainly never meant to cast aspirations on your manhood."

"Funny, that's not how I remember the conversation going."

She patted his arm. "That's because your memory is starting to slip, darling. Why, you've forgotten to tell me how pretty I look this evening."

Tom returned her smile and stepped back to give her the once over. Even into her seventies, Sheila McKenzie was a beautiful woman. The café au lait-colored cocktail dress set off her dark eyes and skimmed her petite frame. Her silver-white hair flowed away from her face in thick waves. His smile widened in appreciation as he drew her hand to his lips. "Pretty isn't the word. You're stunning."

"And you are the devil," she said with a laugh.

When she attempted to recover her hand, he held tight. "Run away with me, Sheila. You know you're the only woman for me."

She squeezed his fingers and rewarded him with a dreamy sigh. "If only I were thirty years younger."

"I've always found older women incredibly sexy."

Her bark of laughter caught the attention of a couple nearby. "Bullshit!"

The other couple's jaws dropped. Tom flashed a beaming smile, and they turned away with a sniff. When he glanced at Sheila, the sharp look in her eyes almost made him flinch. "What?"

She graced him with a small, knowing smile. Diamonds glittered bright and hard on her fingers, ears, and at her throat, but her dark eyes melted like bittersweet chocolate. "Come with me. I think it's high time someone introduced you to a more age-appropriate woman."

"This was a set up," he grumbled, standing his ground.

"Of course it was," she said with a tinkling laugh. "Did you really think I cared whether you showed your pretty face or not? I've already deposited your check."

"You are heartless, Sheila."

"And you like that about me," she countered, tucking her hand into his arm again. "Buy me a glass of that god-awful vinegar we're passing off as wine and I'll tell you all about her."

"I love your talent for mocking your own accomplishments."

She squeezed his bicep. "And I love the feel of warm, firm man. Stick close, darling, I want to feel you up a little more before I give you away."

Tom threw his head back and laughed. He may have flexed a little too. "Heartless and shameless."

"You'll thank me," she said with an airy wave of her hand.

They drew to a halt just inside the hotel ballroom. He surveyed the scene laid out before him, picking each detail out in one sweeping glance. The tiny white lights strung through the branches of potted trees were both tasteful and festive. A small orchestra played standards from the low bandstand set up at the far end of the room. The parquet dance floor was already crammed with couples. Uniformed wait-staff circulated with trays of crab puffs and shrimp. A buffet anchored by two artfully carved ice sculptures trailed the length of one wall. Four fully stocked bars beckoned the revelers.

"It's just the usual crap."

Tom acknowledged her assessment with a distracted nod. Then he clicked on the one noticeable difference between this benefit and dozens of others he attended as a part of his duties as a partner. Half of Chicago seemed to be in attendance. "Christ, did you blackmail them all? Is that the mayor?"

"Believe it or not, some people find me charming," she said with a sly smile. When he shot her a dubious glance she shrugged. "The rest…Well, they think I'm too rich to piss off."

His chuckle morphed into a laugh. He led her to the nearest bar where he ordered a glass of white wine. "Are you sure you won't run away with me?" he asked. "We can go someplace warm and sunny. You can oil my back."

"Are you rusting already?" She tsked softly. "Sad for one so young."

Tom eyed the crowd, measured the depth of his patience, then added two fingers of scotch to the mix for safety's sake. "I thought you wanted to feel me up."

"No need to throw yourself at me. I prefer to be more subtle about these things." She searched the crowd as he led her through the milling throng of guests.

Tom smiled a hello to a guy who looked a little familiar. At least, he hoped he managed a smile. It may have fallen a bit short, edging more toward a grimace. He hated these things. He hated the small talk, the business talk, and the intense negotiations masked as polite conversation.

Sheila gave his arm a squeeze and nodded to the room. "Time to mingle."

He sighed and kept his gaze fixed on the bar set up along the far wall, charting his course to the next stop. "So, this woman you're setting me up with… Whose niece is it?"

"I have no idea who her people are." Sheila abandoned his arm to exchange air kisses with a passing blonde.

She reclaimed her hold on him. "I take it she's over thirty?"

"Definitely."

"Forty?"

"I don't think she's there yet."

"Harelip?"

"And a club foot," she retorted. "Can't you give me a little credit? I've known you for years, Tom. I know what a snob you are."

Her words felt like a punch in the gut. "A snob? I'm not a snob."

"When it comes to women you are," she chided. "A snob and an attention whore."

He covered her hand with his and plastered a charming smile to his face. "Careful, Sheila, I'm beginning to think you don't like me."

She snorted, somehow managing to pull the derisive sound off with class and aplomb. If he didn't have a weird prickly sensation tickling the back of his neck, he would have admired the effect. As it was, his Spidey-senses were all a-tingle.

"You forget I've known you since you were a nerdy little intern trailing after Howard picking up his paper-clips." She nodded to a knot of guests standing nearby, flashing a gracious smile.

"I was never nerdy."

She forged ahead, brushing past his objection and slicing through the crowd like a Coast Guard cutter. "He was very fond of you. I am too, but I'm tired of watching you pick up whatever Barbie Doll you think will turn heads." He drew to an abrupt stop but managed to rein in his temper enough to keep from jerking his arm from her grasp. His eyes narrowed to slits. She simply smiled in response. "I understand. Men are horribly vain. Lord, Howard used to spend more time in front of the mirror than I did."

"I'm not vain."

"Aren't you?" Sheila stared up at him with just enough wide-eyed innocence to set alarm bells ringing in his head.

"I'm leaving."

She pursed her lips and dropped all pretense of innocence. "I can't stand watching men I like making fools of themselves. It's maddening."

Apparently, all pretense of teasing was behind them. "How exactly am I making a fool of myself?"

"You're not the young stud about town anymore, Tom. Now, I'll admit there's nothing more amusing than seeing an old fool chasing after young women, but I can't bring myself to laugh at you. I'm nipping it in the bud now, before you become a cocktail party joke," she said, tipping her chin up defiantly.

"I'm only forty-six!"

"You aren't a joke yet, but soon you will be if you aren't stopped." She squeezed his arm and refused to let up. It probably would have hurt if he wasn't already numb.

First Sean, now Sheila. The attack hurt a little more coming from Sheila, though. He was used to ducking the shit Sean threw at him. He didn't expect to be ambushed by his mentor's widow, particularly after he'd shelled out five hundred dollars for the honor of attending the shellacking.

This was the woman who hugged him harder than a sumo wrestler when he was made partner in the firm her husband founded. He glanced down at her tiny hand. It scared him to realize the same frail hand clutched his arm with nearly the same intensity when they lowered Howard McKenzie's casket into his grave.

"Who is she?" he asked at last.

"You'll see." Her grip relaxed on his arm. She waved a greeting to a woman passing by. "She's beautiful. Not one of those skinny colt-like girls you usually go for, though. She's built like a real woman. Smart as a whip. Kind-hearted but strong. Exactly the type of woman you need in your life."

"Says you."

Sheila nodded to the bar, and Tom reluctantly began to move again. "She's done some work for us at Haven House. The women adore her. It's hard not to admire her. She's built her business from the ground up, and she's very successful. Like you, I think she sells herself a bit short on the personal front, but I hope that will change."

Her fingers bit into his sleeve again. For a split second he wondered if she'd leave a bruise. "Now, Tom, she needs a partner, not a knight in shining armor." She searched the crowd at the bar. "My Maggie can rescue herself."

She opened her mouth to continue the lecture, but something beyond his shoulder captured her attention. The gleam in the older woman's eyes melted into a warm smile. Her fingers banded around his arm like a shackle. "There you are!" Sheila extended a bejeweled hand, reaching past him to lay claim to her quarry. "Come here. I want you to meet a dear friend of mine."

Tom tensed, half-afraid to sneak a peek at Sheila's choice. Instead, he fixated on her hand. Knobby, age-speckled fingers closed around equally dainty, albeit smoother digits. She pulled his mystery woman closer. The hand Sheila grasped was connected to a fine-boned wrist that gave way to a softly curved forearm and finally creamy skin stretched over a temptingly silky bicep.

He lifted his gaze slowly, praying he wouldn't have to mask disappointment. After the blows Sheila had dealt his ego, he wasn't quite sure he had the acting chops to pull it off.

The rounded curve of a bare shoulder. So far, so good. The irresistible hollow of a woman's collarbone. Delicious. The sensuous undulation of the pulse quickening in her throat made his mouth water.

He milked the moment, letting anticipation build as his gaze swept higher. A flash of persimmon licked at the edge of awareness. Heat prickled his throat. The hairs on the back of his neck rose. A slash of black satin split the field of ivory. His brain sputtered before kicking into high gear. Anticipation. Milk the moment. Milkmaid skin....

Sheila's fingernails scraped the wool of his suit coat. Her red lips curved into an encouraging smile. She began to speak, but it could have been Swahili for all he cared. He resisted the pull of her smile and stared straight into the sparkling emerald eyes that fueled a thousand fantasies.

"Darling, I'd like you to meet—"

Holy hell..."Hello, Maggie."

****

Tom Sullivan. This had to be some kind of a joke. Two years of near radio silence from Tracy, then her old friend drops a giant bomb. Now suddenly Sullivans were popping out of the woodwork. Freaking Tom Sullivan. And he looked good. Damn good. Damn him.

"Hello, Tom."

She matched his polite smile, going for a cool tone, but Sheila's sharp glance told her she fell short. Not a shocker. Any woman with a pulse would feel a spike in temperature near Tom Sullivan, and Maggie definitely had a pulse. The stupid thing was doing a cha-cha-cha in her throat. She never could pull off the cool bit, but there was something about this guy that made her feel compelled to try.

"You look well," Maggie said, craning her neck to peer past his shoulder. She wanted to kick herself. Such an obvious ploy. Such a ridiculous idea. As if there could be anything better to look at than the man standing right in front of her.

"I see you already know each other," Sheila murmured, glancing from Tom to Maggie and back again.

His head swiveled. The startled widening of those beautiful eyes made Maggie's heart skip two, maybe three, full beats. He'd clearly forgotten they had company.

"Yes, we've known each other for years," Maggie purred. Something hot flashed in his eyes as he turned back to her. Then it was gone. His usual mask of cool indifference slid back into place.

"My brother is married to one of Maggie's friends," he explained, his lips twitching into a smirk. "Or so they claim."

Sheila shot him a puzzled glance, and a slow smile curved Maggie's lips. The devil made her do it. Resistance was futile. A full team of horses—wild, tame, or rabid—couldn't have kept her from resting her hand on his broad shoulder and stretching up to brush an unprecedented kiss to his freshly shaven cheek. She held his gaze, forcing her smile to widen as she wiped away an imaginary smudge of lipstick with the pad of her thumb.

"Yes, Tracy was brave enough to snare one of the elusive Sullivan boys." She turned to Sheila and winked broadly. "Sadly, I hear they don't do well in captivity. Like giant pandas. Cute, but you wouldn't want to keep one in your backyard."

"Excuse me. Mrs. McKenzie?" A young woman sidled up beside Sheila. "I'm sorry to intrude, but there seems to be an issue with Judge Meade's silent auction bids."

Sheila's mouth thinned into a line. She rolled her eyes then closed them tight. "Too much or too little?"

The woman cast a nervous glance over her shoulder then whispered, "He signed each sheet with an opening bid of ten million dollars."

Tom sputtered, and Sheila blew out an exasperated breath. "If I thought for a moment that drunken old coot had ten dollars to his name I'd let each one of those bids stand," she hissed. "Excuse me." She slipped her hand from the crook of Tom's arm and smoothed her hands over the skirt of her dress.

Maggie tried to seize the opportunity to escape. "I was just going—"

"Do not leave," Sheila ordered then turned her sharp gaze on Tom. "Stay here. Entertain Maggie. She hates these things almost as much as you do."

"But—"

"Stay, or I'll order you file suit on Haven House's behalf against a senile old judge. Would you call it malicious mischief or fraud?"

"More than likely Johnnie Walker Black," he muttered.

Sheila set sail, cutting through the throng like a battleship running full steam ahead. Maggie glanced at Tom and raised an eyebrow. "Buy a girl a drink, Sully?"

One corner of his mouth lifted. "My pleasure. *Mags*."

His smirk more closely resembled a sneer. Unfortunately, it didn't detract from the overall effect. He was every bit as gorgeous as she remembered. He offered her a gallant arm, and Maggie slipped her hand into the spot Sheila vacated, reminding herself he was still way too hot for her to handle.

They approached the bar. She dropped her hand from his arm and fiddled with the clasp on her evening bag. He kept his gaze fixed on the bartender as they inched forward.

"What would you like?"

Maggie bit her lip. She wanted the biggest, fattest bottle of Malbec ever made and her hula girl pajamas, but it looked like she was going to get was another dose of Tom Sullivan's infuriating indifference. She snapped her bag shut and tipped her chin up. "Champagne, please."

Without sparing her another glance he stepped to the bar. "Chivas neat and a glass of the bubbly stuff," he muttered, stuffing a bill into the brandy snifter that served as a tip jar. "So, did you and Tracy have a good time the other night?"

She blinked and reared back. "How did you know I saw Tracy?"

He turned at last, shooting her an exasperated glare. "How do you think?"

There were tiny flecks of brown in his deep blue irises. Somehow the disconcerting combination made his eyes as purple as pansies. How had she never noticed that before? Oh yeah, he'd never stood this close before. Maggie frowned as snippets of Tom Sullivan sightings flickered through her brain. They attended the same pre-wedding festivities, three baptisms, and dozens of backyard barbeques over the past decade and a half, but she could have swung all fifteen pounds of Fred and never come close to hitting him.

It was galling. The guy was the consummate player, flirting with every woman from eight to eighty, but he barely ever spoke to her. He screwed his way from Lincoln Park to Lincolnshire, but he never bothered to give her a second look. That fact alone was more than vaguely insulting.

Resisting the urge to smooth her hands over the clingy black dress she wore, Maggie observed others of the species. The bartender blatantly ogled her cleavage as he filled her champagne flute. A guy with a paunch and thinning blond hair practically crawled onto the bar to peek around Tom's arm. Some pervert standing behind her kept trying to grope her ass. She gave brief consideration to hitting the ass grabber with a whirling backhand but dismissed the thought. At the moment she needed every ounce of validation she could get.

Maggie accepted the glass of sparkling wine Tom presented and raised it in a silent toast, inching away from the bar but keeping him in her sights. The bubbles made her tongue tingle. His index finger brushed the bump on the bridge of his nose when he took a greedy slurp of his scotch. The urge to brush her finger over that bump had her tapping a sharp staccato against her glass. He spared her a glance more effective than a cease and desist order and she reined in her nerves.

"How is Sean?" she asked, tracing the rim of the champagne flute with her fingernail.

"How do you think?"

He glowered at her finger. She tapped the glass with her nail to capture his attention and he met her gaze at last. "I hate that this is happening to them," she said softly.

Those indigo eyes flashed hot. Then they froze, icing over like Lake Michigan in January. He drained the rest of his drink. "It isn't happening to *them*. *She's* doing it *to* him."

His glass smacked on the bar, but it was the sharp edge in his voice that made her flinch. Rather than allowing him the pleasure of intimidating her, she bristled. Her fingers tightened around the glass. "It takes two people to make a marriage work."

Tom turned his head, scanning the crowd with supreme indifference. "And only one to blow it all to shit." Before she could work up a suitable retort he pinned her with a challenging glare. "Trust me, I should know. I see it every day."

She pulled her shoulders back, refusing to be the first to look away. "I suppose that's the only angle you would know," she said derisively. "Excuse me. I think I'll slip out while Sheila's not looking."

Her retreat was blocked by the handsy pervert stationed behind her. Maggie planted her stiletto on the toe of the man's gleaming wingtip and whirled to glare at him. "Next time you touch my ass you'll lose a finger. Got me?"

A woman gasped. The rumble of masculine laughter rolled after her. Keeping her head held high, she focused on the ballroom door as she wove her way through the crowd.

"Maggie!"

Tom's voice carried over the hum of conversation, smothering the tinkle of glasses, and cutting through the haze of indignation making her see red. She squeezed past a knot of over-perfumed women and their olfactorally-challenged escorts. Someone grabbed her elbow. Angry, annoyed, and all out of patience, she whirled.

"What?" she hissed. "After fifteen years of pretending I don't exist you finally have something to say to me?"

He dropped her arm, but the square toes of his polished shoes dared to bump her precious Louboutins. His Adam's apple bobbed. Tom spared a quick glance at a cluster of silk and satin-clad women inching closer for better reception. He ran his hand through his thick sable hair. A tiny tuft at his crown broke free from its carefully styled restraint. Maggie curled her fingers into her palms, raking her nails over tender skin to resist the itch to smooth it into place.

"Maggie—" His hand reclaimed her elbow. His palm was disturbingly warm against her cool skin. Long, strong fingers pressed into her arm. Ebony lashes lowered, shielding his vibrant violet eyes. "I'm sorry." His voice was hushed, tinged with a boyish sincerity that caught her off guard. "I'm sorry. I was rude. I just…I know she's your friend, but he's my brother…."

Maggie lowered her gaze. His golden-brown fingers glowed in sharp contrast against the whiteness of her skin. A sprinkling of fine, dark hairs peeked from his cuff. She wet her lips and swallowed the urge to stroke them. The differences between them were too stark. This man was the antithesis of everything she ever wanted. She needed to remember that. She *had* to remember that because his hand looked too damn good on her.

"Sean is my friend too," she managed at last. Maggie chased the simple statement with a defiant lift of her chin and his grip relaxed then fell away. Her arm tingled. Faint pink imprints marked the spot.

His gaze lingered on the marks for a moment before he raised his head. His lips parted. His pupils dilated, inky black overtaking the precious millimeters of midnight blue. "She's the only sister I've ever had."

Maggie took a bracing breath and stared straight into those fathomless eyes. "I'm not Tracy."

The corner of his mouth twitched then lifted. His eyes crinkled at the corners as his smile bloomed. He shook his head slowly, eying her with frank admiration for the first time since they met. "Oh no. I know you're not. You're Maggie McCann, the most dangerous woman in the world."

"Dangerous?" She scoffed.

He took her hand, sandwiching it between his palms and leaning closer. "Hello, Maggie," he said, a laugh coloring his tone. "It's terrifying to see you again." She gaped when he snatched the champagne flute from her fingers and downed its contents in one gulp. "Can I get you a fresh drink?" The devastating dimple in his cheek flashed like a bawdy wink when he handed her the empty glass. "I think we're both gonna need another."

Chapter Five

The proverbial ton of bricks had nothing on seeing Maggie McCann live and in Technicolor. From the moment he dared to lift his gaze to meet hers, he was reeling. What the hell is a guy supposed to do when confronted with a woman who looks like she was conceived while Snow White's animator was busy ogling Jessica Rabbit?

When Sheila started to introduce them a red light flashed in the corner of his mind. He said her name and his brain chirped like a car alarm poised to go off. She spoke and the beeping began, drowning out the low, husky contralto of her voice. She was that Maggie. The one-in-a-hundred-thousand Maggies. The Maggie he'd spent a decade and a half avoiding.

She kissed his cheek, damn her. That was a first. Hopefully a last. Well, not really hopefully, but it would be better if it were the last. Kisses from Maggie, no matter how innocent, were just too damn risky. Her perfume coiled around him, making his head spin and his lungs cease to function, and the alarm in his brain whoop-whooped.

She wasn't his type at all. A good girl. Home, hearth, hearts and flowers—that was Maggie. Jesus, she smelled good. Buzzers, horns, and New Year's Eve noisemakers blared at him. The manic robot from *Lost in Space* was flailing, droning his name in a desperate attempt to warn him. Danger! Danger!

He panicked. Not that he'd ever let her see him sweat. The minute Sheila disappeared into the crowd, he opened his mouth and the snark came pouring out. The old offense as a defense ploy usually worked like a charm for him, but it didn't faze Maggie McCann. She stood at the bar, her emerald eyes shooting off sparks of fiery indignation. Her lips trembled, and he nearly doubled over to stave off the urge to kiss them into stillness.

An image of her pressed up against the bar flashed in his mind's eye. His mouth on her throat, his knee pressing the full skirt of her dress between her legs, his hands overfloweth-ing with Maggie....

Thankfully, the star of the show managed to squelch the vision when she babbled some crap about it taking two people to make a marriage work. Tom had to shove his hands into his pockets to keep from shaking her. Hard. He wanted to shake her, and not just because she was naïve enough to believe the platitudes she was spewing. He could see it in her eyes—the sadness, the disillusionment, the loss of...innocence.

Her eyes. The innocence in her eyes punched him in the gut each time he got within ten feet of her. He wanted to scatter every single one of the pins holding that crimson mane in a sleek, sophisticated twist. He ached to plunge his hands into the flames of her hair just to see if he could stand the heat.

Something flashed in her eyes when he spewed some crap about it taking only one person to blow everything to shit. They stared at one another for a heartbeat, possibly two. Then the golden lights her anger lit sputtered and died, leaving her gaze cool, dull, and flat. For one heart-stopping moment, the Maggie McCann who'd inspired countless fantasies ceased to exist. The threat that had his fight or flight instincts raging had been neutralized. He should have been cheering, but when she murmured her excuses and turned away, he felt oddly bereft.

Her curt dismissal and sudden departure hurt more than he cared to admit. Then, she paused to give the shithead who'd been groping her ass a toe piercing and a piece of her mind, and he couldn't help but laugh. For the first time in he didn't know how long, he laughed. For real. It gathered strength low in his belly, bludgeoned its way through his chest, bubbled up in his throat and burst forth like a geyser.

Those lush hips swayed as she hurried away, a siren song so seductive no mere human could resist. Tom had no choice but to chase after her. He followed her through the crowd, his eyes fixed on the black satin bow tied at the nape of her neck. After he shook the pins from her hair, he'd untie that bow with his teeth and peel that good girl out of her bad girl dress….

Tom called her name, an easy apology ready on his tongue, but it died on his lips when he looked into her eyes. Everything he ever thought he knew crumbled under his Bruno Maglis. Tiny pebbles loosened under his soles when Sean confessed the decay of his marriage. The dust of a hundred half-hearted attempts at relationships made it hard to find his footing. The undisguised pain in Maggie's eyes made him slip, and her harsh assessment of his treatment of her over the years left him teetering on the brink. His hand closed around her elbow and he led her from the ballroom, terrified that if he let go he'd stumble over his own feet.

Ironic that feeling completely off balance was what led him to be balanced on a stool in the dim lobby bar, staring into his scotch and listening with half an ear as Maggie rambled. She spent too many precious minutes dissecting the demise of Tracy and Sean's marriage. He didn't want to hear it. Not just because it hurt to think about it, but because the sharp-edged tone of her voice sliced him to ribbons.

Old habits are hard to break. Tom fell back on the safety net he'd employed for a decade and a half and avoided looking directly at her. Instead, he stared into his scotch, nodding along with whatever she was saying, grunting a response every now and again, and pretending he wasn't imagining birds, bunnies, and other small woodland creatures helping her dress. And undress.

He tossed back his drink and signaled the bartender for another round, letting her go on, listening to her trample all over the only common ground they had. Still, her shocking cynicism gave him hope. He wasn't buying into it, but he'd go along if it got him what he wanted.

And maybe, if she could cling to that tiny spark of skepticism, maybe it could work between them. At least, for a little while. She couldn't be as good as she seemed. Any woman who exuded such raw, earthy sensuality had to be at least a little bad. And he wanted her bad. Really bad.

He scowled at the tragically misplaced canister lighting above the bar, forcing a slight smile when the bartender replaced their empty glasses with another hit of liquid courage. He reached for his glass, surreptitiously nudging the votive on the bar a little closer to Maggie.

"I just…I don't know…" She trailed off, reaching for her wine glass.

The desolation in her voice snagged his attention. He yanked his gaze from the delicate hand cradling the oversized bowl of the glass and focused on her profile. Bingo. Candlelight played over her features, warming cool, creamy skin and picking up pale freckles dancing across her nose. Her hair outshone the cabernet she sipped. Blackened lashes brushed ginger brows when she turned to face him.

"You don't know what? Did Tracy say something?" The question popped out of his mouth before he could cloak the demand in a more palatable tone. Her eyes widened and he winced, cursing the years he'd spent dredging the truth from recalcitrant spouses and their counsel. "I mean, Sean still seems a little hopeful," he offered, hoping it would soften her up enough to spill.

"Tracy didn't say anything other than she was unhappy." She swirled the rich red wine in her glass. The corners of her mouth twisted into a wry smile. She toasted him with the glass then raised it to her lips. "Proving you can't really have it all," she mumbled into her wine.

A frown tugged at his brows. Her remark should have soothed him like a balm. Instead, it rankled. "Maybe it's just a rough patch. Maybe they'll get past it," he said, trying to inject more hope into his tone than he held in his heart.

She snorted softly and fixed him with a bland stare. "She told me they haven't had sex in over two years."

His wince bloomed into a full-blown grimace. "Did *not* need to know that."

Oh hell. Frickin' Snow White was sitting next to him boiling sixteen years of marriage down to that one cold, hard fact. Her conclusion was so much like his own it scared him. Like watching Glenn Close preparing poached Easter Bunny.

But she was right. It was inevitable. The only way any marriage lasts is mutual apathy. Flames burned down. Some people could rouse the embers, but others let them turn to ash. Some were okay with that and others weren't. A giant fist squeezed his heart. He ran a hand down his left arm, checking for telltale tingles. He blew out a breath when he concluded he'd live to see another day.

It's not like he believed in happily ever after. Life didn't work that way. People lie, cheat, steal, and leave. He learned that lesson at ten, and his beliefs were shored up every day he stepped foot into his office. But women like Maggie were meant to wear aprons and pearls and vacuum in high heels. They weren't supposed to run a background check on Prince Charming. They shouldn't expect the villain to win. She shouldn't be like him.

This was bad. Very bad.

Mustering every skill he'd honed in courtrooms and Friday night poker games, he wiped all expression from his face, raised his glass to take another pull, and drained the fiery contents in one long gulp.

****

His lips pressed against the rim of the glass and a hot surge of lust nearly choked her. She swallowed it, forcing the heat into her belly. The tip of his tongue picked up a stray drop and the heat wave rolled steadily southward. She shifted on her stool, trying to wiggle away the sensation.

He turned toward her, his knee brushing hers under the bar. The warmth of his skin seeped through the fabric of his pants. Before he could pull away, she turned too. "Let's talk about something else. Anything else."

"God, you're beautiful."

His voice came in a low, husky rasp and she met his gaze, an amused smile curving her lips. "Are you drunk?"

"No," he answered too quickly. Her smile widened and he shook his head. "Not that drunk."

She held her thumb and forefinger a centimeter apart. "Just a little drunk?"

He laughed and nudged her fingers a little further apart, a boyish smile transforming the hard lines of his face. Maggie bit her lip and rocked back, putting what she hoped would be a safe distance between them. She reached for her glass and shot him a bright smile she hoped covered the singing of her nerves.

"You look like Patrick when you laugh," she observed, referring to his eldest nephew.

Undistracted, he reached for her. His hand cupped the nape of her neck, crushing the bow that held her dress in place. She felt him tug one of the pins holding her hair. "Beautiful, dangerous Maggie McCann."

"Tom…" She caught his hand before he could work the pin loose. Pulling his hand into her lap, she gave his fingers a gentle squeeze before releasing them. "Maybe we should get you a cab."

His hand closed over her thigh. The heat of his palm threatened to singe the satin of her dress. "Are you coming with me?"

Maggie sniffed, checking the air for smoke but coming up with scotch. She deftly removed his hand from her thigh. "I'm too old for you, Tom."

His eyebrows shot up in surprise then collapsed into a frown. "You aren't older than me," he said, clearly puzzled.

"No, but I'm a helluva lot older than most of your girls."

A roguish smile curved those sculpted lips. Heat tingled in her cheeks. Her breath caught in her chest. Her nipples beaded as temptation arrowed straight to the empty, aching spot between her legs. Maggie closed her eyes and allowed herself just one moment to wallow in the wine and want swirling in her belly. It clouded her mind, blurring the sharp edges of reality. The wicked promise she saw in his eyes beckoned to her. He was everything she'd spent a lifetime avoiding.

She clamped down on her lip and raised her eyebrows. He matched her accusing stare with such bland innocence she threw her head back and laughed.

He moved in again. This time his hand closed over her knee. His thumb traced lazy circles on slippery fabric. The crinoline sewn into the dress teased the sensitive crease at the back of her leg. "How do you know anything about most of my girls?"

"I own a spa and salon." Hating the breathlessness she heard in her own voice, she swallowed hard and pinned him with a glare. "Women talk. How does it feel to be the Corbin Bernsen of Chicago law?"

He chuckled and shook his head. "First, I have a lot more hair, and second, I don't Arnie Becker my clients."

"You have to admit, it's a pretty good comparison."

Tom shook his head more adamantly. "No, I don't have to admit anything."

"Pleading the fifth, counselor?"

"How 'bout I throw myself on your mercy?"

She wet her lips, watching his gaze follow the path of her tongue. "Is that what the kids are calling it these days?"

That low, sexy laugh reverberated through her body. His fingers smoothed the creases he'd pressed into her dress. "Maggie, Maggie," he murmured. Those midnight eyes peered at her from under dark lashes. That playful smile flirted at his lips. "Don't you ever want to be just a little bad?"

Oh, Christ on a cracker. Wasn't that the million-dollar question? Want. It's never been a question of want. She grabbed her glass and slurped greedily at her wine. Closing her eyes, she tried to block him out. It was a half-hearted attempt to think straight. But, oh, she didn't want to think straight. She didn't want to be smart, or sensible, or even borderline good. There had been too many safe dates for drinks with the possibility of dinner. She was too impatient to wait for the end of that first date for a dry, undemanding kiss, or the third date for an uninspiring tumble. She wanted more. Now.

She flipped the clasp on her evening bag and pretended to search through the sparse contents. The heat of his gaze warmed her cheeks. She wanted this. She wanted him. Just for one night. Maggie snapped the bag shut with a decisive click. No more waiting. No more wanting. Hadn't she just decided to take action? Hadn't she just spent the last week of her life tossing aside her hopes and dreams and cooking up plans and schemes?

In a few short months, the years of yearning might be a thing of the past. This time next year, the possibilities she thought were no longer possible could be a reality, and that reality would change everything forever. Being good had gotten her nowhere. Her cabernet-coddled common sense had long since passed out. She wanted everything a guy like Tom Sullivan had to offer, and what he was offering her was a night she would never forget.

Maggie drew on her bottom lip as she turned toward him again. Placing her hand high on his thigh, she leaned in and released her lip with a soft pop. His eyes dropped to her mouth, lingering there for a moment before they were caught in the gravitational pull of her cleavage. She laughed and gave his leg a slight squeeze. His gaze popped back up to meet hers.

Hot breath tickled her wet lips—hers, his, it hardly mattered which. She blinked slowly, and his eyes darkened with awareness. Raising one hand to cup his cheek, she smiled when the muscle in his jaw tensed and jumped.

She moved a little closer, her lips hovering a mere inch from his. "Oh, Sully, you have no idea how good I can be when I'm bad."

****

Nothing like the smooth swizzle of Chivas to shift a guy's worldview. Sheila wanted him to go for women more age appropriate? Well, he wanted to be inappropriate, and he couldn't give a good goddamn how old Maggie McCann happened to be. This could be wrong. All wrong. But damn, following her out the door of that hotel felt damn good.

Looked good too. Her hips swayed, but it wasn't the practiced swish of a runway wannabe. No, Maggie moved with the rolling grace of a woman born to have that killer body. She reminded him of the women in those old movies his mother used to watch. A dame. A broad. A woman with a capital 'whoa'.

He stumbled off the curb and into the cab beside her. She laughed, rich and husky, more potent than the whisky burning in his belly and far more intoxicating. "Maybe I should just hand you over to your doorman."

He struggled to straighten his suit coat. "Don't have a doorman. Just a cranky old lady who lives in the apartment below."

"Huh." Maggie sniffled. "Definitely pegged you for the doorman type."

Cracked vinyl creaked when he shifted closer, draping his arm over the back of the seat and nuzzling the tender, pink shell of her ear. "Maybe I'm not what you think."

"I think you're drunk, and I'm pretty sure the cab driver isn't clairvoyant," she retorted. "Damen and Division, please," she called through the Plexiglas window.

"Clark and Armitage," he countered.

"I'm going home."

The stubborn tilt of her chin did him in. He pulled a pin from the sleek coil at the nape of her neck. "With me," he whispered, brushing his lips to the corner of her jaw when she shivered.

"Which is it?" the driver snapped.

He met her wary gaze, holding it as long as he could bear without flinching. "Don't break my heart, Maggie."

"You have no heart."

Her voice was thin and soft, but her jaw was delectably firm. He dove for the safety of sweet skin. He knew how to handle that. "Oh, I have one." Pressing her palm to his chest he whispered, "Come home with me, Maggie." The organ in question thrummed against his ribcage when she blinked her assent. He pulled those delicate fingertips to his lips and turned toward the driver. "Clark and Armitage."

The cab shot from the curb, throwing her into his side. His arm closed around her, holding her close. He wasn't a fool and he was far from immune to the soft, curve of her breast pressing against his chest. He also couldn't help but notice she was damn close to wearing out the snap on the tiny little purse she carried.

"Maggie?"

"Hmm?"

"What do women put in these little things?" he asked, gently removing the purse from her fidgeting fingers.

"Lipstick. ID. A little cash…"

"I always wondered."

She glanced at him from under her lashes. "Did you?"

Tom set the purse in his own lap and shook his head, crooking a finger beneath her chin. She gazed up at him, wide-eyed and wary again. "No. I don't really give a damn."

Her pink tongue darted out to wet her lips. "Yeah, I know you don't."

He wanted to speak—to refute her claim, to prove she didn't know jack squat about him—only the fear that she might be right spurred him into action. He did the one thing he swore he'd never do. He kissed Maggie McCann.

Good God, her lips were soft. Full and plush. The kiss lingered, unhurried and unending. The slick gloss she wore tasted like toasted marshmallow. He savored the corners of her mouth. His tongue brushed her full lower lip and those delicious lips parted. The tang of wine on her tongue made him hum low in his throat.

"Tom," she breathed as they separated.

His fingers grazed the corner of her jaw and slid to the pulse throbbing in her throat. He scooted forward on the slippery seat, unable to resist pressing his lips to that delicious spot. "Yeah?"

She blinked. Her fingernails scraped lightly along his jaw. "I swore I'd never sleep with you."

The words hit him like a splash of ice water. He'd never forced his attentions on a woman. Hell, he'd never even had to coax one. Much. Stunned, he pulled back and met her gaze. "Did you say Damen and Division?"

"Not that it was ever an issue before," she went on as if she hadn't heard him.

Flopping back against the seat, he pushed his hand through his hair. "Maggie, listen—"

"No, I get it. I'm not your type, and frankly, you aren't mine either."

His blood pounded in his ears. "I'm not?"

"I mean…no offense, but I've never been into the guys who are into themselves."

A laugh escaped before he could corral it. The chuckle burned like acid on his tongue. "Okay, I'll try not to be offended by that." He tossed her purse into her lap and rapped on the cloudy partition, startling the driver from his Armenian Idol audition rehearsal. "Change of plans. Two stops. Drop the lady at Division and Damen first."

Maggie slid to the far side of the cab, eying him warily as he tugged on his suit jacket then straightened his tie. "You have to admit, you have a bit of a reputation."

"Oh, I'll even admit I earned it," he grumbled, turning his glare on the passing traffic. "The hard way."

"So dirty," she murmured.

Click…click…click. Again with the clasp on the purse. The damn thing would be worn out before they even made it out of the Loop. If he didn't toss it out of the cab first. He glanced over and saw her gnawing that luscious bottom lip. A surge of anger and envy bubbled up inside him. "I'm not gonna jump you," he growled.

Her eyes grew round as saucers. "I didn't think you would."

"No?"

"I don't think you're a complete asshole, Tom."

Her tone made him want to prove her wrong, but he sucked it up. "You mean I only made partial asshole status? What do I have to do to up my score?"

She shot him a dark look. "You're getting there now."

"You know what, Maggie? You're right. I'm an arrogant, self-absorbed, asshole misogynist suffering from a terminal case of Peter Pan Syndrome."

"Wow. Someone beat me to the punch."

"Many, many people have beaten you to the punch." He stopped to give his scotch-addled brain a moment to catch up with his mouth. "You know what? It doesn't really matter." He blew out a tired sigh, propped his elbow on the door, and rested his head against the heel of his hand.

Maggie snorted. "Is it really that easy for you? That's it? You move on to the next contestant?"

"No means no, Maggie. A guy doesn't need a G.E.D. to learn that lesson."

"I didn't say no," she pointed out, turning to face him.

"Well, hell, I don't want you breaking promises to yourself over me. I think we both know I'm not worth it," he said snidely.

She clammed up and turned her attention to the buildings and businesses whizzing past her window. Eastern European pop drifted through the speaker holes in the partition, saving them from total silence. Tom rubbed his forehead and wished he could switch it off.

"Fuck it," she muttered.

His head swiveled. She turned back to him and he blinked, still trying to ascertain if he heard her correctly. "What?"

“I said fuck it,” she enunciated.

He couldn’t stifle his laugh. Snow White just dropped the f-bomb in the back of a smelly gypsy cab. He had to laugh, and his laughter sent her eyebrows winging for her hairline. Tom tried to muffle his mirth, but she was just so damn incongruous with her neat twist of auburn hair and evening bag clutched primly in her lap.

She stared at him, those green cat’s eyes light with a mischievous glow that should have warned him. “Fuck me.”

Those full lips deliberately formed both syllables and his laughter croaked in his throat. His mouth went dry. He had to remind himself to blink. “Huh?”

Yes, brilliant. He was a master of seduction. A regular fucking wordsmith. Luckily, she didn’t seem to care. Maggie slid across the cracked seat and winced. She raised her luscious bottom, rubbed the spot where a piece of cracked vinyl snagged her nylons, and moved closer, plopping herself down right next to him on the rump-sprung seat.

Tom pressed against the door, frantically trying to recall if he’d slammed it hard enough when he crawled in after her. Her thigh brushed his. The hem of her dress inched up over her knee. Black satin swayed with the weight of her breasts when she leaned in closer. She brushed her thumb over his bottom lip and his autonomic system went on strike. It would have been complete and total system failure if not for the telltale tingling in his crotch.

Her breath grazed his lips and his elbow slipped from the door. She held him still with one knuckle curled beneath his jaw, her thumb pressing into his chin. “Fuck me,” she whispered.

Tom would have swallowed his tongue if he wasn’t acutely aware he might need it soon. His dick practically jumped for joy.

“It’s perfect. I don’t need any entanglements right now, and you avoid them like the plague,” she continued. As if he gave a damn about her reasoning. "One night. You. Me." Her thumb brushed his lip again, tugging it into a pout. "I'm gonna be bad this one time, and then I'll be so good," she promised.

Her lips touched his in the barest of kisses. The artful tendril that curled at her ear tickled his cheek. His lungs expanded, dragging in her cinnamon-tinged scent. His brain screamed at him, demanding negotiation. "What if one night's not enough?"

"One night."

She kissed him again, the tip of her tongue teasing the corners of his mouth. She traced the seam of his lips, and he was held captive by one of his favorite weapons. Sweet, slow seduction. She tried to pull away, but he caught her. His fingers sank into her hair, mussing the smooth coil. His thumb caressed her cheek. "Counteroffer…"

"Hmm?"

"One night and one day."

Maggie reared back. "One day?"

He held firm, drawing her close once more. His palm closed over her knee. He teased the sensitive nylon-clad crease behind her leg with the pad of his middle finger. "Tomorrow's Sunday. Tonight might not be long enough."

"Long enough for what?" she asked with a breathless laugh.

"Everything," he murmured. "Everything, Maggie."

Her laughter drifted away and her smile faded. She wet her lips then nodded. "One night, one day."

He couldn't resist pushing for a little more. He checked his watch then turned his wrist so she could read the dial. "Twenty-four hours from now."

"Now it's twenty-four hours?"

The cab pulled to the curb. The pink flush coloring her cheeks was only enhanced by the glow of the red light. He brushed his thumb over the heated skin then caressed the smattering of freckles dusting her nose with one finger, drawing it down to her moist, parted lips. "You won't regret it."

Maggie averted her eyes, fumbling with the clasp on her purse again. She extracted a twenty and inched forward to push it through the slot for the driver.

"No. I'll get it." Tom fumbled in his coat pocket for his wallet, but she pressed her hand to his chest to stop him.

Meeting his gaze solemnly, she shook her head. "I'm not cooking, so you're covering take-out for the next twenty-four hours."

He plucked the bill from her fingers, tucked it back in the ridiculous little purse, and snapped it shut once and for all. "Tell me there's decent Chinese around here," he mumbled, thumbing through his wallet for the fare.

"I have it on speed dial."

He shoved some cash through the slot. "Thai?"

"To die for."

Tom opened the door and planted one foot in the gutter to keep his mind company. Then a terrifying thought struck. All the merit badges he'd ever earned scouting girls could be ripped from his grasp. Just when he was finally going to get his hands on Maggie McCann, she could slip through his fingers. His heart clenched and he froze, turning to look at her. "Twenty-four hour pharmacy?" She nudged him and he crawled from the cab, mentally kicking his own ass as he offered her a steadying hand.

"Got you covered there too," she purred, brushing past him onto the sidewalk.

The cab took off and Tom hopped to the curb, a grin splitting his face. "You're a hell of a girl, Maggie McCann."

****

Maggie made it about twenty steps into the block-long walk before she started having second thoughts. He chuckled, and her head jerked up. She glanced up to see if he'd somehow picked up on her misgivings, but his gaze was riveted on her shoes.

"I always wondered how women walk in those things."

Tom wrapped his arm around her waist, snuggling her up against his side. The second thoughts were chased off by a swarm of butterflies taking flight in her stomach. "Kind of like the purse thing?"

He laughed again and his warm fingers closed around her ribcage. "No, this is for real."

"Practice," she murmured.

A gust of cool November wind cut through her thin wrap, carrying the stench of uncollected trash. She turned her head, burying her nose in the lapel of his jacket and inhaled deeply. The scent of expensive cologne, aged whisky, and a hint of bar soap made her head swim. His lips brushed her hair, and she nearly blew years of training by tripping over her feet.

"Easy," he crooned, tightening his hold on her.

Easy. Oh God, she was being too easy. "It's just up ahead," she murmured. "The red awning."

"The Glass Slipper?" That low, husky laugh rumbled again. "Someone got a Cinderella complex?"

A cab cruised toward them, its light gleaming like a beacon. Maggie briefly contemplated hailing the driver and shoving Tom into the back seat. "Watch it, Peter Pan. I can still ship you off to Never-Neverland."

"Or is it because you go in feeling like a drudge and come out a princess?"

Her steps faltered. She spared a glance at his profile and found him giving the rouge red awning careful consideration. The cab slipped past. "Something like that," she murmured. When his serious frown gave way to that boyish smile, her heart skipped in her chest. "Been keeping up with your fairy tales, have you?"

"Erin suckered me into taking her to Disney on Ice every year for five years running," he confessed.

A startled laugh tripped from her lips. "Disney on Ice?"

He slowed as they approached the door. "Hey, she liked it."

"I bet she did." The thought of Tom Sullivan sitting through hours of costumed figure skating to make his niece happy made her stomach flip. She pulled her key from her purse and nodded to the door to the left of the salon's entrance. "Sucker."

He gently took the key from her hand and inserted it into the deadbolt lock. "Yeah, well, what can I say? I am the ultimate uncle."

His cocky grin was infectious. She found herself returning it automatically. "I bet you are."

He stood aside, letting her lead the way. Maggie started for the narrow staircase, but her step wavered when she heard him jiggle the door to be sure the locks caught. Within seconds his hands were on her hips. Hot, moist breath seeped through her wrap, sending shivers down her spine. Biting her lip, she resisted the urge to dash up the steps, knowing that would put her ass right at eye level. Not her best angle.

"This is nice."

She ignored the obvious leer in his voice, opting to play oblivious. "Angelini Restoration did the renovation work," she said, referring to the company his uncle founded and his brother now ran.

"Uh-huh."

"The place was pretty much trashed, but Sean managed a minor miracle," she babbled.

"He's good at those."

The door at the top of the steps loomed. She searched her memory, trying to recall the exact state of her apartment. There were clothes strewn all over the bedroom floor. Had she changed her sheets this week? Would he care? Oh God, had she cleaned the litter box? She hesitated at the threshold, jingling her keys in her palm.

"As a matter of fact, it might be pretty trashed right now," she said, sneaking a glance at him from under her lashes as she separated her house key from the rest. "I usually clean on Sundays."

Tom ducked his head, grazing her cheek with the barest of kisses and pulling the pin he'd loosened earlier from her hair. "Unless I'm gonna need a tracking device to follow you through a maze of stacked up newspapers and magazines, I couldn't really give a damn."

She sucked in a breath, trying to ignore the riot of tingles his touch incited. Her fingers trembled when she slid the key into the lock. He pulled a curl loose from her sleek up-do. Maggie made a stab at the second lock as he wound her hair around his finger. The heat gathering low in her belly coiled a bit tighter.

He moved closer. The hard planes of his chest and stomach teased her back. Her bottom nestled against his thighs. His hand covered hers and the key slid home. The doorknob slipped in her damp palm. The warped wood was stuck, as always.

Flashing a sheepish smile, she nudged him away with her elbow. He conceded the space, his eyebrows shooting up as she threw her hip into the effort. The door swung open wide. "Takes a magic touch."

The surprise in his violet eyes melted into admiration then flared to something hotter, deeper, more urgent. He advanced on her. "Do it again."

Maggie stumbled into the apartment, her eyes locked on his. He stepped into her space, his stride confident and purposeful. A tinkling laugh gave her nervousness away. She wanted to clamp a hand over her mouth, but a low growl cut the tension like a machete.

Tom whirled, searching out the source of the threat. Keeping her knees primly pressed together, Maggie lowered herself to the floor and ran her hand over her cat's arched back. "Fred this is Tom. Don't eat him," she whispered to the cat then straightened. "Tom, this is Fred."

The two men in her life sized each other up. She was pleased when Tom met her rotund roommate's unblinking stare without a flinch. "Fred," he acknowledged with a nod.

Fred turned his attention to Maggie, winding his way around her ankles. "I should give him a little food. Otherwise, he won't leave us alone."

Her wrap slid from her shoulders. One end drifted to the floor when she tossed her purse onto the hall table. Fred promptly pounced. A stack of unopened mail slithered from the table, falling to the floor with a splat. She gently but firmly removed the butter-soft cashmere from the cat's claws. She looked up and found Tom grinning at her. "What?"

"You're a slob, Cinderella."

"I told you I clean on Sundays."

She spun away from the cocky man crowding her entry and sashayed toward the kitchen, hoping to distract him from her lack of housekeeping. It worked like a charm. She pulled a can of cat food from the cabinet, simultaneously opening the drawer that held her fancy new can opener. When she removed the opener from the drawer his fingers closed around hers again.

"Let me."

His breath stirred the tendrils he'd loosened. She stared at the counter, trying to blink away the swirl of desire and confusion his proximity stirred. He freed the opener from her grasp but didn't step back. Instead he planted one shiny shoe on either side of hers, reached around her for the can of cat food, and set to work, trapping her in his embrace.

"You keep taking things away from me," she observed.

"A princess shouldn't have to do the drudge work."

"I'm no princess." She felt him tense then the lid popped free from the can. Tom set the can opener on the counter. She hoped for a little breathing room, but at the same time she prayed he wouldn't give it to her. Her prayers were answered.

Tom snatched the can from the counter and slid it across the floor. Fred chased after his late-night snack, but Maggie stood still. Waiting. Wanting. He was just behind her, his body warm, solid, and tempting. Oh-so-tempting.

Without warning, he pushed both hands into her hair, loosening the bobby pins that anchored the elaborate twist. A moan tangled with a groan and cushioned by a sigh filled the room. A full ten seconds passed before she realized it came from her.

His breathing grew rough and raspy, but his fingers gentled. His lapels brushed her shoulder blades with each rough inhalation, sending shivers down her spine. He plucked each pin from her hair one by one. Hairspray starched tresses tumbled to her shoulders, their natural wave tamed by hours of captivity. She closed her eyes when she heard the patter of pins pinging off the floor.

Long, strong fingers massaged her scalp, trailed the length, and fanned tickling ends across her bare back and shoulders. "Your hair is beautiful."

Unabashed desire weighed his words with knee-buckling gravity. Maggie clutched the counter and bowed her head, surrendering to the master. "Keep talking."

He gathered her hair with both hands, winding the ends around his fists as he leaned forward, letting his weight pin her to the counter. His breath bubbled over the exposed skin of her neck, raising goose bumps. She felt him tug at the bow tied at the nape of her neck. It wasn't until the knot gave way that she realized his hands were still tangled in her hair. His tongue brushed her skin, lifting the fabric. Moments later, he growled low in his throat as the black satin fell away from her breasts, pooling on the counter in front of her. She blinked in astonishment, gaping at the inky fabric.

His mouth claimed the spot the bow had covered. He drew her flesh against his tongue, sucking gently. This time she flat-out moaned, and she'd admit as much before a judge and jury. His teeth scraped the sensitive skin and his hands tightened in her hair. Tom unfurled his fingers and slipped away.

A strangled sob rose in her throat. Her mangled hair swirled around her shoulders. She relinquished her grip on the counter and groped behind her, determined to hang on to him. Her fingers closed around his forearm. He chuckled. The vibration of the laugh boomeranged inside her.

"Not a princess," he murmured, nipping playfully at the curve of one shoulder.

"No," she breathed.

His hot, wet tongue swirled around the tip of her spine. He began to slide down, licking, kissing, and teasing his way to the thick elastic strap that bound her long-line bra at her waist. Maggie flew into panic mode. Visions of her writhing on the bed earlier that night sprang to mind. The span of super-sucking-spandex encasing her body from waist to mid-thigh could be a deal breaker.

He knelt behind her, his hands spanning her waist. "Turn around." Maggie swallowed hard, squeezing her eyes shut as she forced her feet to move, turning to face him. His thumbs traced the boning of the bra, skirting along her stomach to the curve of her breasts. "Maggie."

When had her name become a question, an order, a plea? She clung to the safety of her closed eyelids, desperately searching for an excuse, any excuse, to excuse herself long enough to lose the gargantuan girdle he was about to encounter.

The blunt tips of his fingers pressed into the curve of her waist. "Maggie," he said more forcefully. She pried her eyes open only to find herself rendered speechless at the sight of Tom Sullivan kneeling before her. The desire in his eyes scorched her, a bright blue flame setting her blood to simmer. "Not a princess." He pressed a hot, open-mouthed kiss to the silky fabric covering her stomach. "A goddess."

The words soaked through to her skin. Maggie broke, giving in to the urge that gnawed at her since he caught up to her in that fairy-lit ballroom. She smoothed the tuft of sable-brown hair that sprung up at his crown.

The tips of his ears turned pink. He smiled and pressed his nose to her stomach. "Cowlick," he murmured against her skin.

"That's okay," she whispered. "I'm wearing the biggest, ugliest, super-sucker-inner, granny panties you've ever seen."

Tom reared back, his face lighting with that boyish smile. "Are you kidding me?"

She rolled her eyes. "Why would I kid about that?"

He dove for her skirt, batting the froth of satin-covered crinoline out of his way. His hand closed over her thigh, sliding higher until he hit the hem of her body shaper. Tom closed his eyes, a rough chuckle rumbling up from his chest. She planted her hands on his shoulders and tried to shove him away, but he just shook his head and fell forward pressing his cheek to the crumpled bodice of her dress. "Oh God, I'm sick…"

Panic shot through her. She pushed harder, trying to pry him from her legs before the Chivas hit the fan. "Sick?"

"Not that kind of sick," he protested. Rocking back on his knees, he grasped her wrists and pried them from his shoulders. He stared up at her, waiting patiently until she dared to meet his eyes. "Don't you see, Maggie? For fifteen years I've been trying not to think about getting into your pants, and now that I'm here, you're telling me I'll need a crowbar to get you out of them."

"You won't need a crowbar—"

"And the sick part about it is I couldn't be more turned on if you told me you were naked under there," he said, cutting off her protests.

Maggie raised a cautious eyebrow. "Yeah?"

Rising from his knees with a groan, he caught her lips in a hard, urgent kiss that left them both breathless. When he pulled away, Tom glanced over his shoulder. "We don't have much time. I've gotta get you out of those things."

Maggie pushed away from the counter. "It won't take that long."

"Bedroom. Stat. I only have twenty-four hours," he pressed, urging her from the room.

"Or, I could tell you to leave now."

Tom shook his head and kissed her again, propelling along the narrow hall to the bedroom. "You can't do that. You need me."

She paused at the open doorway to survey the wreckage. "I do?"

Oblivious to the mess, he nudged her into the room, walking her back until her thighs bumped her unmade bed. She dropped to the mattress in a swirl of excess clothing. He shrugged out of his suit coat, yanking his arms from the sleeves and trying to land another kiss all at the same time. Stumbling, he shook the jacket from his wrists and dropped to his knees in front of her again, a wicked grin playing at those sculpted lips.

"Yep. You need me, Maggie." He cupped her calves, sliding his hands higher and higher. "You're trapped. Girdle lock. Like gridlock, but far more frustrating." A rakish grin lit his face. "Lucky for you, I've got the jaws of life."

Chapter Six

Sunlight teased his eyelids, but he resisted. Pigeons cooed on the windowsill. A low, rumbling motor hummed. Satiated and supremely comfortable, Tom saw no reason to invite the outside world into his cocoon. The dull ache in his back tried to nudge him into moving, but a warm, soft weight on his chest anchored him to the bed. He sniffed then smiled, remembering where he was and why he was waking up in sheets that were anything but April fresh. He breathed a sigh of relief. He wouldn't have to fire his cleaning lady after all.

A smooth arch caressed his instep. Concentrating all his energy, he raised one hand from the mattress then lowered it to his chest, itching to pet Maggie's silky hair. Instead, he got a handful of fur.

The motor cut out and Tom's eyes popped open. He stared into slumberous green eyes, but they weren't the pair he expected. "Fred," he croaked.

The cat blinked and he treated the third member of their ménage to a desultory scratch behind the ears. The motor roared to life again, vibrating through his chest like a Harley Davidson. Fred stared him down. "I'm not scared of you, cat," he whispered.

"Yes, you are." The muffled reply came from deep in the pillow next to his.

Tom chuckled. "Maybe a little." He stroked the cat's enormous head then added another ear scratch for good measure. "I don't suppose he's been declawed...."

Beside him, Maggie stirred, pushing a mass of sleep-crumpled red waves from her face. "Don't make any sudden moves."

The husky timbre of her voice was like a shot of adrenaline to the heart. Sluggish blood warmed and raced for the southern hemisphere. His moves weren't as sudden as they would have been twenty years before, but all in all, Tom was fairly impressed with his body's response to her call of action. He turned his head, meeting a much more desirable set of grass green eyes. "Too late."

Maggie rolled onto her back. The tangled and twisted sheet molded to the curves of her body. One silky-smooth leg escaped. She raised her arms over her head and the sheet slipped, clinging to the rosy tips of her breasts as she stretched.

Fred emitted a low growl of warning, and Tom quickly ran his hand over the cat's head. "Sorry, big guy, got distracted."

Maggie clutched the sheet, pulling it up to her throat with a giggle. He shook his head. "Too late for that too."

She blushed. A delicious pink crept up her throat and bloomed in her cheeks. He would have chased it with his lips if her bulky bodyguard wasn't pinning him down.

"Sleep okay?" she asked.

"Better than okay."

Tom made a grab for the edge of the sheet with his left hand, but she held firm. The giggle turned to a sultry laugh as she wriggled from his reach. "Nuh-uh. You have to go get breakfast."

"Breakfast?"

"There's a Polish bakery around the corner."

He blinked at her then Fred leaned into his palm, demanding the return of his attentions. "You don't have any food in the house?"

"I usually grocery shop on Sundays too."

"I can make us some eggs, if you've got them," he offered.

She shook her head. "Fred will be having salmon."

"Is it smoked?"

"No, and you can probably tell he's not big on sharing."

His eyes narrowed to slits. "You only lured me up here so I'd feed you."

She let the sheet fall, revealing a tantalizing hint of the tops of those glorious breasts. "Possibly. I want a bear claw and the biggest coffee you can get. Maybe two."

"If I wanted to starve I coulda stayed home," he grumbled to Fred.

Maggie snickered, rolling onto her side and snuggling into her pillow. "I'll be right here waiting for you."

He swallowed hard then nodded. "Anything else?"

"The Sunday paper."

Tom cast a wary glance at his feline friend. "What do I do about the enforcer?"

Maggie's smile rivaled the sun streaming through the slats of the blinds. She reached for Fred, deftly lifting the gazillion-pound cat and pulling the lucky bastard into her warm embrace. "There. I won't let the mean, old pussy-cat hurt you," she cooed, stroking the length of Fred's body.

Smug. He'd swear the cat's smile turned smug when he stretched out beside her. Tom glowered at the pair of them. Maggie met his gaze, her lips twitching into the same smug smile.

"Bear claw, huh?" he asked, swinging his legs over the side of the bed. He hung his head for a moment, pressing his knuckles into the mattress as he tried to gather his wits. Her fingernails skittered along the length of his spine and his head swiveled. She smiled and drew back, pressing her palm to the crown of Fred's fat head and burying those delicate fingers in orange fur. "Lots of almonds."

"Got it." Tom rummaged through the knots of discarded clothing on the floor until he located his pants and underwear. As he dressed, he thought about the gluttonous, gourmet, morning-after meals other women had prepared for him in the past and chuckled.

"What's so funny?" she asked.

"Nothing." He shrugged into his rumpled shirt and let the tails hang open as he bent to capture her lips in a searing kiss. "You'll be right here?"

"Why would I move? You're bringing me breakfast and the paper," she answered with a sly smile.

****

The moment the door closed behind him, Maggie launched herself from the bed. Fred yowled in protest, but she shushed him as she made a beeline for the bathroom. She peed, started the shower, squeezed toothpaste onto her brush, and popped it into her mouth before leaping into the tub. Exactly three minutes later, she wrapped a turquoise bath sheet around her body and peered into the cloudy mirror above the sink.

"Ten minutes, right?" she asked Fred. "It'll take at least ten. Fifteen or twenty if Mrs. Diminski is feeling chatty."

She yanked her blow dryer from the cabinet under the sink, jammed the plug into the wall, and bent over, shooting her wet tresses with a damaging blast of hot air. "Come on, come on," she muttered, finger combing the damp curls. A minute and a half later, she stashed the dryer under the sink and dashed back to the bedroom.

The towel slipped when she pulled the corner of the fitted sheet from the mattress. Maggie cursed under her breath and let it fall to the floor in a heap. Naked but for goose bumps, she stripped the bed then rummaged through her closet for a fresh set of sheets that weren't too flowery. She had to settle for pink rosebuds printed on ivory cotton.

The front door slammed just as she tucked the flat sheet under the end of the mattress. Maggie flung the duvet onto the bed and ignored Fred's howl of protest when she dove for the covers. "In a minute," she hissed at the bossy feline.

She plumped the pillows and propped them against the headboard, sinking against them as the lock on the apartment door tumbled. Fred leapt onto the freshly made bed and voiced his opinion in no uncertain terms. Tom appeared in the doorway holding a cardboard carry-out tray loaded with cups and a waxy bakery bag. The Sunday *Tribune* was three inches thick and tucked under his arm.

His jaw dropped and his shoulders slumped. "You said you were staying in bed."

Maggie shrugged. "No. I said I'd be right here, and here I am."

Stepping over her damp towel, he skirted the clothes strewn across the floor and slid their breakfast onto the nightstand. The newspaper hit the floor with a *splat*. The Styrofoam cup squeaked when he pried it from the carrier. He peeled the lid from the cup and handed it to her. "I didn't know how you take it, so there's sugar and cream and stuff in the bag."

The hot flush scalding her cheeks had nothing to do with the steam rising from the cup and everything to do with the virtual stranger standing beside her bed. She lowered her gaze and inhaled deeply, hoping a hit of caffeine by osmosis would help her power through the rush of Catholic guilt. Every muscle in her body ached. When she opened her eyes she thought it was a good ache, but now she wasn't so sure. Now she was sitting in bed stark naked staring at a man who didn't know it took at least two doses of Nutra-Sweet and a half-pint of milk to make coffee tolerable.

"Are you okay?"

The sincerity in his tone startled her. Her head jerked up and she blinked to clear her thoughts. "What? Yeah. I'm, uh…" Maggie took a quick sip of her coffee and grimaced when the bitter brew burned her tongue. "Waking up," she mumbled.

Tom smiled and began to unbutton his shirt. "Good."

The shirt hit the floor as he toed off his shoes. She tried not the stare. Hell, she'd been eyeballing, kissing, licking, and stroking that same bare chest for the past ten hours. The allure should have worn off by now. But it hadn't. She ogled the man as if he were a pastry in a glass case. A thatch of lustrous brown hair curled between his pecs. It straightened into silky strands of sable as it narrowed to a fine line bisecting the hard ripples of his stomach. The tempting trail disappeared into the waistband of his pants, beckoning to her like a flashing neon 'Follow Me!' sign.

Maggie tried to rein her lustful thoughts in. After all, she already tumbled into that particular rabbit hole. A couple of times. She glanced at the clock. If he didn't wuss out, she still had over thirteen hours of completely mad and astoundingly passionate tea partying to go. She needed to pace herself.

Bare-chested and beautiful, Tom moved the tray of drinks aside and opened the bakery bag. "Your bear claw, madam," he said, presenting the flaky pastry to her wrapped in a sheet of waxed paper.

"Thank you, kind sir."

Perched on the edge of the mattress, he bent to strip off his socks. In profile, the bump on his otherwise perfect nose was slightly more noticeable. She cocked her head, gazing at him intently as he sat up. He unhooked his suit pants then paused, a worried frown furrowing his brow when he caught her stare.

"Is this okay?" he asked, nodding to his pants.

"Taking them off?" She raised one shoulder in a shrug. "Why wouldn't it be okay?"

"You're looking at me funny. Do you want me to leave?"

Startled that he'd ask, she blinked. "Do you want to leave?"

"No, but…What?" He shook his head. "What's wrong?"

"Nothing's wrong. I was just looking at you."

Tom rolled his eyes. Nodded to the orange cat curled at the foot of the bed. "Wondering if you can toss me out without the help of your bodyguard?"

"Wondering how you broke your nose," she said, hoping her shrug conveyed just the right amount of nonchalance.

"Sean."

"Sean broke your nose? How?"

He chuckled. "He has a mean right."

She kept her eyes locked on him as she took a dainty bite. A flurry of tiny almond pieces freckled her chest. His gaze locked on them like a tractor beam. Maggie wet the tip of one finger and collected the stray slivers. "He hit you?"

She smiled as she sucked the tiny morsels from her finger, watching his eyes darken to indigo. "We've hit each other lots of times. That time, he got lucky."

She laughed. "He's bigger than you."

"Taller," he countered.

"Taller, bulkier, bigger."

He snorted. "Taller and bulkier, but definitely not bigger," he asserted, fixing her with a meaningful glare.

Maggie laughed. "Well, I wouldn't know about that, so I'll have to take your word for it."

Tom grinned and rubbed the bump with his knuckle. "Actually, he hit me with a two-by-four."

"I hope not on purpose."

He twisted his torso to face her, propping one knee on the bed. Maggie eyed the tiny bulge of flesh above his waistband and smiled. She plucked an almond from her pastry and popped it into her mouth, pleased with the knowledge that the studly Mr. Sullivan wasn't immune to a little middle-aged spread.

"I have my suspicions, but he claimed it was an accident. I worked for Uncle George during college and law school."

She grinned, trying to picture the delightfully rumpled but normally spit polished and urbane attorney sitting on her bed wearing a hard hat and a tool belt. "I can't picture you working construction."

His smile widened and his eyes lit with a wicked gleam. "Destruction. I was the demolition man."

She laughed. "Okay. That I can see."

"Unlike Sean, I hate the fixing, building, and restoring parts, but tearing things to pieces? I'm all over that."

Something about what he said struck a nerve. Maggie pressed her lips together, staring at the bear claw in her hand as if she were plotting her next bite, and parsing his simple statement for tone and subtext.

"Maggie?"

Her head jerked up. She met his gaze and found only frank appreciation shining in his dark blue eyes. "Hmm?"

"Pants on or off?"

"Well, if you're keeping them on, then I get your shirt," she bargained, testing out a teasing smile.

"Off," he said with a decisive nod, launching himself from the bed and fumbling with his zipper.

Maggie laughed. She had to laugh. Despite her uncertainty about his motives, she had none about her own. She needed this. She wanted him. A last hurrah. The fling to end all flings. In just a few short hours he'd be a memory. A hot, happy memory to warm cold, lonely nights.

Naked, he reclaimed his spot on the edge of the bed, bracing his arms on either side of her hips. A self-conscious blush burned her cheeks, but Maggie took a defiant bite of her pastry. A hailstorm of sliced almonds sprinkled her chest and slithered under the sheet.

"Want me to get those?"

The deep, rumbling rasp in his voice rolled through her. Her fingers closed around the flaky pastry. She snagged a sliver of almond from the corner of her mouth with the tip of her tongue then nodded slowly. "Why, yes. Yes, I do."

A devilish gleam burned in his eyes when he leaned in. Hummingbirds took flight in her stomach. His lips parted. The tip of his tongue grazed the edge of his teeth, and she held her breath.

He lunged, those sparkling white teeth sinking into the edge of her bear claw. Maggie gasped at the injustice as he consumed a third of her breakfast. Her hand jerked and she opened her mouth to protest, but the pastry sailed across the room, hit the wall, then plummeted to the floor.

A streak of orange sailed from the bed. Fred pounced on his prey, nipping and licking at the remainder with gusto.

"Look what you made me do!" Maggie cried.

The deep rumble of his laugh bounced off the bedroom walls. His chest heaved as he pressed sticky lips to the hollow at the base of her throat. Short, hot strokes of his wet tongue collected stray slivers of almond, teasing the tops of her breasts. He grasped her wrists and pressed them into the pillow, working his way back up her throat. His lips closed over the pulse throbbing beneath her ear. Her breath caught. He drew the sensitive skin into his mouth, laving it with his talented tongue. A tremulous breath seeped from her lungs.

Tom nipped her jaw. Moist, hot breath tickled her ear. "There's a cherry danish in the bag," he murmured. "Wrestle you for it."

****

A crab…No…Flower. One of those big poofy mum things guys used to give girls for the big homecoming game. Tom blinked and tried to focus the Rorschach blob, but his vision remained too blurred to make heads or tails of it. A swarm of bees buzzed in his head. He gave it an experimental shake, but they refused to be dislodged. A laugh clutched his stomach, rolling through his chest then tickling his throat, but he couldn't catch his breath. Mustering what little strength he had left, he stared at the blob. Plumbing. Rain. Roof leak. Water spot.

The rustle of paper shooed the buzzing bees. His hair scraped the cotton pillowcase. He blinked, and Maggie swam into focus.

Her cheeks glowed with a rosy flush. Acres of alabaster skin were semi-cloaked by the color comics from the Sunday paper. She chuckled and took a healthy bite of the cherry danish balanced on her fingertips. He tried to snatch it from her hand, only to be caught up short when his necktie tightened around his right wrist. She raised one knee and the flimsy newsprint draped one succulent thigh.

He gave the tie another half-hearted tug then rolled onto his side to face her. "I let you win."

Her green gaze flickered over his face and she smirked, swirling the pad of her finger in the pool of cherry glaze then popping it into her mouth. Her eyes locked on his as she slowly withdrew the damp digit. "You got a little something in exchange."

Another laugh bubbled in his belly. He clenched his abs, trying to stave it off. His muscles ached. They weren't used to this abuse. Crunches, yes. Those sadistic rowing machines at the gym they could handle. Laughing like he'd laughed in the past twelve or so hours? He couldn't remember ever laughing this much.

"Don't you want a little somethin' in return?"

His voice sounded strange to his own ears—throaty and rough. A thread of promise wound its way into the words that rolled off his tongue so easily. It was a far cry from the calm, practiced tone he employed every day. This wasn't just any day. This was a day with Maggie. And, if it was possible, the day with Maggie was proving to be even better than the night.

"I'm good." She took another huge bite of the pastry, smiling as she chewed. He almost purred like Fred when she reached over and smoothed his hair into place. "Want me to read the comics to you?"

His eyelids drooped. The warm, fuzzy buzz of post-orgasmic bliss threatened to pull him under. He struggled to keep his eyes open. He didn't want to miss a minute of his time with her and he didn't have the energy or the heart to peek at his clock. Burrowing into the pillow, he stared up at her. "You gonna untie me?"

"You've got one hand free," she pointed out.

"If you don't untie me, I'm going to assume you plan to have your way with me again." Her smile blossomed. Color bloomed in her cheeks, pretty and pink and perfect. His smile faded, and he stared at her solemnly. "Why didn't we do this a long time ago?"

The question seemed to surprise her as much as it stunned him. He wasn't exactly sure where it came from, and he didn't know if he wanted to know the answer. Maggie set the comics aside and slid down on the pillow, breaking off a chunk of pastry and holding it to his lips. Tom took it, chewing slowly as he waited for her response.

"Well, I think part of it was because you were trying to screw your way through every blonde bimbo on the north side."

"I don't do bimbos," he grumbled.

"From what I hear, you do just about anything."

He raised an eyebrow. "You don't think very highly of yourself, do you?"

Maggie shrugged and took another bite. "I know I'm an anomaly for you," she mumbled through stuffed cheeks.

He opened his mouth to retort, but a muffled buzz distracted him. For a moment he wondered if there really was a swarm of bees in the room. Maggie read the confusion on his face and nodded to the floor.

"Your phone. You forget a date today? Your phone has been seeing more action in the last hour than my vibrator has in a year."

He rolled over and glared at the crumpled suit jacket on the floor. "No, I didn't forget a date. Listen, I don't know what you think you know about me…Oh, shit!" He lunged for the phone, only to fall back on the pillow when his shoulder nearly popped out of its socket. "Crap," he grunted, fumbling with the knot in his tie.

She stared at him impassively. "You *did* forget a date?"

The frost in her voice nearly froze him to the spot. Her green eyes were cool as glass. The tail of the tie slipped free and he yanked his arm from the headboard. "With my mother," he muttered. He lurched from the bed and snagged the collar of his jacket, shaking out the worst of the wrinkles as he searched the pockets. "I was supposed to clean her gutters today."

"Gutters? You do gutters?"

The marked disbelief in her voice stung his masculine pride. He scanned the list of missed calls then glanced at the bedside clock. His mother had called six times in forty-five minutes. He pushed a hand through his hair, pulled the sheet over his crotch, and punched a button. "Yes, I can do gutters." The petulance in his tone would have embarrassed him if she wasn't staring at him with those luscious lips parted in shock. He pressed the phone to his ear and grumbled, "I can do all sorts of things."

His mother answered on the first ring. "Hi, Ma. Sorry…." He sneaked a glance at Maggie. "I got tied up trying to work out some custody thing."

That shut Maggie's mouth. Of course, those lips just curved into a smug smirk. The urge to kiss it off of her made his foot twitch with impatience. He let his mother ramble on a bit, knowing he couldn't squeeze a word in without using a machete to cut her off. Maggie plucked the Sunday comics from her lap and folded them neatly. She set them aside, slipped from the bed, and reached into the closet. He followed her every move with interest. She belted a long, fuzzy robe securely at her waist and he snapped from his stupor.

"No. Leave the ladder alone," he ordered. Running his hand over his face, he shot Maggie an apologetic glance. "I'll be there in about an hour or so." Thick terry cloth swirled around slender ankles when Maggie swept from the room with Fred hot on her heels. Tom pinched the bridge of his nose and closed his eyes, wishing he could block out the sound of his mother's voice and ignore the guilt snaking through his gut. "Sorry, Ma. Be there as soon as I can," he said then ended the call.

Tossing the sheet back, he scooped his pants and underwear from the floor and started to pull them on. Dread pooled in his belly. The abrupt end to their conversation would give Katie Sullivan plenty of ammo to unleash on him when he showed up.

He grabbed his shirt and gave it a sharp shake before shoving his arms into the sleeves. Guilt clogged his throat. His mother was old. And alone. And yes, a giant pain in his ass, but she was his mother. If he didn't show up to do the job, she was just stubborn enough to try to wrestle the ladder from her tiny garage. Then she'd fall, break a hip, and he'd never hear the end of it. Tom had learned at a young age that accommodation was the best form of self-defense.

The weight of his guilt and disappointment bogged him down. Moving in slow motion, he picked up his shoes and socks, slung his suit jacket over his arm, and padded from the bedroom in search of Maggie.

He found her in the kitchen. Her fat cat wound his way between her ankles. Flame red hair tumbled down her back. Wavy curls tangled and tousled by his hands spilled onto celery-colored terrycloth. He held his breath, allowing himself the luxury of just a few extra moments. An odd, unidentifiable ache gnawed at him.

A soft click echoed in the empty apartment. A can of cat food clattered to the counter. Maggie held an unwieldy-looking can opener aloft and grinned down at the cat. "See? I'm getting faster with it," she assured her feline friend.

Fred growled a meow and sat beside his food bowl, curling his tail around his haunches and staring up at her with barely contained exasperation.

Tom stifled a chuckle. Then he squelched a surge of lust when she bent to scrape the contents of the can into the dish. He cleared his throat. "Think that'll hold him?"

She straightened, smoothing her palm over the front of her robe. "For a few minutes," she replied, flashing a sheepish smile. Maggie turned to face him and the ache he'd felt a moment before morphed into a full-fledged pang of regret.

"I'm sorry." He stepped into the room and tossed his jacket over the back of a kitchen chair. Dropping into the seat, he released a huff of breath and looked up at her. "I have to go."

"I figured."

He shook out one of his socks and bent at his waist. "My mother can be a little high maintenance." He yanked the sock over his toes.

"I know. I've met her."

Startled, he jerked his head up to find her watching him with a small smile. She *had* met his mother. This woman he'd violated in a half dozen ways in the past fourteen hours had met his mother at least a dozen times. Tom blinked when he realized she was the only woman he'd ever been with who had the dubious honor. He busied himself with the other sock. "That's right."

"She's a piece of work," she said with a laugh.

"Putting it mildly."

"And you're her fair-haired boy."

Tom sneered as he pulled the second sock into place. He tugged at the hem of his pants and reached for a shoe. "Lucky me. Why couldn't I have inherited the Sullivan hair?"

She smiled and leaned against the counter, crossing her arms over her chest. His brother's hair had once been jet black, but not anymore. "At least you're not turning prematurely gray, like Sean."

He gave the laces a good yank and quickly tied a knot. "If Sean had to deal with her as much as I do, he'd be snow white by now."

Snow White. A pang of regret zinged through him. He had to leave. He didn't want to, but he had to. Tom looked up, searching her face for any hint of the same disappointment. All he could find was calm acceptance. That puzzled him even more. The only time he had ever discussed his relationship with his mother with a woman, it ended in a huge fight followed by a much quicker break-up than even he anticipated. Maggie didn't look as though she was prepared to fight. As a matter of fact, she seemed oddly relieved.

That confused him even more. Wriggling his heel into the other shoe, he quickly knotted the laces and stood up, grabbing his coat from the back of the chair. "Can I have a rain check on the other ten hours?"

She smiled as he shrugged into his jacket. And blushed. Just seeing that petal pink made his pulse quicken. Now he knew that when Maggie McCann blushed, she flushed that pretty, pretty pink all over. It was a glorious sight, and he wanted to see it again so badly his mouth went dry. One hand slid to her throat. Her fingers closed around the lapels of her robe, holding it closed. She kept smiling, but she didn't answer.

He patted his pockets, checking for his wallet and keys. A strange lump in his left pocket puzzled him. He reached in and extracted her key ring. "Oh." He stared at them blankly for a second. Had it just been a couple of hours since he'd dashed out her door on a quest for breakfast? "Here."

"Thank you." She dropped the ring into the pocket of her robe and ushered him toward the door.

He stood his ground, watching as she twisted the locks and gave the stubborn door a full-body yank. "Maggie?"

"Hmm?"

"The other ten hours?"

She wouldn't meet his gaze. Instead, she seemed to take sudden interest in the peeling paint along the door jamb. The rain check wasn't going to be honored. "Okay, not ten hours. Dinner," he negotiated.

"Thanks, but that's okay."

He crossed to the threshold, planting himself between Maggie and the strips of wood and paint she found so damn fascinating. "I want to see you again."

"Oh, I'm sure we will. Patrick's birthday is in a few months. The big one-six. I'm sure Tracy and Sean will have a party or something."

He reached for her elbow. The muscles in her arm tensed, but she didn't pull away. Nor did she meet his eyes. "I'm sure Sean could whip up a mean birthday cake in the next five months, but I was thinking sooner and I was thinking more along the lines of a date."

Maggie wet her lips, lifting her head until their gazes met and held. A small smile curved her lips. "I had a great time, Tom. Thank you."

Anger and confusion ruled his better judgment. "If you had such a great time, we should do it again," he snapped.

"I think it's better if we don't."

"Why?"

"Why ruin it?" She took a small step back. Her fingers tightened on the doorknob. He watched the blood flee from the death grip, leaving her knuckles a ghostly white. "Let's just let this be a nice memory. The next time we run into each other, you can smile at me and I can smile at you, and no one else ever has to know we've seen each other naked."

"What did I do wrong?"

Her eyes widened. "Nothing. You did everything right. It is what it is, Tom. Let's not pretend it'll ever be anything more, okay? That'll just make one of us look like a fool." She gave him a not-so-gentle shove and he stumbled into the hall. "The downstairs door will lock behind you. Just make sure you pull it closed."

"Maggie!"

She shook her head and murmured a soft, "Goodbye, Tom," before closing the door in his face.

His jaw hit the floor. She pushed him out the door. That never happened to him before. Women usually clung to his ankles as he tried to beat a path to the nearest exit. Okay. The ankle thing only happened once, and his niece was only four at the time, but still….

He raised his clenched fist and rapped on the door. "Maggie?"

No answer. No shuffling footsteps. No movement within at all. He knocked harder.

"Maggie!"

Fred answered his call with a curious meow. The healthy ego dozens of women had fed and nurtured over the course of his adult life quaked. His forehead puckered into a frown. He pulled his hand back and scrubbed his face. A grim smirk twisted his lips when he lowered his hand. His fingers curled. The blunt tips of his fingernails bit into the meat of his palm as he stared at the door.

"I'll call you!"

Whether it was a promise or a threat, he wasn't sure. How Maggie would take it, if she even heard him, was anyone's guess. His phone vibrated. He fumbled in his jacket pocket trying to pull it free. His mother's number scrolled across the display. Tom exhaled through his nose, punched the button to ignore the call, and then dropped it back into his pocket as he turned toward the stairs.

The front door slammed behind him and Tom dragged in a breath of crisp morning air. He pushed on the door to be certain the locks caught, then shivered when he realized he didn't even have Maggie's phone number.

The bright red awning above the door snapped in the autumn breeze. Glancing up, a slow smile crept across his face. He spotted a cab meandering down the street, cruising in his direction. Tom flung his arm up to hail the driver then hurried for the curb. As he slipped into the back seat, he spared the plate-glass windows another glance. Relief coursed through him and he left his head fall back against the stiff vinyl seat.

He knew how to find her. The Glass Slipper. Her business would be listed in the book, and the Yellow Pages beat the hell out of trying to beat her information out of Sean—or worse, beg it from Sheila.

Chapter Seven

Maggie spent the rest of Sunday doing all the things she should have done in the first place. Her apartment was now sparkling clean and clutter-free and both sets of sheets were tumbling in her dryer. As a matter of fact, her evening of indulgence unleashed a fresh burst of determination. Maggie McCann's road to self-containment was paved with the very best of intentions. She was feeling pretty smug as the evening wound down. Her fridge and cabinets were bursting with food, there wasn't a bottle of wine within a three-block radius, and the sweet scent of lilac wafted from the steaming bathtub.

Ignoring the book she'd carried into the bathroom with her, she opted to close her eyes and drift away on a cloud of bubbles. Her fingers fluttered through the water. They stirred tiny waves that lapped at her belly and breasts. She sighed, pretending the caress of bathwater was a suitable stand-in for the heat of Tom Sullivan's talented tongue.

She pushed him out the door. Hours later, she was still stunned. That was a first. Hell, usually she was trying to lure men into her web. She could tell by the startled disbelief on Tom's face that it was a first for him too. But it was pure self-defense. She had to do it. He stood there in his wrinkled suit, his hair mussed, a dark shadow of beard stubbling his jaw… Rude or not, she had to do something, anything, to keep from prolonging the moment.

Maggie forced herself to resist the temptation of his offer of dinner. She couldn't take the sincerity shimmering in those vibrant blue eyes. Each minute they spent together stripped away another illusion, making him more human and more likeable. And when that stubborn cowlick on the crown of his head popped up, he was almost…lovable.

Her eyes snapped open and she fumbled for a loofah. Loving Tom Sullivan was not and never would be an option. She bit the inside of her cheek and started to scrub the last vestiges of him from her body. No, another ten hours in his company would have been too dangerous.

She almost made a mental note to send Mrs. Sullivan a little thank you gift. She discarded flowers or candy and considered sending his mother a gift certificate to the spa before she remembered that doing so would mean that Maggie would have to deal with Katie Sullivan and her running litany of complaints. It was a close call. Too damn close for comfort. After fifteen years of flitting around the edges of the Sullivan family, Maggie knew enough to steer clear of that. A smirk curled her lip. She chuckled when she envisioned Tom on a ladder patiently ignoring his mother's harangue while he scraped leaves and twigs and gunk from her gutters.

Restless, she pulled herself up and climbed from the tub with a groan. Her stomach muscles griped. Of course, they were only one item on the laundry list of aches and pains. She was too long out of practice, and her poor body had been well and truly abused in the best possible way. Maggie wrapped a towel around her body, tucking the end between her breasts.

From his usual spot on the bathmat, Fred watched as she reached for the clip that held her hair and shook the heavy curls free. She snapped the clip to the edge of the shower curtain and turned to face the mirror. Fingertips grazed the pale pink patches of razor burn his whiskers left on her throat. She squinted at her reflection, noting every fine line and furrow on her freshly washed face. Those lines marked nearly four decades of living, but they didn't seem to appear any deeper than they had the day before. It seemed impossible. Never had she felt more alive than she had last night.

She drew a deep breath and tugged the edge of the towel. It fell to her feet in a heap. Cupping her breasts, she pushed the soft mounds high like Tom had just before he buried his lips in the valley between them. The look in his eyes when he gazed up at her almost did her in. Wonder. Reverence. Unabashed desire.

Men had lusted after her body before. When a girl is fitted for her first training bra in the fourth grade, those looks start way too early and continue with mind-numbing frequency. In fact, she hardly noticed them anymore. Still, she hadn't expected it from Tom. It was funny to her that a man with a known predisposition for stick women seemed to relish the bountiful curves of a woman without a single straight line.

Shaking her head she released her breasts, grimacing when gravity took over again. Maggie snatched her robe from the back of the door and cinched the belt at her waist. She would store these memories away for another night, another time when her body wasn't sore from his loving, her skin didn't prickle from his caresses, and her mind wasn't clouded with misty wisps of daydreams. She had more important things to think about.

Worn out in mind, body and spirit, she shuffled toward the bedroom. Her gaze landed on the unmade bed. The hum of the dryer filled the apartment. Fred leapt onto the bare mattress with a grace belying his bulk. Sighing, she scooped the rumpled duvet from the floor, wrapping it around her body like a cloak then falling onto the bed. The scratchy cotton shell of the bare pillow rasped against her cheek. She curled into a ball and waited for the cat to settle into the crook of her bent knees.

Closing her eyes, she ran through the list of her new hopes and dreams. The plans she was determined to build on using the rubble of the fairy tales she once believed. A house with a little yard… Maybe a dog one day… Fred's claws tested the duvet's resilience and she chuckled. Okay, no dog… And no prince.

Maggie flung one arm over her head. Her fingers grazed the headboard. Soft, slippery silk brushed her knuckles. She pulled Tom's necktie from the rungs, scowling as it slipped through her fingers.

He wasn't a prince. And even if he was, Sheila was right. Princes were unreliable. No, she didn't need a prince, but she wouldn't mind having someone to serve as consort every once in a while—if for no other reason than to conserve batteries. But guys like Tom Sullivan were not consorts fit for a queen. They were men born to be a fling. And she was a girl who no longer believed in happily ever after. She just wanted to be flung every now and again.

****

Tom dropped the receiver onto the cradle and scowled at the leather blotter on his desk. No answer. His pen beat a steady staccato on a thick stack of files. He jiggled his knee. Thinking he was being clever, he purposefully waited until the clock struck twelve on Monday afternoon to call. Now he felt like a fool.

He snatched up the receiver again and jabbed at the keys, punching out his brother's cell number. Tucking the phone under his chin, he leaned back in his chair and turned to face his office window. The moment Sean answered he blurted, "Hey. Do you have Maggie McCann's cell number?"

"Who?"

"Maggie. Maggie McCann… Tracy's friend," he clarified impatiently.

"Uh…no. Why would I have Maggie's cell number?"

"Didn't you do the work on her building?"

Sean laughed. "Five or six years ago, yeah… Why do you need it, anyway?"

"I, uh…" He tipped his head back, trying to come up with a plausible excuse that wouldn't lead to more questions. "I ran into her the other night. She mentioned something about needing some legal advice."

Sean didn't answer right away, and the stretch of silence made Tom nervous. "Since when do people need a divorce lawyer when they've never been married?" his brother asked at last.

He twirled his pen between his fingers. "I didn't say she needed a divorce lawyer. I was just going to answer her questions for her."

"Uh-huh. And you forgot to give her your card?"

"Yeah."

His brother's snort was impressive. "I've seen you hand those things out like an ambulance chaser at a fifteen car pile-up."

His patience snapped. "You don't have her number?"

Sean hesitated only a moment. "You can call Tracy at work," he offered in a gruff grumble.

"Never mind." Tom swiveled back to his desk. "I have to go. I've got a lunch appointment."

He hung up before Sean could squeeze in another word and shot from his chair. Running an agitated hand through his hair, he turned his glare on the bustling street four stories below his window. He couldn't call Sheila. She'd be even quicker to pounce than Sean. Biting the inside of his cheek, he perched on the edge of his desk and crossed his arms over his chest.

The pose lasted about one minute. He hit the button for the speaker and dialed The Glass Slipper's number again. The phone rang and rang. He let it go on, stubbornly refusing to give up. Once it hit an even dozen, he had to concede defeat. Something he wasn't particularly fond of doing.

He glowered at the blank display and his stomach growled. Lunchtime. Maybe she closed the salon during the lunch hour. He checked his watch, smoothed a hand over his tie, and pushed away from the desk. He fumbled with the buttons on his suit jacket as he crossed his office. His secretary, Mrs. Osgood, jumped when the door opened. "I'm going out," he announced, striding past her desk.

"You're due in court at two," she called after him.

He raised one hand in silent acknowledgement and strode through reception, trying to resist the urge to break into a jog.

The elevator took too long. Every damn cab seemed to be taken. He finally snagged a ride north by jamming a five dollar bill into the fare box on a city bus. Clamping down on his impatience meant he ground his teeth at every damn stop. By the time the bus crossed from the Loop into the River North area, he lost it. Spotting a line of cabs queued in front of a hotel, he bounded from the bus the moment it stopped at a red light.

Mid-day traffic snarls held him up. Tom slid forward on the duct-taped seat, checking his watch and trying to gain a little forward momentum through sheer force of will. By the time he sprung from the cab at Damen and Division, the big hand was inching toward straight up one o'clock. The soles of his shoes slapped pavement. A disgruntled panhandler voiced his displeasure when Tom dashed past without sparing him a glance, much less some change.

He arrived at The Glass Slipper to find a darkened storefront. With a growl of frustration, he jammed his thumb to the buzzer for her apartment. He checked his watch, mentally calculating the time it would take to get back downtown, grab his briefcase, and make it to court on time.

"Come on, Maggie," he hissed, laying into the buzzer again.

"Tom?" He whirled to find Maggie standing on the sidewalk. A handful of shopping bags bumped her shins. "What are you doing here?"

His eyebrows rose as he took in the faded jeans and nubby sweater she wore. "Why aren't you open?"

"It's Monday," she answered, shifting the bags to one hand. "The spa is closed on Mondays."

Like that explained anything. He scowled when the wind caught her hair, tossing the riotous red curls. "I've been trying to call."

The tiny furrow bisecting her brows was nearly irresistible. "Because you need a facial?"

A thousand crude thoughts flitted through his brain, but he clamped the filter in place. "No."

"Actually, you do. Your pores are clogged."

He rolled his eyes. "I'll take some sandpaper to them." He checked his watch again and figured he had about five minutes to convince her to have dinner with him. "Listen, about that dinner—"

"I thought I was pretty clear about that."

Frost sparkled around the edges of her tone, but he was nothing if not determined. "I was hoping I could get you to change your mind." He added what he hoped was a charming smile to sweeten the deal. It never failed him before.

"No, thank you."

Her simple refusal hit him like a baseball bat to the knees. She made it seem so easy. Too easy. He focused all his energy on keeping the smile in place. "No? Come on, Mags, give a guy a chance."

Her lips pursed. Color rose in her cheeks. He tried to parse the blush, searching for clues on which way the emotional wind blew, but Maggie just shook her head. Those crimson curls danced over her sweater, catching on knots of yarn and springing free. He coiled his fingers into his palm to keep from fisting his hand in her hair and kissing her stubborn refusal into a resounding yes.

"Why?"

"What's the point?" she asked.

"The point is I like you. I want to spend more time with you."

Maggie looked away, drawing a deep breath and staring at the trash wafting along the gutter. "I don't have time," she said quietly.

He crossed the sidewalk and took his stand right in front of her. "Any time you're free."

She shook her head harder. "No, Tom. I don't have time to play games anymore. I'm done."

"I'm not playing a game."

A derisive snort erupted from her freckle-dusted nose. "Listen, it was fun. It was great. You were great, okay? You're one hell of a last fling. I'll even provide a testimonial to any future women of the moment you want to refer, just make sure they book a couple of services with us," she said in a low, firm voice.

"I don't need your help, thanks. And last fling? What's that about? Are you dying or something?" he asked in a snide tone.

Maggie met his gaze head-on at last, her emerald eyes narrowing to slits as she tried to stare him down. Tom raised one eyebrow and crossed his arms over his chest, prepared to stand his ground.

"I'm going to have a baby."

The pavement dropped out from under him. Good thing, otherwise his jaw would have been scraping sidewalk. "You're pregnant?" he managed to croak.

Tipping her chin up, she shrugged as she pushed past him. "Not yet, but I will be."

His stomach dropped, pooling around his Italian loafers. He glanced down just to be sure he hadn't just pissed himself. "But… But we used—"

"Oh. No!" She held her keys up in one hand. "Don't stroke out, Sully. I'm not planning on having *your* baby," she said with a smirk. "I'm picking my donor daddy by number. Well, number and a few other considerations."

"Donor?"

She nodded once then slid her key into the lock, favoring him with a sunny smile. "Tick-tock, you know. Gonna be forty next year. I can't keep waiting for Prince Charming to mount that white charger." The locks tumbled and his world tilted, spinning off-axis. Maggie shot him a glance over her shoulder then pushed through the door. "So, uh, thanks for a good time, okay? I'm sure I'll see you at some Sullivan soiree or another, but if not…Have a nice life, Tom."

Before he could pull his tongue out of his throat the door closed between them. Locks snicked into place, and it all clicked. A passing cab blasted its horn and a city bus belched black exhaust. Reeling, he slumped against a metal trashcan embedded in the sidewalk. Fate must have been keeping a watchful eye on him, because the moment he mustered the strength to look up, a Yellow Cab pulled to a stop just down the block.

He sprinted for it, grabbing the door handle before a portly man in a cheap suit pried himself from the seat. Once the cab pulled away he let his head fall back and blew out a breath. Blinking at the stained headliner, he waited for the wash of relief he was certain should follow such a narrow escape. It never came.

The driver blasted the horn as they soared through an intersection. Startled, Tom glanced at his watch. Pulling his phone from his pocket, he dialed his office and briskly instructed Mrs. Osgood to send his paralegal to the courthouse with his briefcase. He ended the call, dropped his phone into the pocket of his suit coat, and let his head fall once again.

"A baby," he whispered to the mottled felt above his head. "Holy hell."

****

Maggie paused in the entryway to catch her breath. Heat flooded her cheeks. Her blood rushed in her ears. She pressed her fingertips to the wall, steadying herself on wobbly legs. Then she took off.

She didn't look back. She refused to acknowledge the twinge of regret pinging away at her stomach. Dashing to the top of the steps, she fumbled with the locks and hip-checked the door. The bags flew from her hand. A set of snowman-printed hand towels skittered across the floor. She leaned against the solid oak door and pressed her fingers to her lips.

Fred greeted her with an impassive gaze. She wrestled with the locks. Once she was secure in the safety of her apartment she gave it another shot. "I'm going to have a baby," she whispered to her companion.

Until today, she never said it out loud. Not to anyone. Not even her doctor. They made it through the entire consultation speaking only in the most detached, clinical terms. It took some amazing skill, really. She visited the fertility clinic her doctor recommended and repeated the entire process, asking questions, filing away information for reference, and mapping out a timeline to turn her life upside-down without actually stating her intention. That is, until she stared into Tom Sullivan's earnest blue eyes in broad daylight and announced it without missing a beat.

A giggle bubbled from her lips, seeping through her fingers and spilling into the room. Her heart beat a pitter-pat. The throb of her pulse roared in her ears. She could feel the blood whooshing through her veins.

"I'm going to have a baby," she asserted, throwing her shoulders back. Unimpressed, Fred sauntered into the living room. She chased after him, needing to share the joy with someone who wouldn't look like they were about to pass out. "A baby, Fred! A baby!"

She hauled the obese cat from his perch on the ottoman and whirled around the room. Her giddy laugh mingled with Fred's protests. She stumbled on the bags strewn across the floor and clutched the furry feline to her chest.

"A baby of my own. All mine," she murmured into his fur. Pressing a kiss to the cat's broad forehead, she cuddled him close and sank onto the couch. "We're going to be a family, Fred. You, me, and a baby. It doesn't matter what the turkeys say. We can do this. We don't need anyone else."

Fred emitted a growly purr and nuzzled her chin. He also pierced her thigh with his claws. "Gah!" Maggie ejected the cat from her lap. "Dammit, Fred! Why'd you have to do that?" Twitching his tail, Fred sniffed and prowled toward the kitchen.

"Typical man. You're getting dry food tonight!" she called after him.

Rubbing the afflicted spot, Maggie flopped back against the cushions, blowing her hair from her face in an exasperated huff. "Ungrateful…Arrogant…" She traced the weave of her jeans with her thumbnail and checked the fabric for a tear. "We were having a moment, you shit!"

She let her head fall back and stared at the ceiling. "And now I'm talking to the cat."

A throw pillow nudged her ribs. She yanked it free, flung it at the opposite end of the couch, and followed it down, closing her eyes before her head hit the pillow. Her thigh throbbed. Silence strummed in her ears. The prickle of a headache took root behind her eyes. She pressed the heel of her hand to the center of her forehead, but nothing could block the image of Tom standing on the sidewalk looking like she'd just hit him with a battering ram.

All she could see was the flicker of hope in his blue eyes melting into fear and confusion. Her heart beat a dull thud against her breastbone. That twinge of regret was back, squeezing her lungs. Maggie swallowed hard and lowered her hand to her stomach, stroking the soft curve.

She didn't wait to watch him walk away. Something told her that might be too much to bear. She liked him. Too much. She liked his cowlick, his smile, and the rumble of his laugh. She liked the way his deep blue eyes crinkled at the corners, fanning his cheeks with lines earned by a man who enjoyed life. A man who would never settle down, never make a commitment beyond dinner and the possibility of dessert.

It hurt to see him go. About as much as she was afraid it would. But Maggie couldn't afford the luxury of indulging any further. Spending any time with Tom was dangerous. More time would only lead to disaster. She tried for a snort, but it came out in a half-hearted sniff.

"Yeah, best to make a run for it before your super sperm get me."

She knew herself well enough to know she wouldn't be able to keep it casual. Each time she saw him, she'd fall a little for that boyish smile. Each time she talked to him, she'd remember what it was like to laugh that much. Each time he drew near, she'd be unable to resist mussing his hair just so she could smooth that cowlick into place.

No. She had a plan, and Tom Sullivan had no business showing up anywhere but in her daydreams. And maybe a few dreams at night, particularly the X-rated variety, but no more than that. That night was a fluke. A fling. A sort of a farewell to living for herself. Soon she would be living for someone else.

The thought filled her with warmth. She tipped her head back, peering at the dusty windows lining the living room wall, absently rubbing her belly as she stared at the crystal star suspended in the window. Her grandmother hung it in Maggie's bedroom decades before and promised her that wishes could come true.

For too long, Maggie clung to the tattered shreds of her illusions. She nurtured them the same way her grandmother had nurtured her. In the days, weeks, and months following her parents' deaths in a car accident, Mary Elizabeth McCann weaved a gossamer web of wonder in a frightened little girl's world.

A pastel pink fantasy of a bedroom became her reality. Sugary sweet cookies chased away the bitter taste of loneliness. Tales of princes on gleaming white chargers and an unshakable belief in the power of true love's kiss forged an unbreakable bond between two women who should have been separated by the span of decades and the ache of loss. Her grandmother taught her to find joy in little things, and hope in the promise of bigger things to come.

Lately, she couldn't help but feel she let her grandmother down. The hopes and dreams she held onto for so long never came to fruition. The knowledge that it would soon be too late twisted her heart into a tangled knot. The acrid taste of failure chased by a bottle of wine left a lingering taste on her tongue. That crystal star symbolized all of her girlish illusions, and every dream she was letting go in order to take a chance on another dream.

Maggie stared at the sparkling hunk of cut glass. "Is it too much to ask?" she whispered to her wishing star. "It's all I ever wanted."

Pale autumn sunlight filtered through the city grime and into the room. Maggie held her breath, waiting for it to reach just the right angle. In just eighteen days she'd start taking the Clomid. That meant that in about a month she could expect to be ovulating. There was a possibility—a very slim possibility, but still a possibility—that she could be pregnant by the New Year.

All of the twinges, tweaks, and pangs of regret she ever felt pushed her deeper into the couch cushions. She gasped for a breath but choked on the sob that rose in her throat. Her eyelashes fluttered, blinking away the tears gathering on the spiky tips. She wet her lips, covering her stomach with both hands. Sunlight streamed through the windows, catching the facets of her wishing star. Bright rainbows of light danced across the walls, splashing onto the floor. Maggie drew a sharp breath then whispered, "I wish I may, I wish I might…."

Chapter Eight

Three days. For three days he was a complete and total train wreck. The first day was the worst. He flubbed his way through his court appearance, going through the motions of making motions. When opposing counsel asked for yet another continuance, he barely mustered up a weak objection. He could hardly remember if he bothered to say anything more to his client before he snatched his briefcase full of legal gobbledy-gook and bolted for the door.

The next day, he brought a bottle of John Jameson's Irish whisky home with him. The only thing he got out of the visit was a pathetic case of the drunk-sads and a raging hangover the next morning. On the third day, he decided to switch medications by calling the perky blonde who worked at his bank.

The date was a disaster. Another night, another restaurant too cheap to pay the electric to light the place decently, and another three hours of his life he'd never get back. It wasn't Jessica's fault. She was just as perky, blonde, and beautiful as he remembered, and he was just as distracted as he had been since the moment Maggie dropped the bomb. He might have kissed her goodnight at her door, but in all honesty he couldn't remember. So much for perky Jessica.

His keys clattered into the dish on the hall table. Tom stood in his living room, trying to get his bearings. The hum of the refrigerator greeted him. He scanned the room, trying to pick out every item he'd chosen himself. The television, the couch, and the glass-top coffee table…Everything else seemed to have magically appeared over the years.

Dropping onto the couch, he toed off his shoes and tugged at the knot in his tie. His palm brushed the supple leather of the couch cushion. Tom had to screw his eyes shut as tight as he could to keep the image of Maggie naked, flushed, and panting from flooding his overflowing brain, but it was no good.

He let his head fall back, too tired to fight it any longer. The bitterness that ate at his gut was replaced by the memory of the sweet tang of damp, heated skin. The choking confusion that plagued him eased a little when he recalled the fresh lemon-y scent of her soap. He rubbed his chest, trying to soothe away the ache. Being with Maggie shouldn't have hurt, she made him laugh. But without Maggie, he hadn't managed so much as a chuckle for three days. It was ridiculous, spending hour after hour thinking about a woman he never let himself think about outside of his fantasies. What was worse, the more he thought about Maggie, the more afraid he was that the gnawing pain eating away at his heart might actually be jealousy.

Tom launched himself from the couch and stumbled to the foyer. He snagged his briefcase and strode down the hall to the spare bedroom he used as a home office. Seated in the cushy leather chair, he dropped the case onto the desk Marcella Sebastiani found at an estate sale and insisted was perfect for him. He pulled a handful of files from the cordovan attaché—a gift from a woman named Susan Brightman—and plopped the pile onto the polished mahogany surface.

He plucked a pen from the center drawer and grabbed the nearest yellow legal pad. Gnawing his bottom lip, he tapped the heavy fountain pen against the binding of the tablet. He blew out a breath, tossed the pad aside and flipped open the top file. About six words into the document he realized that only one actually made sense. For some reason, the word 'Custody' came across loud and clear.

The fact that his mind automatically latched onto that one disgusted him. Why couldn't he have picked 'whereas' or 'herein'. Those were both perfectly harmless words. Words that wouldn't make him start thinking about Maggie. And her baby.

Of course, with a donor father Maggie would never have to deal with messy custody issues. She wouldn't have to share her child on Wednesday nights and alternating weekends. Neither would she end up spending an inordinate amount of time in the McDonald's Playland trying to squeeze in as many nuggets and minutes of fun into a weekend or Wednesday as she possibly could.

Maybe she was being smart. Maybe she wasn't as crazy as he first thought. Okay, he didn't really think she was crazy. Mildly delusional, perhaps, but not certifiable. She had a point. She wasn't getting any younger, and if anyone was meant to be a mom, Maggie would be the one. Not *The One* for him. The one who should have a baby. Not *his* baby. *A* baby.

He snatched up the legal pad. The cap of his pen clattered to the desk then rolled off the edge. His jaw set in a firm line, he decided to take Sheila's advice to heart. He started to make a list of more 'age appropriate' women who would also qualify as 'Tom appropriate'. Women with no designs on marriage and children or one without the other. Women who were invested in their careers. Women who might be open to the type of relationship he could tolerate.

Ink flowed onto the page, but instead of forming a letter, all he got was a black splotch. He closed his eyes and focused with all his might, scrolling through his mental rolodex. The only candidate that sprung to mind happened to be opposing counsel on the custody case he nearly blew two days before.

Sharon Kincaid fit the bill. She was attractive enough, in an uptight, poker-up-the-ass kind of way. Of course, she could be a barrel of chuckles outside of the courtroom for all he knew, but he doubted it. Something told him that her hair stayed ramrod straight even when it was released from that god-awful bun. He had a feeling those boxy suits she wore weren't hiding lacy scraps of lingerie and a killer figure. Tom chewed the inside of his cheek and tapped his pen. He wrote her name on the pad, but he knew it wouldn't matter. His gut told him it was a no-go.

He had a hunch the woman was drier than the sliced white meat that hung around in his refrigerator for a week after Thanksgiving. After feasting on the bounty of Maggie McCann, Counselor Kincaid would be the caloric equivalent of a Lean Cuisine. It would never work. He wasn't opposed to frozen foods, but as a guy, he felt they should damn well be the full-flavored variety.

Full-flavored. Full-figured. Hands full of Maggie's breasts. Milky white skin so translucent he could map the pale blue veins beneath the surface. Taut, beaded nipples. The delightful rasp of pebbled flesh against his tongue. Those tight buds rosy as ripe raspberries and infinitely sweeter.

The pen fell to the desk then rolled to the floor. He pressed his lips together. His chest felt tight. His pants were even tighter. Planting his elbows on the edge of the desk, he let his head fall into his hands and pushed the heels of his palms into his eyes.

A baby. The woman wants to have a baby. There was nothing wrong with that. Lots of people want kids. Hell, he loved kids. His niece and nephews knew they had their Uncle Tom wrapped around their fingers. He wouldn't want it any other way. Sean's kids were the kids he'd never have.

His head jerked up. He blinked to clear the spots from his eyes. The yellow legal pad with its ink blot and single name mocked him. He lowered his left hand to the tablet, tearing the sheet from the perforations and crumpling it. His fingers worked the paper into a ball, squeezing it in his palm until it formed a tight knot. Raising his fist to his mouth, he brushed his knuckles against his lip, waiting for whatever it was his muddled mind was trying to sort to crystallize.

The gnawing pain was back. The seething ooze of jealousy pooled in his stomach began to simmer. He lowered his hand to the desk, the wad of crumpled paper rolling off his fingertips forgotten. Tom pressed his palm to the clean, lined pad of paper, splaying his fingers wide. Fine, dark hairs curled between the knuckles of his bare ring finger. The finger he vowed would never sport a band of gold.

The jealousy bubbled up inside of him, burning in his chest, scorching his throat. Marriage—and the whole archaic idea of binding your life to one person—was a farce. He knew that. He tasted the bitterness of the cold ash left behind when his father left. His mother's disappointment became his oxygen. Extracting people from those binding ties with some semblance of dignity became his life's work.

The dregs of his Irish-Italian-Catholic upbringing must be to blame for his blind assumptions. Until that moment, he truly thought Maggie had lost it. A decision fueled by some kind of delusional desperation brought on by the prospect of too many candles stuck in a cake. He sat up straight, rubbing his bare ring finger. Suddenly, the merit in her decision became clear.

His smile teetered on the brink of a smirk. He rocked back in his chair, lacing his fingers behind his head. "Brilliant," he whispered to the ceiling. He shook his head slowly, the smile widening into a grin. A laugh burbled from his throat, punctuating the compliment. He stretched his arms above his head, staring up at his unmarred hands. "Fucking brilliant. Brava, Maggie."

****

This time, he was prepared. Tom strolled into the coffee house across from The Glass Slipper at exactly seven-thirty Thursday night. The air was perfumed with fresh-ground coffee. When he stepped to the counter, he picked up hints of cinnamon and sugar and the cloying scent of freshly fired marijuana.

He eyed the pierced and tattooed twenty-something who took his order. The guy moved with the easy grace of a trained dancer. A telltale waft of patchouli tickled his nostrils. Tom produced a ten in exchange for the large paper cup of caffeine and tamped down the surge of envy the guy's mellow smile engendered.

Change in pocket and coffee in hand, he moved to a tiny table situated at the plate glass window and took up his vigil. Four or five scrubs-clad women made the circuit to the spa's reception area in the fifteen minutes he'd been watching, but none of them were Maggie.

A young woman with Whoopi Goldberg dreads and café au lait skin sauntered into reception and leaned against the counter. Tom nearly dropped his coffee when Reefer Boy heaved a gusty sigh. He jumped and twisted in the chair, shooting the younger man a glare that bounced right off the kid's pot-induced haze.

"Now, that's what I'm talkin' about," Cannabis Coffee-guy murmured, nodding to the shop across the street.

Tom couldn't help but smile his commiseration. "Oh yeah?"

The kid nodded. "Dude, her name is Sharita, but I'm bettin' she can shake that ass like Shakira."

Eying the young woman in question, Tom tried for a little objectivity but fell into the age-old habit of masculine objectification. "You're probably right," he concluded.

Patchouli Punk dropped a towel onto a perfectly clean table and began to wipe it down again, his gaze fixed on the lady in The Glass Slipper. "You waitin' on your lady?"

The question jolted Tom from his bemused observation. "Oh, uh… Yeah. A friend, I mean. I'm waiting to talk to a friend who works over there."

The Java Junkie straightened up and gave him a speculative once-over. "Well, three of them are married, and one is barely old enough to drink, so unless you're stalking the redhead who owns the place, you must be talkin' about Sharita," he concluded with startling alacrity.

Taken aback, Tom laughed. "Um, the redhead."

The Caffeine King's smile came slow. His bloodshot eyes narrowed and he nodded his head approvingly. "Dude, excellent choice."

"Uh…Thank you?"

"Seriously. Miss Maggie's hot. Pretty too, for a lady her age. Not all stretched tight and pushed up like a cougar. Fresh and clean, like…grass or a princess or something…" The guy actually snapped his fingers, trying to drum up the right word.

"Snow White," Tom mumbled.

"Dude! Exactly!" The kid guffawed and slapped the towel against his leg. "Snow White, but with red hair and a luscious ass. Nice tits too." He turned his gaze to the window, and his tone grew wistful. "Old or not, if she even looked at me twice, I'd so hit that."

Tom's hand curled into a fist. He clamped down on his lip, trying to stave off the urge to clobber his new best buddy. Instead, he lifted his wrist, checked his watch, and rose. He snagged his cup and stalked to the door. "I'll pass your offer along," he called over the chime of the bell.

"Wha? Dude, I was just kidding…."

Scanning the traffic, he wove his way behind a passing cab and trotted across the street. He dumped the coffee cup in the trashcan he'd used as a crutch just days before and made a beeline for the door to the spa. A dazed-looking woman with greasy hair and beatific smile blew past him clutching a bottle of water. A quick side step saved his toes. He rushed into the salon then drew up short. The bravado that fueled him through a day of plotting, planning, and prepping his arguments wafted away on a eucalyptus-scented cloud.

The young receptionist's eyebrows rose. His lips parted, but words escaped him. The pretty girl with the dreadlocks—Sharita, if his buddy Java Jones could be trusted—turned and gave him a slow once-over.

"May we help you?" she asked, an amused smile quirking her lush lips.

"Uh, Maggie… Is Maggie McCann in?"

"We don't accept sales calls during business hours," the receptionist chirped.

Tom glanced down, smoothing his hand over his tie as he gathered his scattered wits. "I'm not a salesman. I'm a friend of Maggie's."

Sharita pushed away from the reception desk, smoothing her tunic top over her hips. "A friend of Maggie's?"

He managed a nod, trying to hold his ground under her intense scrutiny. "Tom Sullivan."

A bemused smile lifted her lips. She sashayed to the curtain that draped the entrance to the spa. "She just finished with her last client. I'll let her know you're here, friend of Maggie's, Tom Sullivan."

To keep from fidgeting, he tore his gaze from the swaying curtain and shoved his hands into his pockets. The jingling of loose change gave him away as he feigned fascination with the tastefully printed list of salon services.

"We do have quite a few male clients," the receptionist volunteered.

He dropped the brochure like a hot coal. "No, uh…I just need to talk to Maggie." Shuffling a few feet away from the desk, he turned his attention to the display of hair and skin care products lined on the glass shelves. A can of shave cream caught his eye. He snatched it from the shelf and scanned the back of the package.

"You'll like that. It warms when you apply it."

Maggie's voice startled him. He jumped and thrust the can onto the shelf, knocking over a row of lotions. Bottles rolled from the display, falling at his feet. "Shit," he hissed, dropping to a squat to gather the wayward bottles. He rose, cradling the plastic jugs of virulent blue girl goop in his palms. "I'll pay for them."

She chuckled and plucked one bottle from his hand, holding it up so he could read the label. "Do you suffer from razor burn and ingrown hairs around your bikini line?"

"No."

"If you do, you really should use this," she persisted. "It has aloe and a touch of lidocaine. Very soothing."

"Ha. Ha."

One by one, Maggie realigned the bottles on the shelf. "What are you doing here, Tom?" she asked in a low voice.

He matched her tone, leaning a little closer to her as he handed over the last of his victims. "I want to talk to you."

"No point. My mind is made up." She straightened the row of shave cream and stepped back from the display, gently pulling him out of the danger zone.

The girl behind the desk didn't bother to pretend she wasn't listening. The sexy hairdresser leaned against the doorway with her arms crossed over her chest, holding the silky drape back with her hip. He dared a glance at Maggie's impassive face and sighed.

"Fifteen minutes. Is that too much to ask?" Her emerald gaze skittered over the rows of product as if she'd find the answer there. "Maggie, please."

Without glancing in his direction she nodded once and spun on her heel. But instead of leading him out to the stairs to her apartment, she dove into the depths of the spa, leaving him gaping in her wake.

****

The curtain swished between them when Sharita rushed after her. "Do you want me to hang around?"

Maggie shook her head. "No. You guys can go on. He's harmless." She looked up and met his gaze. The man clearly wasn't a fan of being called harmless. She quirked an eyebrow in his direction and shrugged. "Give her your card so she'll know who to sic the cops on if I turn up missing," she instructed.

Tom blinked in surprise but didn't move. Sharita held her hand out palm up, waggling her fingers. He huffed and flipped the tail of his suit coat and rooted for his wallet. "Make up your mind. Am I harmless or not?"

"I think you are, but Shar's a lot more suspicious than I am," Maggie answered.

Tom pulled a business card from his wallet and handed it over. "Want my cell number too?"

Sharita laughed and tucked his card into her bra, adding a bawdy wink. "If Maggie wants me to have it, she'll give it to me." She sauntered past him, flashing a wicked smile. "Not that it matters. I don't call men. Men call me." At the curtain, she glanced over her shoulder. "Night, Mags. Call me if you need help hiding the body."

The batik drape swished into place. Maggie and Tom locked eyes from opposite ends of the narrow hallway. A wry smile twitched his lips. "I'm not sure if she was trying to seduce me or scare me."

Maggie wet her lips. "Probably both."

She ducked into the small treatment room and switched on a dim lamp. Unlike her apartment, she kept her room neat as a pin. The treatment table was draped in fresh sheets and a thermal knit blanket. Her instruments were sterilized and lined up between two clean towels. The rolling stool she used was stowed at the head of the table. Her business cards were splayed in a perfect fan on the small table next to an overstuffed chair. Stacks of cotton squares stood ready and waiting on the rolling table against the wall.

Tom stepped through the doorway and she had to force herself to draw breath. His broad shoulders crowded the room. His scent flooded her nostrils. His midnight eyes locked on her, determination darkening the blue flame that leapt when their gazes met. She took an involuntary step back then forced herself to regroup. This was her territory. If he wanted to talk, he'd have to do it on her terms.

She patted the padded table. "Take your shirt off and hop up here." Maggie fluttered about the room, switching machines on, re-lighting a candle, and reaching for a stack of towels.

"What?"

"You can leave your pants on, but lose the jacket and shirt and lay down on your back."

He squinted at her. "Why?"

She snapped open a towel with a flick of her wrist. "You want to talk? Fine. But I can't stop staring at your pores, so strip and hop up on the table."

"I'm not…."

She cut him off with one arched eyebrow. "You don't want to talk?"

Tom shucked his jacket and tossed it at the chair in the corner. "This better not hurt."

Maggie rolled her eyes. "Got it. No extractions. I'll leave the giant blackhead on your nose alone."

He abandoned the button on his cuff and covered his nose with his hand. "Blackhead?"

"Yes. Very attractive. I bet it makes all the girls swoon."

Without another word, he stripped out of his shirt, tugged his wallet from his back pocket and tossed it onto the chair, and perched on the edge of the table. His head drooped and his muscled shoulders slumped. After about ten seconds, he glanced up with a puzzled frown. "Is this thing heated?"

She smiled and tugged the sheet trapped under him. "You can lose the pants and slide in if you want."

The corner of his mouth lifted. "For some reason, I don't think you meant that the way it sounded to me," he said dryly.

The soles of his shiny black shoes slapped tile and Maggie fumbled with the sheet and blanket, attempting to get the perfect forty-five degree fold she usually made so effortlessly. His belt buckle clinked and she looked up. He was staring at her, toeing off his shoes as he unzipped his pants. A hot flash of memory scorched her cheeks. The knowing smirk that lifted one side of his mouth only helped to fuel the fire. She glanced at the table then back at him, meeting his gaze boldly.

"You were so much faster with this the other night." She crossed her arms over her chest, feigning impatience.

He stripped off his pants and socks, holding them in front of him as he shifted from foot to foot on the cool tile floor. "I was motivated. Tonight, I'm not exactly sure what I'm getting into."

Again she held the sheet up. "Get into this."

Tom grumbled a little but added the pants and socks to the growing pile on the chair. He made his way to the table with all of the enthusiasm of a man expecting a lethal injection. Taking advantage, she admired the long, lean lines of muscle that played under taut skin and the way the snug cotton knit of his boxer briefs clung to his ass. By the time he climbed between the sheets, she'd moved past admiration and into ogling, but that was okay. The uncertainty in his usually confident gaze made her feel powerful.

Maggie lowered herself to the rolling stool and pressed her fingertips to his temples, reminding herself that power needed to be tempered with a bit of benevolence. "I won't hurt you," she promised in a whisper.

She traced gentle circles, applying just enough pressure to ease the tense muscles in his cheeks and working her way to his jaw. Tom closed his eyes when she slid her fingers into his dark hair. "Feel good?"

"Mmm…."

She smiled. The short stands of his bittersweet chocolate hair tickled her palms. She slid her hands under his head, cupping his skull in one hand while kneading the nape of his neck with her knuckles. "Just relax," she murmured. "This is going to feel so good." She drew back, preparing to begin the treatment. A frown furrowed his brow. "Are you warm enough?"

"Fine," he answered, shifting down on the table slightly.

"If you get too hot, let me know." His soft snort made her smile. She wriggled her fingers into a sterile glove and snapped the band around her wrist.

Tom shot straight up, dislodging the sheet and glancing around wild-eyed. "What are you doing?"

She waggled her fingers at him. "It's a surgical glove."

"I know the sound. Why? And why only one?"

She couldn't help it; his abject fear made her laugh. "Relax, Sully. I'm about as far from your prostate as I can get." She held up a second glove and smirked. "Health regulations frown on going for the Michael Jackson look." She placed her gloved hand on his bare shoulder and pulled him back to the table. "You bolted before I got to the second one."

"Yeah, well, the snap of a rubber glove does that to a guy."

She chuckled as she worked her fingers into the second glove. Tom folded his hands over his chest and closed his eyes again, breathing slow and deep through his nose. Moistening two cotton squares, she began to bathe his chin and cheeks with warm water. A moment later, she tossed the squares and pumped a dollop of cleanser onto the fingertips. "This is just a mild cleanser," she said, keeping her voice calm and impersonal. She worked the cleanser in tiny circles from his chin to his forehead. "When you leave I'll give you some samples. Stop using the Irish Spring on your face."

"How do you know I use Irish Spring?"

"I can smell it."

"You don't like it? I think it smells good. It's manly, but ladies are supposed to like it too."

She snorted and began to rinse away the cleanser. "It does smell good. Just not on your face." Moving the steam closer, she smoothed exfoliating cream over his skin. His eyelashes fluttered when the exfoliating brush whirred to life. "Just going to slough off some of the dead skin," she murmured.

He cracked open one eye. "Sounds disgusting."

"Feels great." She touched the rotating brush to his jawline and was rewarded with a low hum of pleasure. "See?" The tension eased in his shoulders. His biceps quivered then relaxed. The clasped fingers on his chest grew lax with each passing circle. "Let me do the extractions," she coaxed in a low, seductive tone. "You'll thank me."

"Okay."

Grinning, Maggie set the exfoliating brush aside and fished two more cleansing cloths from the bowl of warm water. With practiced strokes, she wiped away the residue and tossed them into the tiny can at her feet. She grabbed the cotton and her comedo extractor before he could change his mind.

"So, you wanted to talk?" she asked, hoping to keep him distracted while she went to town on his nose. He tried to nod, but she gripped his head. "Just hold still."

"What made you decide to do this?"

Maggie bit her lip, zeroing in on the worst of the miniscule blemishes marring that perfect Roman nose. She knew damn well what he was asking. Just as she knew she had one shot at getting that blackhead out before he bolted. The problem was, she didn't want to answer his question. At least, not the question she thought he was asking.

Maggie leaned in closer, pressing her cotton-wrapped fingertips to his nose and began to talk about the semester she spent in community college while she put the squeeze on him. "I met Tracy and Shel at Lakeshore," she said, ignoring his wince. "But I only lasted one semester. I couldn't give a damn about U.S. history before eighteen-eighty." Tom yelped as she cleared the pore. Before he could wriggle away, she moved on to the next. "I dropped out and went to Cosmetology school. I was going to be a hairdresser, but then I found out that aestheticians can make a lot more per hour, so that's what I did."

"Christ Almighty, that hurts!"

"Hang tough, big guy. You're not actually all that bad. Just a few more minutes."

"You're just doing this to get your jollies," he ground out between clenched teeth.

She laughed and moved on to the next one. "Well, there are some perks to the job. When I'm feeling particularly bitchy, I make sure I have plenty of bikini waxes on the schedule."

He grimaced, his fingers clawing at the sheet as she moved quickly and methodically from one spot to the next. "You're like that dentist in *Little Shop of Horrors*, or the Nazi guy in *Marathon Man*."

She chuckled and set her instruments aside. "And I thought you thought I was pretty." She swiped a dampened sponge over his nose. "There, all done. You were very brave."

Tom opened his eyes and stared up at her. His upside-down smile packed an even more powerful punch than when it was right-side-up. "You're beautiful, Maggie."

Biting her lip, she turned away. "Back to the fun stuff. A massage and a mask."

"I'll take the massage, but I've never worn a mask. You into that kinky stuff?"

Rolling her eyes, she squeezed a blob of massage oil onto her fingers. Pressing them gently to his forehead, she took a deep breath and started with small circles. "Anyway, I worked at a spa off Oak Street for almost ten years. Very chi-chi, very exclusive and stuffy. When my grandmother passed away, she left me everything. Her house, her savings… She never touched the money my parents left. I had a nice nest egg, so I decided to give it a shot on my own."

Silence shimmered around them as she worked her way steadily around his eyes, down his nose, to his mouth and chin. Tom moaned soft and deep when she massaged the length of his jawline. She stroked his throat. Tiny prickles of five o'clock shadow caught her gloved fingertips and clung. Maggie laughed softly and worked her way back up to his cheeks. "I don't get to give many men facials. The beard feels funny."

Those dark lashes fluttered a bit, but he kept his eyes closed. "Feels good."

A genuine smile warmed her face. "I'm glad you like it. Makes up for the nasty extractions?"

"What happened to your parents?"

Her fingers froze, pressing gently on his temples. Blinking away the jolt of shock his abrupt question caused, she raked her fingers through his thick hair, brushing it over his ears. "They died when I was six. A wreck on the Dan Ryan," she said softly. "My dad's mom raised me."

He reached up and covered her hands, pressing them firmly against his head. He opened his eyes, peering up at her intently. "I'm sorry, Maggie."

A ghost of a smile curved her lips. "Thank you, but it was a long time ago." She wriggled her hands out from under his, grasped his wrists, and moved them back to his chest. "My grandmother was great," she continued briskly. "Funny and smart. She could be tough when she wanted to be, but the best part was she didn't want to be very often. I might have been a bit spoiled." Tom closed his eyes and sighed as she rubbed his ears between her thumb and index finger. "She'd make these incredible sugar cookies whenever I did something good."

"So you always did good," he concluded.

Maggie studied his relaxed features for a moment then nodded slowly. "I tried to."

"And you bought this place with your inheritance."

Again she nodded then turned to grab another tube. "The building was pretty beat up, but Sean and George checked it out before I signed the papers."

She slathered his skin with the hydrating mask, painting it onto his skin with deft strokes. Once it was applied, she rinsed her fingertips and opened a jar of massage cream. The cream warmed between her palms. She spread it across his broad shoulders, pressing firmly against warm, taut muscle. Tom groaned. The deep rumble rolled from his parted lips, carrying the sound long after she began to work the cream into the tight knots at the base of his skull.

"You did good, Maggie. I'd bake you some cookies, but I don't know how."

"It seems to be working out," she murmured, kneading his neck gently but firmly. "So, Sean was the only Sullivan to inherit any kitchen skills?"

"He's a little fruity that way. Plus, when he married Tracy it became a matter of self-defense."

Almost of their own accord, her hands slithered over his shoulders and smoothed the slick cream across his chest. "True. I can't tell you how many times she tried to blow up the microwave when we lived together."

Her breasts brushed the crown of his head. Greedy hands slipped beneath the sheet, massaging his pecs and stroking the ripples of his abs. Her thumbs tweaked flat nipples as she worked her way back to the safety of his shoulders.

"Wow, I had no idea a facial involved a full body massage."

His voice came low and gravelly, the same whisky-soaked timbre that made her drop her granny panties. Heat flamed in her cheeks, but it wasn't all embarrassment. Maggie pulled her hands back as if she'd been scorched. "Sorry. Probably a good thing I don't get too many men in here, huh?"

Tom grabbed her wrists and pulled her hands back to his chest, holding them there as he peered up at her. "I meant the baby, Maggie. What made you decide about the baby?"

Game over. A lump rose in her throat. She swallowed hard but refused to look away. "I told you. Tick-tock. Time's running out."

"I mean the donor thing."

She swiped the last of the sponges from the bowl and squeezed the excess water onto his forehead. "We're done talking." Tom sputtered and reared up, but she pushed him back to the table and deftly swabbed the mask from his face.

"Come on, Maggie, you have to admit it's a little odd—"

"It's none of your damn business."

"Donor sperm. How do you know for sure who the guy is—"

"I'm dealing with a reputable clinic. Each donor is rigorously screened," she said, subjecting his cheeks and forehead to an equally rigorous scrubbing.

"Doing it this way is for when the guy can't do the job or for women who can't get a man."

Maggie tossed a dry towel at his face and pushed back from the table. "I guess I fall into the second category."

Tom mopped his face and sat up, clutching the towel to his chest. "Why aren't you married?"

She gaped at him, her mind racing. "What kind of question is that?"

"I'm assuming it's by choice. It can't be because you can't find a guy."

"You assume wrong."

"Bullshit. Jesus, look at you! You're beautiful, intelligent, successful… What guy wouldn't want you?"

"You think I haven't tried?" she cried, exasperated. "I've been dating since I was sixteen! I've done it all! Church groups, the bar scene, personal ads, online dating… Hell, I was even engaged once—for about five minutes!"

"Really?"

"I was so careful. I was so good. I chose the right guys, I said the right things, I did everything right!"

"What happened? Why didn't you marry him?"

Pushing, pushing… Maggie knew he had to be great in the courtroom, he just kept pushing. "Because I didn't love him!"

Tom blew out a breath, shaking his head. "Really? Did that matter?"

"What do you mean 'Did it matter?' Of course it mattered!"

"Were you compatible? Did you like spending time with him? Did he make you laugh?"

Maggie crossed her arms over her chest. "What's it to you?"

"Love," he murmured, savoring the word like wine. "Love doesn't last, Maggie. You know that as well as I do. You said you were good. You said you did everything right—"

"I don't have to listen to this. Get dressed. We talked. I answered your nosy questions. We're done."

She tried to brush past him, but the damn room was too small. He snagged her wrist and pulled her close. "Stop trying so hard to get it right, Maggie." His voice was deep and seductive, those eyes dark and penetrating. "Don't you know that being good never gets you what you want?"

Her voice cracked. "What do you want me to do?"

"Get it wrong, Maggie. Pick me."

Her blood buzzed in her ears. "Pick you for what?"

"Let me be the one."

"The one to what?" she cried.

Tom loosened his hold on her wrist and gathered her hand in both of his. "Choose me. Don't pick a stranger. You know me… You know my family…."

She blinked, trying to chase away the swarm of bees making it hard to think clearly. "What are you asking me?"

Tom clasped her hand tightly and stared into her eyes. "Maggie McCann, will you have my baby?"

Chapter Nine

Tom wasn't sure what reaction he expected from Maggie, but he sure as shit didn't think she'd slap his face, toss his clothes at him, and kick him out. He fell into his empty bed that night and stared up at the ceiling. He wasn't sure when he eventually drifted off, but the last time he checked the clock he'd passed the four hour mark—a new record for sleeplessness in an otherwise sleep-filled life.

His cell rang, vibrating its way across the nightstand. Tom groaned but rolled over. Whatever doze he had managed was blown. Panic gripped him. Middle of the night phone calls never brought good news. An image of his elderly mother flashed in his head. He was wide awake before the phone touched his ear.

"Ma?"

"No. And if I agree to this cockamamie scheme of yours, you do not get to refer to me as Ma, Mother, or Mommy," Maggie said without preamble.

"Maggie?" He sat up and rubbed the cheek he swore still stung with the imprint of her hand.

"Why are you doing this, Tom?"

The creak in her voice made his chest ache. "Maggie, I—"

"Is my life some kind of joke to you?"

"No!"

He huffed, elbowing the pillow out of his way and wincing when his bare back hit the cool wood of the headboard. "I just…I got to thinking…" Tom let stale oxygen seep from his lungs and struggled to draw fresh breath. "Women can do that. Guys can't. You decide you want a kid, you just go make one and have one."

"It's not that easy."

"For a guy it's impossible."

Maggie hummed softly. "There are ways."

"But not ways of my choosing." He stared into the dark, blank void of the flat screen TV atop the dresser. Taking a deep breath, he forged ahead. "Maggie, I knew from the time I was fifteen I'd never get married. Everything I've seen since then… Well, I think it's the right decision for me. But I never really thought about…kids."

He ran his hand through his hair and switched the phone to the opposite ear. "And you know what? That sucks. I love kids. You know I do. Sean and Tracy's kids…I always thought I'd be to them what my Uncle George was to me and Sean. But they don't need a George-type person in their lives. Hell, not only do they have the real Uncle George, they have both Sean and Tracy, and no matter how screwed up things are between them, that will never change."

"No, it won't."

"And I want that for them. I don't ever want them to need me the way Sean and I needed George."

"I know you don't."

"When you said you were having a baby…"

Maggie chuckled. "You freaked."

Tom laughed too. "I did. But after I was done freaking, I was…jealous."

"You were?"

He closed his eyes and bit his cheek, nodding mutely. The silence stretched for a moment before it occurred to him that she couldn't see him. "So jealous."

"Of the baby?"

Opening his eyes, he searched the gloom of the room. "Of you. You have a choice. You can do this if you want."

"There's no guarantee it'll work."

"You still have a better shot at it than I do."

Silence stretched taut between them. Tom smiled when he picked up the faint hum of Fred's motor running.

"When Tracy told me she and Sean were having trouble…for just one minute…I was happy," Maggie admitted in a whisper.

Tom sank down onto the pillow once more. "I'll deny it if you ever repeat this, but…me too. With Sean…."

"Are we horrible people?"

"No," he breathed. "Just human."

"I wanted it all so bad… Everything Tracy had… Everything she's throwing away."

"I wanted to be right. I wanted Sean to have to step out of his self-righteous little bubble and admit he was wrong."

"About?" she prompted.

He ran his thumbnail along the seam of the duvet bunched around his hips. "The happily ever after crap."

"You don't think they can fix it?"

"Do you?"

She hesitated, and he winced for her when he heard the breath catch in her throat. The wince turned into a full-blown grimace at the tears in her voice. "Tracy wants to," she croaked. "She just doesn't know how."

He blew out a breath and switched ears, sinking deeper into his pillow. "Well, maybe they will, then. I know Sean isn't leaving." Her quiet hum of acknowledgement soothed him. He let his drooping eyelids fall, welcoming the relief of darkness but clinging to the thread of her voice. "Tell me about the donor guy."

Her smile bounced off the satellite signal and trickled through the earpiece. "I've narrowed it down to three."

"Leading characteristics?"

"Red hair and green eyes," she answered.

His eyes popped open. "Genetic engineering, Ms. McCann?"

She laughed. "Well, I don't remember much from seventh-grade science, but I do know I'm a mass of recessive genes. I thought I'd give it my best shot."

"Again, no guarantees," he pointed out.

"Yeah, well…That's life, right?"

His fingers tightened on the phone. "Just hear what I have to say, Maggie," he coaxed in a low voice. "You can still say no. Just hear me out."

She chuckled softly, but it didn't ring true. "This is like one of those pacts you make with your guy friend when you're twenty. You know, the 'If you're not married and I'm not married' thing."

"Neither of us is married and neither of us has kids, but I'm not talking in hypotheticals, Maggie."

"That's what I'm afraid of," she whispered.

"Have dinner with me, and we can talk." He stared at the ceiling, searching his mental rolodex for a fresh, new, tragically ill-lit and hip restaurant to tempt her. "Hey, there's that new Brazilian-Thai place on Ontario. We could go there…."

She snorted. "Brazilian-Thai? No thanks. I don't like my food fused."

Tom perked up a bit. "How do you feel about lighting that actually lets you read the menu?"

"I like it. I figure those other places are either too cheap to play the electric, or they don't want you to know what you're actually ordering."

"Gianetti's?" he asked, hoping she'd bite. The family-style Italian restaurant was sufficiently bright and boasted a menu of good old-fashioned comfort food in case things didn't go well. "I can pick you up or meet you there."

"I'll meet you. What time?"

"Would seven work?"

"Seven would work," she conceded.

"Good." Tom pulled the comforter over his stomach. "So, while I have you, can I ask you something?"

"I'm wearing pajamas."

Tom laughed, and damn it was good. Even better, she joined him with a rich, husky chuckle that tickled his eardrum. "Damn."

"Goodnight, Tom."

"Sweet dreams, Maggie."

****

Maggie studied the menu even though most of it was committed to memory long ago. Gianetti's ranked number two on her speed dial, just after her voicemail, but there was no need for Tom to know that. Gnawing her lip, she wavered between the five-cheese lasagna she really wanted and the chopped salad her hip-span deserved. She glanced up when their waiter approached, drink tray in hand. A beer for Tom, water with lemon for her, and two glasses of chianti for the lucky couple at the next table.

"Order a glass." His voice jolted her from her grape-lust. When her startled gaze met his, he shrugged. "You're not pregnant yet."

"The water's fine." She flashed a bright smile when the waiter deposited her glass.

Tom closed his menu. "Just so you know, if you want the garlic bread you'll have to order your own. I don't share."

She chuckled and shook her head. "Chopped salad. House Italian, please."

Her dinner companion rolled his eyes. "I'll have the five-cheese lasagna and an order of garlic bread. Oh, and bring an extra plate too, will you?"

When the waiter disappeared, she raised an eyebrow. "Extra plate?"

He shook his head. "I know what's gonna happen when you get *your* food, and I get *mine*."

"I thought you didn't share."

"I'd make an effort to share with *you*."

She shifted in her seat and turned her attention to a small group of women cozied around a table in the bar. "I need to watch what I eat, or I blow up like a balloon."

"You're perfect the way you are, and I like watching you eat."

The simple statement captured her attention. "Watching me eat?"

His charming smile did nothing to mask the gleam in his eyes. "You have no idea."

"What? Are you some kind of freaky foodie?"

He leaned in, bracing his elbows on the wobbly table and staring at her intently. "There's something incredibly sexy about the way you eat." She snorted, but he held up a finger to halt her protest. "You forget, I've seen it. Lots of times. You make birthday cake look like there's an orgy going on in your mouth. Burnt hot dogs, creamy potato salad…Nothing is safe. You break cookies into tiny chunks before you eat them…like the bear claw." His blue gaze grew soft and hazy. "Your lips closing around your fingers, a fork, a spoon…" He huffed and shook his head. A sheepish grin chased the clouds from his eyes. "Hell, you practically made love to the rubber chicken they served at Sean and Tracy's rehearsal dinner. That's when I knew I had to avoid you at all costs."

"For fear that I'd devour you?"

He reached across the table, the tips of his fingers skimming across her knuckles before coming to rest on the checkered cloth mere millimeters from hers. "Something like that."

Energy flowed from him, warm and tempting. She stared at the tiny gap, half-expecting to see sparks arcing between them. Her blood sang in her veins, but she refused to close the gap. Awareness prickled the nape of her neck. She blinked, a Jeannie-like effort to vanquish the pesky space between them, but she couldn't make the move. Clearing the lump of lust from her throat, she met his gaze. "It's a good thing we're just here to talk, then."

Tom sighed and sat back, those dangerous fingertips trailing over the oh-so-lucky red and white cloth. He reached into his coat pocket and pulled out a pen and a small pad. "Tell me about the process."

Her jaw dropped as he flipped to a blank page and uncapped the pen. "You're going to take notes? Is this a deposition?"

"I think better when I write things down."

"There's nothing for you to think about."

The muscle in his jaw jumped. Those warm indigo eyes turned cool and remote. "Fine." He capped the pen and pushed the pad aside. "Are the salads here good? I've never bothered with them."

"Was that supposed to be a segue?"

"I'm making polite conversation."

Pushing her hair back from her face, a growl of frustration escaped her. "I don't know why you think you can pry into my life. It's not like we're friends, Tom. We never have been. As a matter of fact, until last Saturday night, I don't think you ever said more than ten words to me."

"And that's my fault?" He sat up, stuffing the pad and pen back into his jacket pocket. "You never talked to me either, Maggie. Why is that?"

"Probably for the same reason."

"You thought I was off-limits?"

"Why would you think *I* was off-limits?" she asked.

"Well, you were off-limits to me."

Maggie yanked her napkin from her lap and tossed it onto the table. "Who set the damn limits?"

He lurched from his chair before she could rise. "Oh no. Uh-uh. You are not walking out on me."

"Walking out?" Nodding toward the rear of the restaurant, she gathered her purse, and stood. "I was going to the ladies room." Maggie cocked her head, studying him as he sank back into his seat. "Do women walk out on you a lot?"

"Enough," he grumbled.

Clutching her bag to her chest, she peered down at the top of his bowed head. Without thinking, she ran her hand over his crown. The tip of her index finger swirled his cowlick, freeing it from the protective seal of hair product.

Tom glanced up from under thick lashes. "I'd like us to be friends."

A wry smile curved her lips. "Friends, huh? Sounds like you're trying to negotiate some benefits too."

"You gonna climb out the bathroom window?"

Her smile grew when he tipped his head back and the cowlick bobbed. "Order me some Chianti and a side of tiramisu. I'll be back."

****

Tom held his tongue when she reached for another piece of garlic bread. In truth, he would have given her the whole basket if it meant she'd stay right where she was, laughing, talking, and relaxing for the first time since she sank her teeth into his danish Sunday morning. Crumbs trickled to her top. The memory of slivered almonds licked from her warm skin assaulted his psyche. He fought back the urge to lunge across the table and lap them up with his tongue. Reaching for the last slice of bread, he realized he'd lost the thread of the conversation.

"So I said, 'Sure, come on by and bring your monkey. I've always wanted a threesome with two of the hairiest beasts in the world' and that was that," she concluded with an emphatic nod.

His head jerked up. "Huh?"

"Am I boring you already?"

"Distracting," he corrected. "Distracting me." He nodded to the bits of crust clinging to her celery green sweater. "You have, uh…I'm having a flashback."

"Oh." She glanced down and immediately swiped at the crumbs, a pink flush creeping high in her cheeks. She flashed a quick smile, but it failed to cover her discomfiture. "Sorry to trigger the post-traumatic stress."

"That was the best morning I've had in years. At least, until my mom called."

The embarrassment that colored her cheeks morphed into a pleased blush. "How were the gutters?"

"Clogged."

"And your mom? How is she?"

"The same as she's always been."

Maggie quickly dissected the remainder of the garlic bread, plucking off bite-sized pieces and slipping them between those lush lips. "Have you told her the golden boy is considering becoming a father outside of the sacrament of Holy Matrimony?"

Tom quirked an eyebrow. "I never tip my hand before a negotiation is complete." He wiped his mouth and set the napkin aside. "Can we talk about it?"

Her green eyes glowed, wary and watchful. She abandoned the bread in favor of toying with the stem of her wine glass. "Fine. Give me your pitch."

"I'm not a salesman, I'm an attorney. We argue our case."

"Okay, counselor. Give me your opening argument."

Tom nudged his plate aside and reached for her hand, smiling when she invested little resistance. "You don't have to do this alone, Maggie." She caught her bottom lip between her teeth and he took advantage of the opportunity her silence afforded. "We can be friends. Hell, Maggie, I've laughed more with you this week than I've laughed in a year. I like you."

She met his gaze and those grass green eyes pierced him. "I like you too. More than I think I should."

He nodded once. "I understand." When she raised an eyebrow, he laughed. "I do understand. I think maybe we both might have been a little wrong about each other."

"Or totally right."

"Possibly. But you have to admit, we seem to fit fairly well together. That is, when you're not letting your temper get the best of you."

"My temper?"

"The red hair…."

Her eyes flashed and her jaw dropped in indignation. He could almost see the angry retort on the tip of her tongue. She caught it at the last second, withdrawing her hand and swirling the dregs of her wine as she raised the glass to her lips. "I'm sure I don't know what you mean."

She sounded cool and prim, but flames licked her cheeks. "I'm sure you don't," he murmured. Retreating into casual flirtation, he dropped a broad wink. "You pack a wallop, Maggie." Her indelicate snort only made his smile widen.

Temper flashed again, but she reined it in. "Get to the point."

"Shared parenting, co-parenting, whatever you want to call it." She opened her mouth, but he held up a hand to stop her. "Hear me out."

She sank back in her chair. The play of emotion across her face ran the gamut from annoyed to agitated. Figuring that was the best he could hope for at the moment, he plunged ahead. "I'd pay half of all your out-of-pocket medical expenses during the pregnancy, monthly child support after the baby is born, and half of all the expenses for the child—medical, dental, education…everything."

"Like a divorce without the pesky marriage," she muttered. She twisted her fingers together and asked in a taut voice, "And you'd want…?"

"You'd have full custody, Maggie." He toyed with the edge of his napkin, worrying a loose thread with his thumbnail. "I'd like to have regular visitation, of course. The norm would call for every other weekend, but since you work Saturdays and I don't, I was thinking Saturdays could be mine. Maybe we can split Sunday, or make a point of doing something together on Sundays…The three of us…I don't know." He waved the thought away. "We can work that out. I'd want one night during the week, too. Maybe Thursday, since you work later on Thursdays…."

"You researched my hours? Have you had me investigated too?"

"Should I?" The smart-ass retort slipped out before he could stop it. He shook his head. "They're on the door, Maggie. Your website and the ad in the *Yellow Pages,* too," he pointed out. He dragged a hand over his face, tugging at his cheeks. "Wow. You really do think the worst of me, don't you?"

Maggie averted her gaze. "I don't know you. Not really…"

"You wouldn't know a donor at all," he pointed out. The stubborn jut of her chin pulled him back from the brink. Tom abandoned the napkin and reached across the table, offering his hand palm-up.

"Get to know me, Maggie," he coaxed. "I'm not a bad guy, no matter what you think you know. I take good care of my mother. I love my brother, my uncle, and my niece and nephews. Even my sister-in-law, although I think she's lost her mind…" His fingers twitched, curling toward his palm. "I like dogs. And cats. Fred even liked me. I think…"

He wanted to fidget. To wriggle in his seat like his six-year-old nephew. She just stared at him, not saying a word. Tom figured she'd make an awesome mother. After all, she already had the penetrating stare down pat.

"Why did you think I was off-limits?"

The question winged him, making his head spin. "Huh?"

"You said I was off limits." Maggie circled her hand, urging him to take the leap with her. "Why?"

Tom blinked. "You know why."

"No, I don't."

"Just…because, Maggie."

"Are you six?"

Rolling his eyes, Tom growled his frustration as he straightened in his seat. "Come on." When she crossed her arms over her chest, he sighed. "Because we were looking for different things, okay? You…You're the kind of girl who wants to get married, join the PTA, and drive a minivan."

She didn't bother refuting his assessment. "And what's changed?"

"You're willing to have a baby without getting married."

Maggie shook her head, disbelief etched into the tiny furrow between her brows. "You're really that anti-marriage?"

"Yes."

His simple answer seemed to give her a jolt. The sinking sensation in his stomach said he'd blown it. He gripped the table, prepared to brace the remains of their first and last supper together when she bolted. Instead, she blinked the confusion from her eyes, folded her forearms on the checked tablecloth, and fixed him with a steady stare.

"So, how do you think this would work?"

The soft-spoken question made him jump. The quiver in her voice made him ache. The overwhelming urge to touch her prickled his skin. He released his hold on the table and flexed his fingers, beckoning to her. Until his fingers closed around hers, he hadn't realized how much he needed to hold onto her to steady his own nerves. "I'm not really sure." He flashed a nervous smile. "The only thing I know is that I'm scared as hell."

A bubble of laughter burst from her lips. "Me, too."

"A part of me can't believe I'm even thinking about this, but Maggie…" He waited until their gazes met and held. "Maggie, it feels right."

"I know," she breathed. "I've wanted to have a baby since…forever, but even though I'd discussed with my doctor and the clinic it didn't feel real. Not until I told you. That was the first time I actually said it out loud."

He cradled her hand between his palms, holding her there with him. "You know what I'm feeling, then. It's like getting hit by a bus, or a train, or a damn asteroid…"

Maggie's eyes widened. Her lips parted, and the pink tip of her tongue darted out to wet them. "I know." She stared at their clasped hands. "So, what do you think we should do?"

"Well, if you insist, we can go through with the insemination thing, but I think the old-fashioned way would be a lot more fun…"

His mouth was off and running before her use of the word 'we' registered with his brain. It took a full minute for that one little word to hit him harder than a bus, a train, and an asteroid combined. For once in his life, Tom lost all power of speech, but his smile was irrepressible as he slid from his chair. Still holding her hand trapped in his, he pulled her to her feet. Maggie stared at him, her eyes locked on his as she swayed toward him. He released her hand to gather her into his arms and planted an exuberant kiss on her parted lips.

"Tom…"

"Say yes, Maggie. Everything else…we'll work things out. Just say yes," he prompted.

"Yes."

The word popped from her mouth. Judging from her stunned expression, she hadn't given it permission to escape, but Tom was all for aiding and abetting the wayward syllable. He kissed her again, his hand sinking into the mass of paprika-colored curls, his lips melting against the plush heat of hers. The dregs of her wine intoxicated him. His head spun. The tang of garlic set his blood afire. Her scent swirled through his senses, enveloping him in a fog of vanilla, cinnamon, and sugar. She smelled delicious. Comforting. Like home and hearth and…Maggie.

A discretely muffled cough yanked him back into the here and now. He blinked at the hovering waiter then glanced around, realizing half the restaurant was watching them with unabashed interest. Maggie ducked her head, nudging his shoulder with her forehead, her face veiled by flame-kissed curls.

"We're having a baby!" he announced to the crowd.

Her head popped up, chucking him on the chin. His teeth clacked together as she hissed, "Tom!"

He staggered back, but the blow couldn't wipe the smile from his face when their fellow diners clapped and called their congratulations. A smile tugged at Maggie's lips as she shook her head and slumped into her seat, her face crimson but her eyes sparkling.

"Your tiramisu," the waiter announced, placing the frothy confection in front of her. "Will there be anything else?"

Tom leaned down and whispered, "Do you want to get out of here?" She nodded mutely, and he brushed his hand over her springy curls. "Can we have a box for that, please? And the check?"

The waiter smiled and whisked the plate away, winking when he caught Tom's eye. "Of course. I'll be right back."

Maggie made a show of rummaging through her purse, keeping her head down. "That wasn't mortifying at all."

He slid back into his chair and stared at her gleaming curls until she dared to peek at him. "I'm so happy, Maggie."

A worried frown creased her brow. "You know I'm not pregnant yet, right?"

Tom laughed, slouching in his seat and tugging at the knot in his tie. "I think I know how it works, Mags." Patiently, he waited until her eyes met his. He tossed her a leer, waggling his eyebrows suggestively. "I think we're gonna have a helluva lot of fun getting there."

The crease between her eyebrows disappeared. She blinked, and her bottle-green gaze cooled. "If you really think jerking off into a cup is a good time, who am I to spoil your fun," she said with a shrug.

Pretty sure his heart came to a full and complete stop, he forced a breath. "You're kidding, right?" he asked slowly. When she barely even blinked, panic set in. "Please tell me you're kidding…"

"Oh, look! Here's our check and my cake," she cooed as the waiter rushed back to the table.

He rooted for his wallet, watching her carefully and praying she would crack. "Maggie?"

She gathered her purse and the to-go box, fixing him with a bland stare as she rose. "I have a full day tomorrow. Saturdays are our busiest day."

Dropping a fifty in the folder, he nearly toppled his chair when he shot to his feet, his gaze locked on the sway of her hips. "Maggie," he hissed, winding his way through the tables in hot pursuit.

She stumbled through the door, pulling her jacket closer and tipping her head back to peer at the night sky.

The sharp autumn wind tossed her hair and stole his breath. Or maybe it was the sight of her moonlit profile. "What are you doing?"

"Trying to find a star," she answered, as if it should have been obvious to him.

Willing to go along with whatever she wanted at that point, he tipped his head back. "There." He nodded to the one twinkling speck of white that dared to defy the glow of a million and one city lights.

She smirked and pointed to the pinpoint of light. "That one?"

"Yeah." Her lush, vibrant chortle made his heart flip-flop. He stared at the sky, trying to locate the flickering light again. "What? Not good enough?" Her fingers curled around his and he turned toward her. Maggie's answering smile was brilliant, pouring over him like moonlight but as warm as a ray of summer sun.

"Tom?"

Her porcelain skin distracted him. The smattering of pale freckles dusting her nose held him in thrall. She squeezed his hand, anchoring him to the cracked sidewalk. "Hmm?"

"That's an airplane."

A weak smile accompanied his chuckle of embarrassment. He glanced up, scanning the sky for the phantom star. When he came up empty, he met her amused gaze once again. "I'll get better at this. I promise."

Maggie squeezed his hand again, stretching onto her toes to peck a soft kiss to his lips. She pulled away, and he swayed like an oak. "We can work on it." Settling back on her heels, she heaved a sigh and cast another glance at the sky. "Come on. We've got a lot to talk about."

He held tight, unwilling to relinquish her hand when he stepped to the curb to search for a passing cab. "I don't suppose you'll share that tiramisu," he ventured.

"What? A baby isn't enough?" She laughed, and Tom was willing to bet the sound was sweeter and richer than the Marsala-drenched cake she clutched to her chest. "Don't push your luck, buddy."

****

He was pushing his luck. Maggie dragged the tines of her fork through the tiramisu, tracking white lines through the dusting of cocoa. Every instinct screamed at her. This wasn't safe. This wasn't smart. This could all end in heartbreak. She ignored those pesky instincts. They couldn't be trusted, anyway. All following her instincts had gotten her were a fat cat who terrorized her and a hot date with a turkey baster. Okay, she knew they didn't really use a baster, but the image of one was burned on her brain now and it wouldn't be erased without benefit of a sandblaster.

The open collar of Tom's shirt called to her. Gold-tinged skin shadowed with dark stubble made her mouth water. The hollow of his throat proved infinitely more tempting than the coffee-soaked cake in front of her. She forced herself to take a tiny bite of creamy goodness, but it was hard to concentrate. His suit jacket was slung over the back of the chair. The tie he wore at dinner trailed from his pocket, snaking across the worn linoleum. Fred kept a close eye on it from his spot near his food dish. She kept a close eye on Tom as he scrawled on the tiny pad he kept in his coat pocket.

He looked up and caught her staring. His Adam's apple bobbed, and, oh, she wanted to take a bite out of him. Instead, she sneaked a peek at his notes. Her eyebrows shot up as she read the words 'blood test' and 'sperm count' near the top of the page.

She stole a glance at him. "Blood test?"

He flinched. When she nodded to the notepad, he tried to recover with a nonchalant shrug. "I just figure it's a good idea. Not that I'm worried about anything. I haven't had unprotected sex since nineteen-eighty-seven."

She snorted. "Those 'No glove, no love' ads really got to you, huh?"

"A girlfriend who wasn't doing due diligence with the birth control pills got to me, but the threat of disease and death didn't hurt." Ducking his head, he went back to work.

His long leg brushed hers when he shifted on the hard wooden seat, stretching beneath the scarred table. Neat block letters filled the lined pages of his tiny notebook. Ink flowed from his pen, making the barest of scratches against the paper. He chewed his bottom lip. His cowlick wobbled as he nodded to himself, adding another item to the pages-long list. His forehead puckered as he glanced around. "Do you think you'll want to stay here?"

Plunging the fork into the soft cake, she collected a hefty bite. "Huh?"

"I mean, I'm sure it'll be fine while the baby's little, but aren't you gonna want a yard? Someplace with some room to run?"

She shoveled the cake into her mouth and chewed slowly, pretending she hadn't asked herself the same question a dozen times. Her shrug came off herky-jerky. Nonchalance wasn't her strong suit, but having a mouthful of cake helped a bit. "I guess. Eventually," she mumbled.

The cowlick fluttered when he nodded. "I'll put that in here too. I can help with a down payment on a house."

Licking a stray bit of fluffy cream from the corner of her mouth, Maggie glared at his tiny notebook. "Sounds like you want me to be a kept woman. Like I'm some kind of brood mare you're buying." The injury she inflicted flickered across his face. Before he could school his features she was regretting her comment. "Joke," she offered with a lame laugh.

Too late. Mr. Excited-possible-baby-daddy was gone and Mr. Cool-and-aloof was back. "These are all just options available to you, Maggie. You can choose to use them or not. I'm just putting them out there."

"I know," she whispered. "I'm just… Sorry. I'm used to doing things on my own."

Tom set the pen aside and waited until she met his gaze. "Isn't that the point of this whole discussion? You don't have to do this alone. Neither would I. We'd be in this together."

"Like a partnership."

Tom hesitated for a split second then nodded. "Yeah, like a partnership."

Taking her fork, she sliced the remainder of her cake neatly in half, separating the two pieces. He raised a curious eyebrow and she smiled. "Should we seal the deal with some cake?"

A slow, sexy smile curved his mouth. "How about a kiss?"

"After the cake," she countered, offering him the fork. "And maybe the blood test."

Chapter Ten

After nearly a week of radio silence, Tom Sullivan had the audacity to tap on The Glass Slipper's window just after closing time. Maggie looked up from re-stocking the retail shelves and there he was, wearing a smile that made his blue eyes twinkle and crinkle. He had the balls to stand there, briefcase in hand, grinning a grin which reeked of boyish charm. She wanted to slap him almost as much as she ached to kiss him.

Perhaps it was force of habit. Confusion was her new best friend. One minute she was so sure, the next, she didn't have a clue about anything. A girl doesn't just forget nearly forty years playing it safe and trying to be good because a guy licks bits of fluff and crumbs from her lips. A woman who is giving serious consideration to setting up a life-long partnership with a man known for ditching previous relationships in accordance with the phases of the moon doesn't dive in head first, hoping to tread water. Okay, maybe she did once, but at the time she truly thought the night they spent together would be a fling, a fluke, a hot memory to warm cold nights.

He mapped it all out for her the night she'd agreed to think about it. He laid out his strategy for this 'co-parenting' thing, adding point after point to the notes he scrawled on that tiny pad of paper. She had to kick him out. She had to make it clear she wasn't buying what he was selling. He didn't play fair. One minute he picked apart every detail of her future, the next he drugged her with molten kisses designed to melt all resistance. Scorching heat wafted off him when he pulled her into his lap, intent on devouring her share of their dessert any way he could get it. He cupped her bottom, groaning into her mouth as he pulled her tight against the bulge in his pants.

She almost gave in. Hell, she almost cleared the table with one arm and begged him to take her there and then. Only the flash of red emergency lights and the wail of a siren from the street below saved her. Maggie leapt from his lap, grabbing the back of the chair she'd abandoned along with her inhibitions, and dragging in a steadying breath.

The wooden chair screeched against linoleum. Tom lunged for her and Fred lunged for the necktie trailing from his jacket pocket. The cat swung too wide, catching Tom's ankle. He yelped, the cat pounced, and the silk tie came out looking like silk shantung. As soon as she was capable of exhaling, Maggie mumbled a litany of excuses and practically pushed him out the apartment door. Again.

He didn't call the next day or the day after. By the time the third day passed, her hormones had her zigzagging all over the place. Maggie wasn't quite sure if Mother Nature was impressed with her forbearance or punishing her for prudery. Either way, as day four began she was full-tilt-boogying toward miserable, and hormones or no, Maggie knew being miserable over Tom Sullivan was definitely not smart.

Now, he was standing there, smiling, twinkling, and crinkling at her. Maggie pursed her lips, ignoring the twinge of nerves tweaking her stomach and the pang of something she didn't want to think about pooling low in her belly.

"What are you doing here?" she asked by way of greeting. "You decide to let me wax your back hair?"

He laughed. "No. I came to give you something." Tom reached into the breast pocket of his coat and started to remove a folded sheet of paper. He paused, his brows drawing together in consternation. "Back hair? I don't have back hair, do I?"

She cocked an eyebrow. "Well, you aren't Sasquatch yet, but…."

"Really?" He cocked his arm, groping at the small of his back. "Where?"

She nodded to the sheet of paper. "You were going to give me something?"

"Oh!" He presented it to her with a flourish. "Healthy, clean, and locked and loaded," he said, recovering his boyish grin. "Reporting for duty, ma'am."

Maggie snorted softly as she unfolded the page. She made a show of scanning the medical mumbo-jumbo then closed it again, setting the creases with her thumbnail. "Well, stand down, solider. We're in a demilitarized zone."

"Huh?"

She thought of the prescription bottle sitting on her kitchen counter. "It's not the time to mobilize the troops."

"Why not? I thought you were all gung-ho to get this going."

"Gung-ho?"

"Hey, you were the one who started the Patton bit," he retorted. His fingers fluttered through his hair. The cowlick popped up. The crinkles around his eyes morphed into weary wrinkles. Lines of strain bracketed his mouth.

A twinge of sympathy tweaked her stomach, only to be overpowered by a killer cramp. She snatched the last two bottles of aromatherapy bath gel from the box and plunked them on the shelf. "Yeah, well, you didn't even give me the courtesy of a MacArthur."

"A MacArthur?"

"I shall return," she intoned. Snatching the box from the counter, she stalked toward the storage room.

Tom dropped the briefcase and followed her into the snug space beyond the reception desk. "You had to know I would."

"Did I?"

"Shit, Maggie, we're having a baby together." Maggie didn't answer. Instead she grabbed a box of sterile cotton sponges from the shelf and brushed past him. "And maybe I'm tired of having you slam doors in my face," he continued, dogging her footsteps as she stopped into the first treatment room.

She shoved a handful of sponges into an already stocked drawer. The damn thing bounced right back at her when she tried to shut it. "Maybe I'm tired of you trying to push your way in."

"If I don't push, you won't let me in!"

The sterile pads flew through the air when she threw her arms up in frustration. "I don't understand why you're doing this."

Tom stepped back and the confetti of cotton fell to the floor at their feet. He stared down at the square-shaped swatches. "Back to square one," he murmured. "It's always back to square one with you."

Ignoring the mess she'd created, she tipped her chin up. "What's that supposed to mean?"

"I don't know how many times I have to say it. I like you, Maggie. You're beautiful. You make me laugh. You're smart, strong, sexy as hell… You're everything you should be, everything any guy would admire," he said, the low timbre of his voice barely ruffling the quiet that surrounded them. "And no matter what you've cooked up in your head, I'm just a guy. My needs are pretty simple."

"You came over here to get laid," she muttered.

He smirked. "You really think getting laid is so hard? You think I went through what I went through this week to get my rocks off? Hell, I already did. Caught it in a cup and rushed over to a lab holding a brown paper bag like I'd packed a peanut butter and jelly sandwich for lunch."

Maggie looked away, battling back the hot rush of tears prickling her eyes. He backed into the hall, his fingers trailing over the doorframe. "I thought we understood each other. I thought we wanted the same thing. A baby…A partner, a friend, someone to count on…."

"You didn't call," she whispered. The mental ass kicking started up the moment the pathos-laced words left her lips.

"I didn't know if you wanted me to call. And…I was a little mad. Hell, twice you've tossed me out of your apartment." He held his palms out in a gesture of futility. "You never gave me your phone number. What was I supposed to do, call you here and hope to catch you between customers?"

She pressed the heel of her hand to the center of her forehead. "You would have had it on your phone. I called you, remember?"

Tom took a cautious step into the room. "I didn't know if I was supposed to use it. I don't know what I'm supposed to be doing, Maggie. Are we dating, or are we just having a baby together? Am I supposed to call you? Why didn't you call me if you wanted to talk to me?" He reached for her but she shook her head and turned away. Warm hands closed over her upper arms. "Tell me, Maggie. Just tell me what you want and I'll do my best, but you're gonna have to be pretty clear. This hot and cold thing is messing with my head."

"Mine too." The tears broke free, spilling onto her cheeks and trickling to her chin. "I'm all over the place," she whispered. She sniffled and his warm, hard chest pressed against her back. She swiped at her cheeks. "Hormones. I have to warn you, they're only going to get worse."

Strong arms taut with tension wound their way around her, pulling her into him, taking some of the weight. "If you can tell me you really want me here, I'll tough them out." His chin came to rest atop her head. He drew a deep breath. "Please, just tell me now. Do you, Maggie?"

The breath caught in her throat, tangled in a knot of hope, fear, optimism and terror. She knew he was right. She had to make up her mind once and for all. She needed to grow up, let go of her girlish dreams, swallow the lump of disappointment that lodged in her throat and get on with her life. Such as it was.

Tom nuzzled her hair. She felt him take a deep breath. As if he needed to drink her in. Like he was parched, and if he had her scent he'd be able to go on. Move forward. And she could move forward with him. Take the chance. The biggest gamble of her life.

She shifted, and he tightened his hold. She chuckled and pushed on his arms, loosening them just enough to turn and face him. His lips twitched. Those dark blue eyes narrowed expectantly, fanning the tiny crinkles again. He wet his lips. She could see the wheels turning in his head and another argument forming in the depths of his eyes. Maggie covered his warm mouth with cool fingertips and shook her head. His lips pursed into a soft kiss, sealing the deal whether she was ready or not.

Maggie was aware that in his own way, he was asking her to share her life with him. All she had to do was say the word. Two words actually. The same two words she'd been dreaming of saying since she was a little girl. Gathering all of her courage, she looked him in the eye and whispered, "I do."

****

The dreamy look in her eyes when she whispered 'I do' should have sent him bolting for the door, but it didn't. Instead, Tom found his feet rooted to the ground. He waited a full minute, just holding her in his arms while ticking off the seconds in his brain. Panic didn't bubble in his gut. His well-honed instincts for fight or flight failed him. The only sensation that registered was her soft warmth melting into him, cloaking him in calm.

A renegade tendril of red hair escaped her low ponytail. He tucked it behind her ear, his knuckles grazing her cheek and jaw. The fuzzy buzzing in his brain was back. Unable to work past it, he gave in to the low hum, gathering her closer and groping for a safe topic. "Are you hungry?"

She caught the edge of his lapel between her teeth and gave it a tug, her answer muffled by his jacket. "Starving."

"Chinese? Pizza? Thai?"

"Perfect."

"All of the above?" he asked as she pulled away.

"Any, not all."

She took his hand to lead him from the room but he pulled back. "Wait." When she turned, he gestured to the cotton-cluttered floor. "Are we going to leave this?"

Maggie huffed and rolled her eyes, bending to scoop up a handful of the decidedly un-sterile sponges. "Are you some kind of neat-freak?"

He laughed. "Not really. I was only thinking about your clients." He gathered as many of the white squares as he could reach. "We need to stop bickering." Straightening to his full height, he found her propped against the table grinning at him. He waved a handful of cotton at her. "Too much clean-up involved."

"I like bickering with you."

"I noticed." He tossed the squares into a tiny trashcan. "Wouldn't be so bad if there were make-up sex involved…"

In a blink, she had him up against the wall and the sponges she gathered fluttered to the floor again. She pinned him with her lush curves. Not that he was resisting. Hell, he forgot how to breathe. Her lips parted, her eyes grew dark and heavy-lidded. She moved, sliding against his body, slow and sinuous, grasping his hands and pressing them to the cool wall.

He ducked his head, trying for a kiss, but she eluded him. Hot, moist breath tickled his throat. His Adam's apple seemed to swell along with the rest of his body, pressing against the knot in his tie. "Maggie," he rasped, wondering if it would be his last word.

Her finger slipped under the knot, gently tugging until she loosened it another inch. "You need to lighten up."

He opened his mouth to protest, but she wriggled again, eliciting a groan instead. "Yes, ma'am." Panting, he wrapped one arm around her waist, binding her to him. "Whatever you say, ma'am…Just don't stop."

He feinted to the left then ducked right, his lips fastening on the smooth skin just beneath her ear. Her pulse throbbed against his tongue. She smelled like sugar cookies and cinnamon. He laved the tender skin with his tongue. Sweet and spice. The scent suited Maggie to a tee.

"I've been dreaming about you, Maggie." His voice rumbled in his chest, trapped there by lack of oxygen and Maggie overload. "I can't wait to be inside you."

A strangled moan, half plea or half protest, it didn't matter. "Can't…Period…" The words escaped in a breathy rush. "Supposed to start taking the Clomid…"

Undeterred, he caught her ear lobe between his teeth, a low growl of frustration punctuating the gentle bite. He set her away from him and glanced down at his heaving chest, wondering if he'd ever draw a peaceful breath again. "Just tell me you want me too," he said, not daring to glance up. "Tell me you feel it. Tell me it's not just me."

"I want you too."

The quiet calm in her voice stilled his jangled nerves. He met her frank gaze. "You feel it too."

"I just pushed you up against a wall," she pointed out.

His nod gained momentum as certainty sank in then stopped abruptly. The back of his head thunked against the wall. He clamped his jaw then had to concentrate on working it free again. A niggling voice in his head told him she didn't feel the same pull he did. She pushed him up against a wall, but she never said she felt it too.

"So, uh…Chinese?"

"You don't have to…If you don't want to stay—"

"We've got some things to go over." He raised one shoulder in a lazy shrug. "Might as well eat."

****

Maggie plucked a pea pod from the container and popped it into her mouth, her lips closing around the chopsticks. She flipped over another page of the document he'd pulled from his overstuffed briefcase and scanned the last paragraph, watching him watching her out of the corner of her eye. He clutched his fork so tight she feared it would bend. "What's the matter? General Tso fighting back?"

Tom gave his head a shake and plunged the fork into the container. "No, just zoning out."

"Got a pen?" she asked, extending one hand palm-up.

He flinched. "You can't sign it now. You need to have an attorney look it over," he said, clearly aghast.

"You're an attorney."

"I'm a party to the agreement."

"You wrote it," she pointed out.

"Which is why you need to have someone else read through it," he retorted.

She rolled her eyes. "It just states everything we talked about."

His eye roll trumped hers. Nodding to the document, he fixed her with a stern glare. "Right, but there might be aspects to what we talked about that you haven't considered."

"Are you trying to rook me out of a baby? You might be good, Tom, but unless you can prove me unfit, you wouldn't stand a chance. Courts still favor the biological mother," she said with a smug smile.

"I don't need you to tell me that."

If his petulant expression were any less appealing, she might have heeded his advice. A part of her knew that she probably should anyway, just to counter-act that little boy sulk he had going on. She sighed and picked through the container again, searching for a cashew she might have missed the first time through. Without glancing in his direction she asked, "If you were my attorney, what would you advise?"

Tom set his container aside and plucked the last egg roll from the box resting on the cushion between them. He pursed his lips as he broke off the end and inspected the roll's contents. "Well, you'd be signing away any possibility of a palimony claim."

"I didn't think they did those much anymore."

"Maybe not, but the precedent is still there."

Maggie slumped onto the arm of the couch and swung her feet onto the cushion, knocking over the empty container. "I don't need your money, Tom."

He snorted softly, fixing her with a bland stare. "It's rarely about money, Maggie."

"Yes, but that's all you get in the end, right?" She stabbed at her dinner, spearing a chunk of chicken with her chopstick. "Any kind of split up is basically a divorce. Someone always comes out worse for it. As long as it's not my baby who suffers, I don't care."

"You say that now."

"And I'll say it later, too," she stated flatly. "It's not like you're gonna set me up in a manner to which I'd like to become accustomed, right?" She sank her teeth into the chunk of chicken and pulled it from the chopstick. "You aren't trying to *Gigi* me, are you?"

"Gigi you? What does that mean?"

"Old musical," she mumbled as she chewed. "A family of French courtesans raise a young girl to be a kept woman…You know, I used to think I wouldn't mind being a kept woman," she mused.

"What changed your mind?"

She shrugged and set the container on the coffee table. "Never met a guy as handsome as Louis Jordan or as charming as Maurice Chevalier."

"This isn't just an agreement, Maggie. I mean, I'm hoping it turns out to be more than this." He waved a hand at the paperwork.

"How so?"

"I'd like us to have…a relationship."

"A relationship?" she asked, raising a querying brow. He shifted and his discomfiture gave her a little rush of pleasure.

"I want to see you. I want to spend time with you. I like talking to you, that is, when we're not bickering."

A pleased blush warmed her cheeks. "You would, huh?"

"If you…" He cleared his throat. "If that's what you want too."

Maggie stacked the pages on her stomach then held them out to him. "I can't sign this, anyway. You got my name wrong."

"I did?"

"Legally, I'm Mary Margaret McCann."

"Mary Margaret," he murmured, as if tasting her name on his tongue. She glanced up and he smiled. "I like that. Mary Margaret. It suits you."

"My parents would be glad you think so." She watched as he devoured the last of the egg roll. "What's your middle name?"

"Daniel," he mumbled through stuffed cheeks.

"Thomas Daniel Sullivan." Maggie wrinkled her nose. "Doesn't really flow."

He wiped his mouth with a paper napkin then crumbled it, tossing it into the empty container before pulling her feet into his lap. "Well, that would make sense. Daniel is my dad's name. Was…Is…I don't even know if he's alive. Anyway, he probably took the flow with him when he left."

His hand closed around her toes, warming them through the fuzzy purple socks she wore. He started to rub and she sighed, closing her eyes and succumbing to the pleasure. "You never heard from him again?"

"He called once on my birthday and talked to Sean. Sent my mother off the deep end," he said gruffly.

"And that was it?"

He snagged his beer from the side table and took a swig. "It was probably better that way." He gasped as he lowered the bottle. "The mere mention of his name could set my mom off for weeks."

"That's horrible! He didn't fight her? He never tried to see you?"

Tom sighed and picked at the label with his thumbnail. "You've met my mom, Maggie. Would you want to deal with her for more than ten minutes?"

"She's not that bad."

He fixed her with a pointed stare. "Yes, she is." Maggie opened her mouth to defend the woman then clamped it shut. "You know she is," he said with a nod. "She shits all over Sean, treats Tracy like she's some hooker her son picked up, and wants the world to believe she thinks the sun shines out of my ass."

"She doesn't think the sun shines out of your ass?"

"Only when she thinks it'll do her some good." He put the bottle back on the table and cupped her foot between his palms again. "My dad left in 1971. My mother wouldn't give him a divorce until 1984."

"Whoa. That's a hell of a separation."

"Yeah, well, he tried, but she made his life a living hell. He finally just gave up and waited for her to divorce him. Of course, she waited until old Danny Sullivan had finally made a little money, and she was able to stick it to him good."

"Jeez." She slumped a little deeper into the cushions. "Is that why you decided to get into family law?"

"No. That's why I'm careful to stay on my mother's good side," he said with a wry smile. "I went into family law because Arnie Becker got laid all the time on *L.A. Law*."

Maggie pulled the throw pillow from under her head and fulfilled its destiny by tossing it straight at his head. He laughed and snagged the pillow, stuffing it under her feet before resuming the foot rub. She hummed her approval and closed her eyes again. "That's why you became a divorce attorney. And why Sean won't leave Tracy," she murmured.

"He'll never leave her. If she wants out, she'll have to walk away. Without the kids," he stated as a matter of fact.

"She'll never leave the kids."

"Then they'd better learn to live with each other, huh?"

She nodded but kept her eyes screwed tightly shut. "She loves him."

"Got a funny way of showing it."

His tone was mild, but she heard the hurt and hope that laced his blithe words. She shook her head. "She's feeling lost. Like she doesn't know who she is anymore." Something in her voice must have caught his attention because those long, strong fingers ground to a halt. "Don't stop," she implored.

Tom pressed his thumbs into her instep, working in a slow circle toward her toes. "And you, Maggie? Have you ever gotten lost?"

A small smile quirked her lips. "I get lost in the grocery store."

"I'm serious."

"So am I." She favored him with a wan smile. "I've never been like Tracy. I didn't have my life all mapped out at eighteen. I never had any designs on conquering the world, or even the metro-Chicago area. I just kind of…floated."

"Is that bad?"

She barked a sharp laugh. "It probably isn't good."

"Don't sell yourself short, Maggie."

His solemn expression tugged at her heart. His frank admiration pleased her more than it should. She wanted flirty, charming Tom back. She could handle him. Sincere, serious Tom was a bit too disconcerting. Needing to regain the upper hand and anxious to get back to more familiar footing, she flashed a bright smile.

"So, Sergeant Sullivan, are you in for the duration, or are you shipping out soon?"

His startled blink made her feel a little more in control. "Huh?"

"You staying here tonight or going home?" she asked, raising an inquisitive eyebrow. "I put in a thirteen hour day and had a foot rub. I think it's time for bed."

His forehead creased. "You'd let me stay here?"

She tossed off a nonchalant shrug. "It's up to you. Just remember, you can't fool with Mother Nature."

His eyes narrowed to slits. "You're not just trying to set me up, are you? You gonna get me stripped down then kick me out again?"

Swinging her legs from the couch, Maggie sat up. "I'm just making the offer. You have to decide if you can take the chance."

"If I stay, what else can I rub?"

Her indelicate snort powered her ascent. "Nothing." A jaw-cracking yawn caught her up short. She pressed her hand to the small of her back and stretched. "Well, maybe my back..." she amended. "You have approximately thirty seconds to decide."

"I'm in," he answered promptly.

She gave a quick nod then strolled over to bolt the door. On her way past the sofa she snagged his hand and pulled him along, leading him toward her bedroom. "You get the crappy pillow and you sleep on Fred's side of the bed."

He wrapped his arm around her waist, pulling her back against his chest and pressing their joined hands to her belly as he shortened his long stride to match hers. "You sure know how to make a guy feel welcome, Ms. McCann."

"Well, nothing's in writing yet. You can still bolt," she said, casting a quick glance over her shoulder.

"Nope. I told you, I'm in. I'm totally in."

Chapter Eleven

He surfaced slowly, his subconscious meandering through a field of wildflowers which seemed to be, oddly enough, scented with cinnamon. Warm. The warmth enveloped him, centering at the small of his back and radiating up his spine. Soft, heavy heat immobilized him, but he wasn't trapped. No, he was right where he was supposed to be, surrounded by spice-laden flowers and anchored by the fuzzy weight of..."Fred," he growled into the pillow.

The cat revved his motor, stretching his front paws until they brushed his bare shoulder blades. Fred's purr did nothing to conceal the silent threat of barely sheathed claws. "Maggie," he murmured, afraid to move a muscle for fear of evisceration. "Move your cat."

No response. He cracked one eye open and licked his parched lips. His tongue picked up the rasp of dried spittle and he winced. He moved his head an experimental half-inch and found his cheek was glued to the pillowcase. Great. Not only had he slept like the dead, but he also managed to nearly drown her too. He licked his lips again. "Maggie?"

She didn't answer. Tom snaked a hand out from under his stomach and groped the tangle of sheets next to him. The threat of stiletto claws was diminished by the brush of cool cotton and the alarming realization that she was gone. He planted both hands on the mattress and reared up, dislodging the corpulent cat before he could engage weaponry.

Fred glared at him, emitting an ominous mixture of meow and growl as he kneaded the knotted blankets, staking out a new spot. Tom glanced around the empty room, taking in the jumble of clothes on the floor, the slanting sunlight filtering through cracked blinds, and the unmistakable absence of Maggie. He ran a hand over the cat's blocky head. "Sorry, bud." Adding a little scratch behind pointy ears for good measure he asked, "Where's our girl?"

Fred deigned to forgive him just enough to let out a piteous meow and lean into Tom's caress. Searching for a clue, Tom followed the cat's green gaze to the digital alarm clock on the nightstand. His jaw dropped when he read the time. "Ten to ten?" The cat celebrated a successful clock reading by stretching his front paws and flipping onto his back, offering up his ample belly for a scratch. Tom obliged. "I can't remember the last time I slept past eight."

The hum of Fred's motor kicked up again, filling the room with its drone. He scrubbed his face with his free hand. The stretched cotton of his boxer briefs pulled taut and the crushing weight in his gut served up reproof from his bladder. With a groan, he swung his legs over the side of the bed.

By the time he emerged from the bathroom, Fred had roused himself to greet him in the hallway. Tom nodded and followed the cat's bobbing tail toward the kitchen. He shot a glance in the direction of Fred's food dish. "I'm betting she already fed you."

The cat stared up at him, employing a mixture of innocence and implied threat to state his case. His own stomach gave a sympathetic grumble. Tom sighed. "Tell you what… If I can find something for me to eat, I might be persuaded to find a little something for you too."

He opened a cabinet door and found only neatly stacked plates and glasses. Fred wound between his ankles, nudging him to the left. More than capable of taking a hint, Tom worked his way down the row of cabinets. He found enough canned soup and cat food to ensure her survival should a freak hurricane blow up on Lake Michigan. He ignored feline cries of protest and moved to the next cabinet. "Me then you, fat cat."

The interior of the next cabinet could have been a depiction of the aftermath of said hurricane. Every package, box, and bag on the shelves appeared to be just shy of total decimation. An empty granola bar box tumbled to the counter. He found one half-eaten victim wrapped in a foil shroud and stuffed between a box of elbow macaroni and a jar of pasta sauce. A torn bag of store-brand spaghetti disgorged its contents onto the flowered shelf paper. Tom shuddered and quickly gathered the dried noodles, stuffing them back into the shredded cellophane. "Your girl is a slob," he informed Fred.

Tipping his head back, Tom scanned the upper shelf with a wary gaze. "Ah ha! Score!" He lunged for the box tucked at the back of the cabinet, shaking it to check the content level as he rocked back on his heels. A satisfied smile curved his lips. He tore open the flaps and wriggled his fingers through the crumpled plastic sleeve and hit pay dirt. He extracted a handful of chocolate-y cereal. "Cocoa Puffs. Gotta love a girl who loves Cocoa Puffs."

Fred meowed piteously, his tail swishing around his haunches. Tom popped a puff into his mouth and found they were only slightly stale. He emptied the rest of the cereal clutched in his palm into his mouth and munched as he moved to the refrigerator.

"What are the odds…" He skimmed the contents of the fridge and found no milk. "I didn't think they'd be very good." The door slammed shut. Tom freed another handful of cocoa-goodness from the box and let one puff plop to the floor. The cat lunged then drew up short, giving the morsel an experimental lick and nibble. "They're good. Trust me."

His orange friend wasn't impressed. Shoveling the rest of the handful into his mouth, he set the box aside. He opened the cabinet of canned goods and selected the seafood medley. "Will this do?" Fred danced a tango around his ankles, so Tom took that as a yes. He found the can opener and studied the contraption until he could figure out the mechanics then went to work. After a full rotation, the can dropped to the counter, seemingly untouched.

"Huh." He scowled at the can, trying to figure out where he went wrong. In his excitement, Fred kicked the tango into a tarantella and was inching dangerously close to segueing into a jitterbug. "I'm workin' on it, buddy." He picked up the can and the lid lifted slightly. "Whoa." He shot the can opener a glance. "Is this thing magic?" he asked his feline friend, prying the loosened lid from the can with his thumbnail.

Fred's meows grew more vocal. Tom stooped to empty the contents into the dish bearing the cat's name. "There. Breakfast is served, your majesty." He was rewarded with a firm head butt and the tickle of a serpentine tail twisting around his calf. "Aw, you're welcome."

Tom hiked the waistband of his boxer-briefs as he straightened. After chucking the can into the trash, he moved to the sink to wash his hands. "This is probably the only time we'll get away with this, you know. If she notices there's a can missing, I can only play dumb once."

Snagging the box of Cocoa Puffs, he left the finicky feline to his meal and wandered into the living room. He trickled another handful into his mouth and glanced around, chewing slowly. His briefcase leaned against the front of the couch, and his suit coat lay draped over the arm. A red chenille throw covered in orange and white fur graced an ancient ottoman with no matching chair. Every table, nook, and cranny was jam packed with framed photos and figurines. Scattered among them was the evidence of what appeared to be an extensive collection of cheesy tourist trap souvenirs.

He moved through the room, picking up a thimble from Tulsa and a picture frame touting Lake Geneva. Tom squinted at the photo, stretching his arm until the faces swam into focus. A smile twitched his lips when he recognized a very young Maggie sandwiched between his sister-in-law, Tracy, and their third roommate, a photographer named Shel. He repositioned the frame precisely on the dust-free spot and turned to scan the room.

Tucking the cereal box under his arm, he gathered the discarded cardboard containers with the remnants of their dinner and snagged his empty beer bottle from the end table. Fred was still savoring his second breakfast when he dumped the lot into the trashcan. He shook his head and gathered another fistful of cereal as he made his way back to the living room.

The agreement he'd drawn up lay forgotten on the couch cushion. He dropped down next to the crumpled pages, reaching blindly to set the cereal box on the end table as he gathered the sheaf of papers. A picture frame toppled and he jumped. The box fell to the floor, scattering sugarcoated puffs of cocoa.

"Crap!"

Tom snatched the box from the floor and propped it against the couch. The picture frame lay face-down on the table. He winced as he lifted it, expecting to find a spider web of shattered glass. Instead he found a grainy photograph of a little red-haired girl in a pink party dress clutching a fairy wand.

He grabbed the frame, stretching his arm to find that magic spot where focus came into play. Frustrated, he dove for his briefcase, groping for the reading glasses few people ever saw him wear. Sliding the glasses onto his nose, he tipped his head back and devoured the suddenly sharp details of the photo.

The dress was pink, but the froth of fluff beneath the skirt was white. Little Maggie's delighted smile outshone the sparkling star affixed to the tip of the magic wand. An older woman wearing a rhinestone tiara beamed her approval. A younger woman, her face partially obscured by rich waves of deep auburn hair, looked on with a tolerant smile. The man in the photograph had his back to the camera and his head bent. His fair hair tumbled forward as he waited on bended knee, as if waiting for the touch of the fairy princess' wand.

The sound of footsteps on the stairs made him jump. Tom hurriedly set the frame on the end table, unable to spare a glance to see if he hit the mark. He gathered the printed pages of his proposed custody agreement from his lap, flipping them right side up just as the apartment door opened.

Maggie slipped inside. "Oh. You're still here."

He looked up, meeting her gaze over the wire rims of his glasses. His fingers clenched the pages and he stifled a wince, trying to resist the urge to yank the frames from his face. "Oh. Yeah. I just woke up."

"Lazy bum." She circled the end of the couch then drew up short, her eyebrows taking flight.

He glanced down. Heat seared his cheeks when he realized he was sitting on her couch practically naked. Maggie laughed and dropped onto the far cushion. "Wow. Not often I walk into my apartment and find a half naked man." He scowled, and her laugh slowed to a throaty chuckle. "I think I like it, though. Maybe if I keep you barefoot, you'll get me pregnant."

Tom mustered up as much cool as a guy caught lounging around in his underpants could manage and stretched his arm across the back of the couch. "I don't have a lot of experience in getting girls knocked up, but I'm pretty sure my feet won't have much to do with it."

Her grin turned soft. The lines of her mouth melted into the same indulgent curve the older woman wore in the photograph. "You look good in the glasses."

Cool be damned, he snatched them from his face, folding the temples into the palm of his hand. "Why aren't you downstairs?"

"My ten-thirty cancelled. I came up to see if you made the bed before you left."

He grinned. "Not yet. You wanna get back in it?"

Maggie heaved a put-upon sigh. "Yes, but I can't. I have to rip someone's pubic hair out in twenty minutes."

His grimace made her laugh, and Tom decided there and then if getting completely grossed out was what it took to elicit that tinkling giggle, he'd let her tell him war stories all day long. "You're a sadist."

Running her hand over his arm and caressing his shoulder, she cooed, "And you keep volunteering to be my victim."

"Do I really have hair on my back?"

Maggie smiled. "You didn't notice me petting you?"

"Seriously…."

"Everyone has hair on their backs, Tom. Even women," she added in a whisper. "The average human body can have over five million hair follicles."

"I'm asking you, as a professional, friend, lover, whatever… Am I turning into a Yeti?"

"Not yet…eee," she answered with a grin.

"You're a funny girl."

Maggie scooted closer, her hand gliding up the side of his neck then cupping the back of his head. Her fingers sank into his hair. He almost purred when her nails scratched his scalp. "You're a pretty boy," she whispered, drawing near.

Her breath tickled his lips, and Tom became acutely aware that he was anything but minty-fresh. He tried to turn his head, but she held firm. "I haven't been a boy for a long time."

"Pretty," she murmured, her lips brushing his. The glancing blow of a kiss made him suck in a breath. "Smooth…" Her hand slid to his shoulder again. Those nimble fingers kneaded the knot of muscle until he relaxed into her touch. "Hard in all the right places." Her mouth grazed his jaw, damp and soft…so soft. As if reading his mind, she nipped at his ear lobe. "Soft in the most delicious spots."

"Let's go back to bed." The words rushed from his mouth as the last of the oxygen caged in his lungs made a break for it.

"We can't…Remember?"

"You're killing me."

She nuzzled his neck, cuddling against his side like a kitten. "Can't have that… I still have plans for you."

"You never answered me—do these plans include a plastic cup?" His voice came out rough and gravelly.

"Now that would be a waste, wouldn't it?"

"I think so."

He curled his arm around her and nearly managed to coax her into his lap. She resisted, breathy chuckles mixing with the soft kisses she trailed along his throat. The jumbled ponytail she wore snaked down her back. A sly smile curved her lips. She raked her fingernails along the inside of his bare thigh and he almost came off the couch. Hell, he almost came in his pants.

In a flash he had her flat on her back, pinned against the couch cushions. She laughed that throaty, full-bodied laugh that rippled through his blood. Her lustrous curls trailed over the edge of the cushion. Tom snaked one hand under her head and started to pull the cloth-covered elastic from her mane.

"What are you doing?" she laughed. "I have to go back to work."

He shook his head and tossed the band onto the coffee table. "Not for a few more minutes."

Straddling her thigh, he pushed up, pulling her with him. She clung to his shoulders for balance and he took full advantage, plunging both hands into the mass of auburn curls and letting his fingers filter through to the ends.

"Are you busy tonight?" he asked, his voice low and husky with suppressed need.

"No."

He started at her scalp again, letting the slippery, silky waves spill over his wrists and tickle his forearms. She moaned softly and he smiled. "Wanna go to a movie or something?"

Maggie blinked. "Are you asking me on a date?"

Tom couldn't help but laugh. "Jeez, Maggie, don't act so surprised. I've only spent the last two weeks trying to get you to spend a little time with me."

Her sheepish chuckle gave him vindication. The pink blush rising in her cheeks signified hope. "A movie?"

"Maybe pizza then a movie?" he asked, feeling compelled to push while luck seemed to be running his way.

Maggie nodded slowly and his fingers clenched the ends of her hair, hanging onto the moment. "Pick you up at about six?"

"Okay."

"Okay." Tom sealed the deal with a sweet, lingering kiss. "Okay," he breathed, reaching for the hair band again.

Maggie blinked at him solemnly as he gathered her hair in one hand, smoothing it with the palm of the other. "Do you know how to do that?" she asked when he stretched the elastic between his fingers.

"I think I can figure it out." He bound her hair in a low ponytail he imagined was a little sloppier than one she could do, but still neater than previous attempts made on his niece's hair. "I might need the practice, right?" Sitting back on his heels, he offered her a lopsided smile.

"Right."

She batted a few stray tendrils from her face, and he caught her hand. Pulling it to his lips, Tom brushed a kiss to her knuckles. "Don't fix it yet, okay? Humor me."

"Okay."

Fred sauntered to the ottoman, inadvertently kicking one of the balls of chocolate-coated puffed grain. The skittering morsel captured his attention and he pounced. Maggie raised an eyebrow. "Problem with the Cocoa Puffs?"

"I'll clean that up," he promised, reluctantly releasing her hand.

She climbed from the couch, pressing the wrinkles from her pink scrubs with her palms. "I need to get back down there."

He nodded. "I'll lock the door behind me when I leave."

"Okay. Uh…thanks."

He smiled at the flustered flutter of her hand. Peering up at her, he tried to play it cool. Of course, there was only so much cool a mostly-naked guy sitting on a floral-print couch sporting a raging hard-on could manage. “See you tonight.”

A smile twitched her lips and she started toward the door. “Don’t forget to get dressed first. It’s chilly out there.”

The door slammed behind her and he released the breath he was holding, frowning down at the burgeoning bulge of his belly. “Yeah. Thanks for the tip.”

****

Pizza, a movie, a warm body in bed next to her, a bakery box filled with bear claws, and the Sunday paper. The whole thing would have been perfect, if only it were real. Maggie tried not to think too hard about it. She flitted about the apartment, stuffing scrubs into the washing machine, running a dusting cloth over tables, chairs, and shelves, and inventorying the depleted contents of her cabinets. All the while, she worked around the immobile lump of man parked on her couch with her cat in his lap.

She dragged a two-wheeled wire cart from the coat closet and propped it against the door. Her hands planted on her hips, she studied the pair with pursed lips. A slightly acidic comment burned on her tongue. She thought about the Clomid pill she gulped that morning and wondered if the mood swings could kick in after only two days. Probably not.

Maggie swallowed the comment, forcing it down and storing it for another day. She drew a deep breath through her nose then opened her mouth to speak. The rustle of the newspaper cut her off. Her jaw dropped when Tom folded the paper, rolled it into a tube, and swatted the coffee table with it. Fred leapt from his lap and shook out his fur, shooting their new companion a nasty glare as he stalked to the opposite side of the room.

The section plopped to the floor, unfurling at Tom’s bare feet. He leaned forward, covering his face with both hands and rubbing vigorously. As she approached, Maggie was momentarily distracted by the strip of gold-tinged skin visible between the bunched cotton of his thermal Henley and the gaping waistband of faded denim. His shoulders slumped in defeat. He rubbed his brow with his thumb and forefinger then clasped his hands, wringing his knuckles.

"Are you okay?"

He jumped, twisting in his seat to peer at her. "Huh? Oh. Yeah. I'm fine." Rising from the couch, he shook out the legs of his jeans. "What's up?"

Maggie forgot about her shopping list and the cart propped against the door. She blocked out the chug of the washing machine, the hum of the dryer, and the annoying prick-prick-prick of Fred's claws piercing the trashed upholstery on her grandmother's ottoman. All she could see was the tension rippling under the broad expanse of combed cotton. She pressed her hand to the center of his back and a shiver danced along his spine. "Sit down," she ordered gently.

"I thought we were going to the store."

"Sit down," she repeated more forcefully. Tom dropped onto the cushions and she smiled, climbing over the arm to sit behind him on the back of the couch. She pressed her thumbs into the muscle at the back of his neck. His head fell forward. The cowlick swirling at his crown popped. She smoothed it with her cheek then kissed the top of his head. "What's got you all wound up?"

He shook his head. "Nothing. Just stupid people shooting their mouths off."

She leaned into him, working her way across his taut shoulders. "Isn't that what stupid people do?"

"What makes people think they can dictate how other people should live?"

"Ah. Are you all worked up over the whole 'don't ask, don't tell' thing?"

He chuckled and a little of the tension seeped from his shoulders. "Yeah. That ticks me off too." She ran her thumbs up his neck and pushed them into the base of his skull. He groaned long and low and his body grew loose and lax. “One of my cases,” he mumbled.

Her eyebrows rose. “In the paper?”

Tom nodded. “It’s a damn mess.”

“Can you talk about it?”

“Not the details, but thanks to this moron most of it’s pretty public anyway,” he grumbled, nodding to the newspaper.

She frowned. “I hope the moron isn’t your client.”

“She’s not.”

Cupping his arms, she pulled him back, settling him between her legs before going to work on his shoulders again. “Give me the Reader’s Digest version.”

He blew out a breath and let his head fall into her lap, blinking up at her. “You don’t wanna hear about this.”

She cocked an eyebrow. “You think I’m too stupid or too delicate?” she asked, pushing her thumbs into the knot of stress.

He yelped and she smiled down at him. With a soft snort he shook his head. “Neither. It’s just… It’s a messy custody case.”

“Oh?”

“A couple who couldn’t have a baby. They were matched with a grad student who mastered everything but birth control. They paid the girl’s medical expenses, contributed money toward her living expenses, the wife took birthing classes with the girl, and stayed with her through labor and delivery. When the baby was three days old, the birth mother signed away her rights and the happy couple took their little girl home.”

Maggie hummed as she raked her nails through his thick hair. “So far, so good.”

He stared up at her. “Fast forward seven years. The couple has been having trouble for a couple of those years, they decide they can’t work it out and file for divorce,” he recited, his voice flat.

“Enter Tom Sullivan, Esquire.”

He sighed and closed his eyes. "Meanwhile, our intrepid grad student grows up to be a banking maven and marries her Prince Charming—not the father of her child—a different model," he explained. "In keeping with the adoption agreement, my client encloses copies of her daughter's second grade picture with a newsy letter keeping her birth mother up to date on all the happenings in their lives. Unfortunately, she decided to include the news about the separation."

She gasped, grasping his shoulders in a vise-like grip. "I read about this! She's fighting them for custody because they're getting a divorce."

"Not anymore, they're not," he mumbled.

"They aren't?"

A bitter laugh escaped him. "The ironic thing? This was going to be one of the friendliest divorces I ever handled." He pressed the heel of his hand to his temple. She batted his hand away and took over, gently massaging his skull. "They had it all worked out—shared custody, he got an apartment practically around the corner from them. They didn't hate each other. They just didn't want to live together anymore."

"Then the birth mother decides to sue for custody," she murmured.

"Yeah."

"Are you really worried that she'll win? I mean, if they've reconciled and the adoption was in order…."

He reached up. His fingers encircled her wrist pulling her hand down to his mouth. He pressed a soft kiss to the center of her palm. "There's always a chance. You said it yourself; the courts tend to favor the mother. That's just the way it is. I guess we'll have to wait and see if they'll favor the mother who gave birth, or the mother who raised that child from the time she was three days old."

"That's awful."

"The awful part is she thinks she can play this out in the court of public opinion, spouting off about the sanctity of marriage and all that crap. She conveniently forgets she's the one who got knocked up without benefit of clergy."

Maggie snickered. "Benefit of clergy. You sound like my grandmother."

"I just love the selective morality people whip out when it suits them," he muttered.

Pressing the heels of her hands between his shoulder blades, Maggie worked the solid ridge of muscle bracketing his spine. "I don't understand why she's doing this. The birth mother, I mean… Can't she have another baby?"

"I don't think that's an issue. I think she thinks my clients breached their agreement. Maybe she wants to prove a point. I don't know what her motivation is. The whole thing is just wrong."

"But they're back together," she objected.

He reached for her hand again. A wry smile twitched his lips. "I think she knows as well as I do that it won't last."

She jerked her hand from his. "How do you know? Maybe it will. Maybe this is what they needed to remind them what's important."

"It's important to lock yourself into a marriage that isn't working?"

"When you commit to raising a child, you do what you have to do to ensure your child's happiness."

"And you think a child can be happy living with parents who are miserable?"

"You said they weren't miserable. You said it was amicable."

"The divorce would have been amicable," he corrected. "Who knows what the marriage is like."

Maggie had to admit he was right. She knew better than anyone that no one knows what goes on behind closed doors. Dejected, she slid from the back cushion, landing with a bounce behind him. He grabbed her ankles and wrapped her legs around his middle, pressing his back to her chest and pinning her to the couch.

"It's a mess."

"Yeah." She pressed her cheek to his shoulder. "So…you like Cocoa Puffs, huh?"

Tom chuckled, rubbing her denim-clad shins. "Who doesn't?"

"Ready to go to the store?"

He nodded. "Wanna take a drive?"

"A drive?"

"We can get out of town for a little while and do our shopping in the suburbs…."

"Our shopping?"

"I eat too," he pointed out.

"Do you have a car?"

He reared back. "Yeah, I have a car. Don't you?"

"Where would I put it?" she asked, gesturing to the apartment.

"Uh, in a garage, like I do."

She snorted. "Why would I pay hundreds of dollars a month to park a car I'd never use?"

Tom pried her legs from his waist and patted her knees as he stood. "So you can go for a drive on a nice fall day." He offered her his hand. "Maybe we'll get ice cream."

She let him pull her from the couch. "Oooh. Ice cream?"

Fred meowed and leapt from the ottoman. "Oh no. You're not hacking hairballs up in my car." Tom hustled her toward the door. "Quick. Before he follows us…."

She chuckled at his antics. "Are you scared of my cat?"

"Yes. You are too."

"You don't have your shoes."

"Crap!" He whirled and scanned.

"Bedroom. I tripped over them three times this morning."

Tom nodded decisively. "Okay. I'll get the shoes and you open a can of food to distract him." He jogged the length of the short hall, skidding to a stop just before he smashed into the doorframe. "Spare no expense! I'll spring for the replacement."

Chapter Twelve

Maggie stared at the plastic shrouded clothing hanging in her coat closet. Lowering her lashes, she stashed the broom in the corner of the closet and sneaked a peek at the man parked on her sofa. The suit pants he wore were a dark gray herringbone. They matched the jacket slung over the back of her kitchen chair. The sleeves of his snowy-white shirt were rolled to the crooks of his elbows, exposing the dark, downy hair that covered his perma-tanned forearms. His chocolate-colored hair showed the furrows of frustration. The tie he'd liberated from her bedpost hung askew at his throat.

She bit her lip and stared at the bags printed with the dry cleaners' name and logo. Four starched and pressed shirts hung alongside three ties clipped to a paper-wrapped hanger. Two more suits, one pearl gray and the other the same midnight blue of his eyes, completed the inventory. She secretly hoped he'd choose the navy suit the next day. With the blue shirt and the burgundy tie.

The door latch caught with a click, and Tom looked up from the brief on his lap, offering a wan smile. "Almost done."

"Take your time."

Maggie cleared the plastic and aluminum carryout containers from the table. He'd brought Thai. The night before dinner had been gyros, and the night before that he showed up holding a pizza box. She stowed the leftovers in the fridge, dropped the empties into the trash, and scowled at Fred.

"The dry food is good for you," she admonished.

Fred meowed in response and Tom chuckled. "The cat equivalent of eating tofu."

She rolled her eyes and wiped down the counters. "He didn't need to scatter it all over the floor."

"We're men. We destroy what we do not understand," he mumbled.

She draped the washcloth over the faucet and glanced up at the cabinets. A soft sigh seeped from her lips. Leaning back against the sink was the perfect vantage point. From there, she could watch him in the reflection of the decorative mirror by the door, but Tom couldn't see her. She'd discovered the magic spot two nights before and made the most of it whenever possible. Luckily, he was unwittingly compliant. He showed up with dinner that first Monday night and stayed, accepting the whole-grain breakfast bar she offered him the next morning with a sheepish smile. The next day was a repeat, and the next… Somehow the man was now a fixture in her apartment.

In just a few minutes, he'd set whatever it was he was working on aside and flash that wicked smile. Within a half-hour, she'd be pinned beneath him, gasping for breath as he smothered her with hot, hungry kisses. In just an hour or so, he'd pull her from the sofa and crawl into her bed beside her.

He kept his hands to himself—damn him and his healthy respect for Mother Nature. Dealing with his cocky self-assurance was so much easier than the perfect gentleman schtick he had going. He waited for the green light, exhibiting a shocking patience she both loathed and admired. Bit by bit, her resistance was wearing thin. Not that it was thick to start. After all, the point of this whole arrangement hinged on them getting naked and getting busy as often as possible. Maggie just wished she wasn't the one who had to make the first move. Stupid Mother Nature put her in this ridiculous position. She should let Mother Nature seduce him.

"What are you doing?"

Maggie pushed away from the sink and straightened the already perfectly aligned refrigerator magnets. "I'm just finishing up." She pulled her shoulders back, took a deep breath, and strolled toward the living room. "You finish what you needed to get done?"

"I just needed to refresh my memory on some stuff," he said, extending a hand to pull her to the couch.

The cushion gave way beneath her weight, nestling her into the crook of his arm. She fit perfectly. Too perfectly for a girl who didn't really belong there. His lips brushed her hair. Maggie swallowed a sigh and placed her hand on his thigh. The muscle tensed under her palm. Her fingers reflexively bit into the taut flesh then slid higher.

His breath caught and she smiled. "Do I need to refresh your memory too?"

"No." The word escaped him in a rush of breath.

"No?"

He covered her hand, pressing it hard against his thigh. "I remember everything," he said, his voice low and husky. "The way you taste. Your skin is so soft… I remember the little noise you make just before you come."

Now he wasn't the only one with a little hitch in his giddy-up. Maggie closed her eyes and forced her lungs to expand and contract. "Do you?"

He crooked one finger beneath her chin and tipped her face up, pulling away just enough to meet her gaze. "You think I'd forget?"

"I was beginning to wonder."

He rolled his eyes. "I was just waiting for you to say go."

"Go." The word clung to her lips for a second too long. He trapped it there, covering her mouth in a kiss so ardent she feared she'd never draw a full breath again. He shifted, pressing a knee into the cushion and angling his body over hers. Their lips parted and she exhaled, "Tom."

"Oh God, don't say stop, Maggie." His fervent whisper carried more than a hint of a plea. "Please don't say stop."

She pressed her fingertips to his mouth, silencing his doubts. "I'm not. I'm just asking for a slight detour."

"Detour?"

"Bedroom."

"Oh." He pulled back, capturing both of her wrists and pulling her upright again. "Right. Bedroom."

The edge of the coffee table took a chunk out of her shin, but she couldn't have cared less. His breath tickled her cheek, hot, moist, and expectant. He kissed her hard. Suppressed desire tasted tangy on his eager tongue. A rush of pure feminine pleasure pulsed through her veins, heating her blood and raising a steamy flush on her skin. His elbow hit the wall in the hall, knocking a picture frame akimbo. They bounced off the doorframe and dove headfirst for the bed.

Clothing flew in every direction. His shirt sailed across the room and landed atop an indignant red tabby. Maggie howled with laughter as Fred growled his displeasure, and Tom tore at the button and hooks on his pants.

His zipper rasped, and she covered his hands with hers. "Easy… We have time."

A wry smile twitched his lips. He pulled her hand to his mouth and kissed her knuckles. "I think I'm just afraid you'll change your mind."

"I thought we both decided," she chided.

"I know." Tom shucked the rest of his clothes then ducked his head, pressing wet, open-mouthed kisses to her neck and throat. "I'm just paranoid."

She framed his head with her hands and urged him to lift his head. "Tom."

"Hmm?"

"Tom," she prompted. When he raised his head, she gave him a shaky smile. "We decided, right?"

He blinked then nodded slowly, his Adam's apple bobbing as he swallowed hard. "We did."

"You sure about this?"

His smile was chased by a weak chuckle. "Mags, it's all I've been thinking about."

"I mean the, uh…possible result."

"Probable," he corrected, pecking a soft kiss to her lips. "I plan to do my damndest to knock you up, Mary Margaret McCann."

Maggie couldn't stifle her smile. "You sure know how to sweet talk a girl, don't you, Sully?"

He laughed and rolled onto his back, pulling her on top of him. Her hair shrouded her face as she pushed up, straddling his trim hips. His fingers were warm and gentle against her cheeks, brushing the curtain of crazy curls back and tucking them securely behind her ears.

"I just want to make my intentions clear."

"Crystal clear," she mumbled, tossing her head back.

His fingers trailed down her cheek skimming her jaw, tickling her throat, and teasing the curve of her breast. "We're gonna make a baby. Beautiful babies, Maggie," he whispered, and she was a goner.

****

Tom fixed his gaze on the water stain above her bed. "Sorry."

It was his third apology in as many minutes. With a wince he realized his remorse officially lasted longer than the act. Maggie chuckled and rolled onto her side, her fingers ruffling the line of hair that led to his crotch. She kissed his bare shoulder, but the soft laugh shredded the tattered remains of his ego.

"It's not funny."

She propped her head on the heel of her palm and grinned at him. "It *is* funny," she insisted. "Stud…" He freed his ankle from the tangled sheet and shifted his weight, preparing to roll off the bed, but Maggie flung herself across his chest, preempting the move. "Nuh-uh." She smoothed the hair on his arm with butterfly light strokes of her fingertips. "I'm taking it as a compliment."

He squinched his eyes shut. "Don't flatter yourself. It's just been a long time since I rode bareback."

She laughed as she pecked a line of soft kisses across his chest. "You'll get the hang of it, cowboy."

"Damn right I will," he growled. He had her on her back before she could land the next kiss. Her throaty laugh filled the room, reverberating off the walls and wrapping him in a shroud of promised pleasure. He cupped one full breast in his hand, testing the weight of her soft flesh in his palm and kneading impossibly silky skin with his fingers. His found the sweet spot just below her ear and sucked gently. Maggie shivered and he smiled. "I just need practice. Lots and lots of practice."

"Planning a trip to Carnegie Hall?"

He cruised the slender column of her throat, nipped his way along her collarbone, and staked a claim on the curve of her shoulder with a playful, smacking kiss. "Planning to make that up to you in every way you can possibly imagine."

She teased the line of his spine with her fingernails. "I don't know if you noticed or not, seeing how you were all wrapped up in your performance issues, but I wasn't complaining."

He raised his head and peered into her grass-green eyes. "You were laughing."

Her response was a negligent shrug. "It was funny." She traced the curve of his bottom lip and he almost moaned. The pad of her finger felt as soft as a flower petal. The fragrance of her skin rose off her heated body, dulling his senses while setting every nerve ending in his body on high alert. "Super-stud, Tom Sullivan, and his alter ego, Quickdraw McGraw."

His brow knit. "Now, hold on there, Baba Looey…."

"Whatcha gonna do? Sic El Kabong on me again?" she taunted.

Tom ran his hand over her ribcage as if committing the lush lines of her curves to memory. He buried his face in the curve of her neck and a tremor of laughter shimmied through him.

"What?" Maggie gave his hair a tug to get his attention, which only made him laugh harder.

He nuzzled her ear and pressed against her. "Olayeee," he crooned in a husky rasp.

She squirmed, immediately responding to his body's battle cry. "Wow. For a guy of your advanced years you have incredible restorative powers, Sherriff McGraw."

"And don't you forget it, Baba Looey," he drawled in an exaggerated Texas twang. He pulled her thigh up to his hip and froze, poised on the brink. Brushing the tangle of wild red curls back from her face, he smiled before branding her with a hard, hot kiss. His eyes closed and he sank into the embrace of her body once more. "Don't you forget it…."

Chapter Thirteen

Maggie pursed her lips and took a step back, surveying the shelf with a critical eye. With a decisive nod, she reached for the neatly stacked cans and plucked two from each row.

Tom peered into the basket. "Go easy on the turkey and giblets. I think he likes the cod, sole, and shrimp ones better."

Cocking a brow, she turned a cool glare in his direction. "Now you're telling me what flavors my cat prefers too?"

He flashed a smug smile. "Yes. You like the non-fruity yogurt better and Fred is into seafood."

Her eyes narrowed to slits. "Who asked you to come along?"

"I have the car, remember?"

"I have a cart. I would have been perfectly happy to do my shopping at the market near my apartment."

He waved a paper-wrapped baguette like a white flag. "Yeah, but then you wouldn't have this delicious seventy-trillion grain artisan bread to go with the two dozen packages of boil and serve pasta we're buying at a drastic discount because I have a shopper's card."

"Who is this 'we' you keep talking about? Do you have a mouse in your pocket?"

His grin widened and his springy cowlick bobbed when he nodded eagerly. "Yes, I do. Wanna see?"

Maggie suppressed a smile as she turned back to the expansive selection of cat food the suburban grocery store offered. "Please." She gave a sniff of distaste and tried to distract him with an airy wave of one hand while reaching for two more cans of the cod, sole, and shrimp flavored cat food. "Been there, done that. Hasn't done me any good."

Quick as a cat, he snatched the cans from her hand, tossed them into the cart, and pulled her into the cradle of his body. "No?" Warm, moist breath tickled her ear and she melted just the teensiest bit. Possessive hands cupped the curve of her stomach. He nuzzled the tender spot below her lobe, his lips whispering across her skin. "These last few weeks haven't done any good at all?"

"Well, maybe some," she conceded. "We'll see sometime next week."

He held her a little tighter, the hard muscle of his thighs pressing into the curve of her bottom. "Who knows, maybe I still haven't peaked. My best work may be yet to come."

The husky timbre of his voice made her quiver. The veiled promise in his words turned her knees to jelly. She swallowed hard. "Oh yeah? I was hoping you hit it when I was ovulating." A shiver raced down her spine when he drew her ear lobe into his hot mouth and sucked gently. She squirmed in response. Her eyelids grew too heavy to hold open one second longer. As they slid shut she whispered, "You should have told me you weren't feeling up to the task."

"Keep rubbing your ass against me and I'll show you how up to it I am," he growled.

Her eyes popped open. Row upon row of florescent bulbs bathed the store in light. The spotless tile floor gleamed in the glare. Perforated metal shelving lined the aisle, but somehow she had no doubt in her mind Tom Sullivan had the will to find a way. Laughing, she tipped her head back to say as much just when a musically lilting voice called out.

"Tommy? Tom Sullivan, is that you?"

Maggie broke from his embrace when his head whipped around. She reached for a shelf to catch her balance but nearly lost her footing when she spotted an elderly woman perched on the seat of a motorized shopping cart sizing them up.

"Tommy! It *is* you." Her blue eyes lit with delight as parchment cheeks folded into well-worn grooves.

"Oh." His dark lashes fluttered. A puzzled frown creased his brow. "Mrs. Murphy? What are you doing here?"

The old woman's gnarled hands fluttered when he bent to kiss her wrinkled cheek. "I live here now," she said, patting his shoulder. "Mairead insisted that I come to live with them after I broke my blasted hip, and, well…here I am."

"You look wonderful, Mrs. Murphy," he said, darting a glance in Maggie's direction.

The old woman's tinkling laugh gave over to a throaty voice tinged with a hint of a brogue. "I look like death warmed over in the Radar Range, you devil, but it's wonderful to see you."

Maggie was feigning interest in the vast array of treats available to suburban felines when a tall, slender woman clad in designer jeans and a cashmere sweater rounded the corner brandishing a cellophane-wrapped roast. "Ma, the brisket doesn't look good. How about a nice ro… Oh. Hello?"

Tom turned toward the woman, his eyes widening slightly as he took a hasty step into the no-man's land between the scooter and the basket he marked with the jumbo box of Cocoa Puffs just minutes before. "Uh, hello, Mari," he said, nodding a greeting.

The younger woman responded as any sane woman would when encountering Tom Sullivan dressed in his Sunday uniform of faded Levi's and snug sweater. Her smile brightened as feminine appreciation flared in her eyes. "Tom Sullivan?"

The overwhelming urge to claim her territory spurred Maggie into action. She snatched a pouch from the shelf. "Here they are!" Hurrying to his side, she held the package out for his inspection and beamed a triumphant smile. "See? I told you these came in a tuna flavor." Ignoring the perplexed glance he shot in her direction, she turned her attention to the elder woman. "He said they stopped making them. Hello, I'm Maggie McCann."

The moment she said her name, Tom seemed to snap out of his stupor. "Oh. Yeah, sorry. Mrs. Murphy, Mairead, this is my…friend, Maggie." He fixed her with a pointed stare as he explained, "The Murphy's lived two doors down from us in Evergreen Park when Sean and I were growing up."

"Oh!" Her smile faltered for just a moment. "But now you're in Northbrook, of all places. Small world," she babbled.

The younger woman turned her preternaturally white smile on her, and Maggie fought the urge to flinch under the glare. "We're in Highland Park, actually, but mother prefers to shop at this store for some reason."

"Usually they have a better selection of meat." The old woman scowled at the roast her daughter deposited in the basket attached to the scooter. "Still, a person can't find a decent corned beef north of Ogden Avenue unless it's two weeks 'til St. Paddy's Day."

Mairead tossed her mane of streaked blonde hair when she laughed. "Oh, mother, I'll be sure to order a nice cut from the meat market next week, I promise."

The old woman sniffed her disdain. "The meat market." She fixed Tom with a piercing blue gaze. "Highway robbery, what they charge for brisket. How's your mother?"

His head bobbed. "Fine, fine. She's doing fine. I'm, uh…I just saw her yesterday."

"Will she be going to Father Corbin's golden jubilee at Saint Rita's next Saturday?"

Tom's broad shoulders hunched as he shoved his hands into the pockets of his jeans and continued to nod. "Um…yes, yes. I told her I'd take her so she could visit a little before four o'clock mass."

Mrs. Murphy beamed up at him. "You're a good boy, Tom." She slid a sly glance in her daughter's direction. "We're going to try to make it if Mari can fit it into her schedule."

The woman in question rolled her eyes. "I said I'd take you if Trevor's game ended in time." She turned to

Maggie. "My oldest started basketball this week and my youngest is in Tae Kwon Do, so weekends are crazier than usual," she explained with a wan smile.

Spotting an opportunity to save him from his obvious discomfort, Maggie nudged Tom with her elbow. "Speaking of schedules…."

Tom shook himself from his slouch. "Right." Favoring the women with a polite smile, he nodded to their abandoned shopping basket. "We need to get this done so we can get back to the city." He pressed his fingertips to the small of her back, propelling her toward the front of the store. "It was nice to see you."

"Nice to see you too, Tom," Mari replied, flashing her blinding smile again.

"Tell your mother I said hello," Mrs. Murphy called after them.

His knuckles glowed against his skin when he gripped the handle. "I will. Take care," he called as he kicked it into gear.

Maggie smirked when the basket cornered on two wheels, then trotted to catch up. "Hang on there, Mario Andretti."

"Great. Just fucking great," he muttered under his breath.

"Whoa." She slowed, taken aback by his vehemence. "Is this a problem?"

He barreled into a checkout lane and relinquished his grip on the cart, plowing his hand through his hair as he cast a glance over his shoulder. "Problem? That was Mary Patricia Murphy. The woman has the biggest mouth in St. Rita's parish, maybe the whole dioceses. My mother is going to know about this within twenty-four hours."

"Know that an old lady saw you in a grocery store?"

He raised his eyebrows. "Know that I was grocery shopping with a woman."

"Is that a big deal?" One eyebrow dipped, but the other remained in an imperious arch. She rolled her eyes as he started slamming cans and boxes onto the convey-

or. "Okay, so you can just tell them that your *friend*, Maggie, needed a ride to the grocery store."

"A ride to a store an hour away from my condo? I'm not that good a *friend*, Mags."

"All right. Fine." She planted her hands on her hips. "Well, she knows you date women, right? I mean, you haven't told her you're saving yourself for marriage or anything…."

"She'll tell my mom, my mom will tell Uncle George, and George will blab to Sean." He placed a loaf of bread onto the belt then tapped a finger to his cheek. "Hmm, who do you think Sean will tell?" He pointed that finger at her. "You're the one who doesn't want to tell anyone."

Maggie tipped her chin up and crossed her arms over her chest. "Please. Sean and Tracy barely speak to each other," she scoffed.

Tom snatched a box of Tic Tacs from the checkout stand and tossed them in with their purchases. "Thank God for the Sullivan family remake of *The War of the Roses*." He scrubbed a hand over his face. When it came away, a wry smirk twitched his lips and he shook his head. "What are the odds, huh? Running into a nice Southside Irish lady like Mrs. Murphy in friggin' Lake County."

Slipping her hand in his, she gave his fingers a gentle squeeze. "No place is safe."

He snorted. "We were probably better off in the city."

She smiled and squeezed his fingers again. "We'll go west. Far west. Like Rockford."

Turning toward her, he pressed his lips to her forehead in a tender apology. "Right. Or there's always Iowa."

****

Tom trudged into his apartment and tossed his keys into the dish on the hall table. He winced when a shard of china chinked from the edge of the bowl and kicked the door shut behind him. Slippery dry-cleaning bags tried to slither from his grasp. Dropping his briefcase, he scowled at the armload of suits and stomped toward his bedroom. Hauling his cleaning home wasn't part of his plan.

No, he planned to hang the freshly laundered suits and shirts draped over his arm in Maggie's closet, just as he had for the past three weeks. Sulking, he shuffled into his walk-in closet and started hooking the wire hangers over the bar.

"See you Sunday," he muttered when a French blue shirt tried to make a break for it. "What if I don't want to see you Sunday? What if I want to see you Friday?"

His grumblings had no effect on his wardrobe. He let the weight of his overcoat pull his suit jacket from his shoulders. They fell to the floor in a twisted heap, fine cashmere slithering against silk linings. He toed off his shoes and shuffled toward the bathroom. Yanking open the shower door, he gave the nozzle a sharp twist. Droplets of water gathered in the fine hair on his arm and soaked into the rolled cuffs of his shirt. He stripped the rumpled cotton from his back, crumpled it into a ball, and heaved the shirt from the room.

Tom eyed the rough beige towel hanging from the rod and took a deep sniff. His scowl deepened when he got a snoot full of mountain fresh scent. The vanity sparkled devoid of cologne bottles, gobs of shaving cream, or speckles of whiskers. His weekly cleaning lady had obviously made the easiest money of her life over the past month. With a smirk, he stripped off the rest of his clothes and kicked them into a pile.

A hiss seeped from his clenched teeth as he stepped into the stinging spray. He closed his eyes and tried to pretend he was in Maggie's pink-tiled bathroom surrounded by pink-smelling Maggie things. His hiss morphed into a sigh. The soap clutched in his hand didn't smell like lemongrass. The shave cream she swiped from the spa for him actually did warm when it touched his skin. The spray from his oversized showerhead was too strong. Maggie's vanity was littered with his whiskers, and he knew how to rock a lavender bath towel. He didn't want to be here. He wanted to be there. With Maggie and her crazy cat.

Reaching for his trusty bar of Irish Spring, Tom quickly lathered away the stench of his usual Friday night poker game with his brother, uncle, and the old man's cronies. The games were instituted just after the New Year began—a valiant effort on George's part to keep his middle-aged nephews out of trouble. For his part, Tom was relieved when his uncle hatched the plan. There was little he found more disturbing than discovering that his baby brother, a man born to be more monogamous than a damn swan, was drowning his sorrows in the local watering holes and possibly the local blonds. The stunning realization that he actually looked forward to the easy camaraderie of the older men was only overshadowed by the pleasure he took in showing up at Maggie's place after the games.

He tipped his face up to the spray and tried not to think of the sexy way Maggie sniffed him when he walked through her door the past few Friday nights. He failed. She seemed to actually like the noxious cloud that followed him home after a night with the Oak Park Mafia. For some ungodly reason, the lingering scent of scotch and cigar smoke seemed to turn her on. Who was he to fight it? Why would he even want to?

Tom braced his hand on the cool tile wall and let his head fall forward. His muscles tightened. That all-too-familiar knot of hunger coiled low in his gut. He stared dispassionately at his dick, a mocking smile twisting his lips. "Not tonight, big guy," he muttered as he snatched the shampoo from the ledge. "She said she'd see us *Sunday*."

Clumps of bubbles trailed down his chest and back and swirled into the drain, but his scotch-fueled resentment stirred to a froth. Tom cranked the handle and the water cut off. He opened the stall door, allowing the cool air to blast the ardor the mere thought of her stirred. Once the boring beige towel was anchored around his waist, he dripped his way out of the bathroom without sparing another glance. He didn't want to stand at that pristine vanity and brush his teeth with the lonely toothbrush standing in the ceramic cup he didn't even choose for himself.

His gaze traveled across the dustless surface of his dresser. A flat tray held a neatly paired set of cufflinks and shiny tie tacks. Tom jerked the towel from his hips and let it fall to the floor. Beige sucked. He wanted enormous bath sheets made of thick, thirsty pink, turquoise, or even purple terrycloth. The bed loomed before him, a yawning stretch of masculine anonymity in boring blue, beige, and brown. He stared into the dimly lit room. Nothing was out of place. Not one bit of clutter crowded the nightstand. Everything was exactly where it belonged. Except for him.

****

Maggie scanned the caller ID and stifled a sigh. "How did the game go? You take their Social Security checks? Are you the stud in Five-card Stud?" she asked by way of greeting.

"I don't want to wait 'til Sunday to see you," Tom answered.

The note of petulance in his voice brought a small smile to her lips. Then the tears she'd been fighting back all afternoon tangled in her throat. She sniffled and pressed the heel of her hand to her forehead, trying to regain a modicum of control. "I have plans with Tracy tomorrow."

"I know; that's fine."

She bristled at his dismissive tone. "Thanks for your approval."

"I'm downstairs. Let me in."

"It's late."

"That's never mattered before."

Maggie bit her lip. The urge to rush to the door made her toes twitch beneath the sheet. The imperious demand made her feel all girly and fluttery deep in her belly despite raising her feminist hackles. Appalled by her own weakness, she twisted rumpled cotton around her hand, and sank deeper into her too-empty bed, desperate to hang onto the last shred of her resolve.

"Maggie?" She squinched her eyes shut and pressed her lips together, a futile attempt to resist his husky siren song.

"Not tonight, Tom."

"Maggie, what's wrong?"

The gentle caress of his words pummeled her, piercing the brittle shell of disappointment shrouding her heart like hollow-tipped bullets. "I'm not pregnant."

Her voice was barely more than a whisper, but they had the impact of a mortar shell. The ringing in her ears almost masked his sharp intake of breath. Almost, but not quite. He hesitated, just for a moment, but it stretched like an eternity. She broke into a thousand bits.

"But, Maggie… I mean, it's early days—"

"I'm sorry," she managed to whisper before a sob escaped and the tears broke free.

"Is that why?" She cried harder. The sound of his fist pounding the exterior door surrounded her, echoing dimly through the stairwell and apartment but with fiber-optic clarity through the receiver. "Let me in, Maggie."

"No!" The word burst from her lips. Sob number seven thousand and sixty-two rose in her throat. "What's the point?"

The words left a dull ache in her chest, but they seemed to stun Tom. The pounding subsided. His rough and ragged breathing filled her ears. "We just started. We knew it probably wouldn't happen right away."

His voice broke just the slightest bit, and it nearly did her in. Maggie tried to answer him, but the words tangled in her throat like congealed pasta. The man thought he could argue her emotional response away. Typical lawyer. She wanted to tell him to stuff his reason and logic up his tight ass. She sniffed again, preparing to do just that, but a fresh round of tears assaulted her.

"And I just… It doesn't matter, Mags. I like being with you," he continued. "I *should* be with you. We're in this together, right? We'll keep trying."

She snuffled, nodding her head even though she knew he couldn't see her. "Kay", she managed to croak.

A horn blared on the street below, and Tom's voice seemed to drop a full octave. "Now let me in."

She wiped her cheeks with the heels of her hands. "No. I'm a mess."

The quiet stretched between them for a heartbeat, then two, and three. "Maybe I'm a mess too," he cajoled. "I might need you to hold me."

The sly smile she heard in his softly spoken words stunned her tears into submission. She took a shaky breath. "Yeah?"

"My bedroom is boring, and the pillows don't smell like you."

"Maybe that's because you've never invited me over."

A smile colored his words. "I like your place better. Besides, Fred would get lonely if we hung out at my place."

"You could invite him too."

"Maybe I will sometime." Tom blew out a sigh and she smiled, picturing his finger-furrowed hair and creased brow. "I *am* sorry, Maggie. I promise I'll try to do better with the whole impregnating you thing."

Maggie chuckled and tossed the blankets aside. "Hang on, I'll buzz you in."

****

An hour later, his head rested on a lilac-printed pillowcase with a fat cat perched on his stomach. He gave Fred's ears a lazy scratch, but his attention was riveted on the woman next to him.

"It was embarrassing," Maggie insisted.

His lips twitched. "Come on, you have to admit it's kind of funny."

"It's not funny at all! She was standing there waiting for me to come out of the bathroom, and, of course, I was a complete mess."

He shifted, giving Fred fair warning of his intentions. The cat issued his own warning by sinking his claws into the thin skin covering Tom's sternum. Before Fred could regroup enough for an all-out attack, Tom gently dislodged him and rolled onto his side facing Maggie. "It's funny."

"You think everything is funny," she complained.

He snagged the end of one tousled red curl and wound it around his finger. "Not everything. Just you."

"It was mortifying. She totally thinks I'm a slut now."

"Sheila doesn't think you're a slut."

"She thinks *you're* a slut," she countered.

"True, but you didn't tell her it was me," he pointed out. Cocking his head, he peered down at her. "Why not?"

She gave his chest an ineffective shove. "It's nobody's business."

Rolling onto her, he squelched her yelp with a hard, fast kiss. "So, you'd rather let her think you were crying in the bathroom at Haven House because you were scared some nameless, faceless guy accidentally shoved a bun in your oven?"

"I just said I thought I was pregnant! She assumed I was upset because I might be baking a bun, not because I'm not." She trailed her fingers over his shoulder. "I just don't want to jinx things before anything even happens." He winced when she jabbed his bicep. "You're not so anxious to tell everyone, either. Has your mom said anything about Mrs. Murphy?"

He nipped her earlobe, tugging the tender skin with his teeth. "Not yet, but she may be saving it up for a full frontal assault tomorrow."

"Such a lovely relationship you have," she said with a sigh.

"It works for us."

"Mama's boy."

He snorted. "Hardly."

Maggie trailed one fingertip along his jaw. "You're a good son."

"No, I'm not."

"Yes, you are. You take good care of your mother."

"I don't have a choice. She won't deal with Sean, and George won't deal with her anymore."

A puzzled frown creased her brow. "I still don't get what her problem is with Sean."

Tom did his best to smooth the lines of worry away with a kiss. "That is a mystery for the ages." He heaved a sigh and nuzzled her tangled curls. "He looks like our dad. That's the best I can figure."

Maggie stiffened beneath him. "That's not Sean's fault."

"Nope." Tom reared back and cocked an eyebrow. "I didn't say it was logical. I just said it was my best theory."

"Crappy theory," she muttered.

"Crappy mother."

"What are you going to tell her about us?"

"As little as possible."

Her scowl deepened. Fixing her with his best assessing lawyer stare, he narrowed his eyes. "You know she treats Tracy like crap, and Sean *married* her, Mags."

"God forbid some slut touch her precious Tommy." She gave a dramatic shudder and rolled her eyes. "Her perfect, virginal baby boy."

"What? You want me to tell her all about you? How we're trying to have a baby without being married? Christ, I can't even imagine how many rosaries that's going to rack up." Blowing out an exasperated breath, he pushed up, relieving her of some of his weight. "I'm not going to lie to her. I'm not gonna lie to Sean or George either, for that matter, but I'm not going to volunteer testimony. When it comes to letting my mother in on my life, I am definitely a hostile witness."

"No one is asking you to lie." She gave him a shove, trying to dislodge him. He laughed a short, bitter bark, set his jaw, and held his ground, causing Maggie to put a little more muscle behind her efforts. "Get off me."

"No."

She grunted with the strain, but the effect was still the same. Well, not quite the same. Her wiggling was turning him on. All the more reason for him to stay put. She huffed, blinking as she fixed him with a defiant glare. "I didn't say you had to lie to them. Maybe it's just best not to advertise our…arrangement."

"Relationship," he corrected. "We're in a relationship, Maggie. People are going to find out. Particularly, if we ever leave this apartment together."

"Maybe we shouldn't do that," she challenged, breathless and flustered.

"You think we can hide out indefinitely? People are going to notice, Maggie. I am going to get you pregnant, you are going to have a big, round belly, and one day a baby is going to come out of that big, round belly." He knew his tone was a tad too patronizing, but he couldn't help himself. Maggie could get his Irish up faster than any woman he'd ever known. "People just might notice, Mags."

She planted the heels of her hands on his shoulders and shoved. Golden shards of anger shot daggers from her emerald eyes. "Get. Off. Me."

"No." Tom smiled but refused to yield. "Christ you're beautiful, Mags."

"I hate you."

He shook his head, an affectionate smile curving his lips. "No, you don't." Tom stifled further protest with a hard, fast kiss. "I'll tell her when there's something to tell. No need to get her all stirred up." She growled low in her throat and he chuckled. "I do love stirring you up, though."

Her eyes narrowed to slits when he settled his weight on her again, nestling his erection into the curve of her hip. Her snarl turned into a smug smile. "You're not getting any tonight."

"I know, but that doesn't mean I can't want you."

"I do hate you sometimes."

He laughed and shook his head, flipping onto his back and taking her with him. "That's okay. I'm crazy about you. I figure it'll all balance out."

Maggie pushed her hair back from her face, rolled her eyes, and glared down at him. "Would you stop arguing with me and go to sleep?"

He grinned. "I'm not tired, and I can't help it. I love baiting you. You always chomp right down on the hook."

"You want me to chomp down on what?"

His smile widened when she smoothed his cowlick and nipped at his bottom lip. Tom closed his eyes, a smug smile twitching the corners of his mouth. "Sweetheart, you can chomp any part of me you want."

Maggie retaliated by pressing a pillow over his face to stifle his laughter.

Chapter Fourteen

Tracy cradled the empty wine bottle like a baby. Maggie pulled it from the crook of her arm and eased a throw pillow under her friend's head. She covered splayed legs with an afghan and stepped back, surveying her passed-out friend with a critical frown. Her guest snorted in her sleep and an affectionate smile curved Maggie's lips. She tiptoed away from the sofa, snagging her cell phone from her purse as she stole from the room. Pressing a speed-dial key, she closed her bedroom door as the call connected.

"Hello?" Tom croaked.

"I woke you." She flopped onto her bed and gazed up at the ceiling. His answering chuckle carried the same sexy rasp. The vibration of it rumbled through the phone, shivered down her spine, and pooled somewhere in the vicinity of her hoo-hah.

"Make it worth my while. Tell me you're drunk and need to talk dirty."

"Not drunk, but I do need to talk."

"Dirty?"

Optimism made his voice rise to a hopeful creak. She closed her eyes, conjuring the devastating image of that stubborn cowlick coupled with his wicked smile. "Not dirty."

"Damn."

Plunging one hand into her hair, she raked her nails against her scalp. "Maybe later."

He cleared the sleep from his throat. "How'd girls' night go?"

"Oh, you know, the usual. I buffed, waxed and polished her to a high sheen. Added a few red highlights to her hair too." She blew out a sigh. "Tracy poured a gallon of wine down her throat, and we talked about porn and how to save failing marriages… Then, I took her out and bought her a vibrator."

His breath caught. "Uh…" He gave a short chuckle of disbelief. "I'm sorry, did you say porn and a vibrator?"

The restless rustle of bedding made her smile. "Didn't you hear the part about the highlights? They turned out great, if I do so myself."

"What kind of vibrator?"

"Does he still love her?"

"Who?"

"Sean! Who else?"

"I'm still trying to get past the porn thing."

"Well, catch up!" She heard a muffled snuffle and smiled, picturing him rubbing his hand over his face. "Does he?"

"Still love her?" he repeated.

"That was the question."

"I didn't think that was ever in question," he retorted. "Your friend was the one with the issues."

Maggie hissed in exasperation. "I guess I'm asking if he *still* loves her after all this…" She waved a hand, certain he'd get her meaning with or without the visual. "Because I think she's starting to realize she still loves him, but I think she thinks it's too late."

He exhaled long and deep. She waited patiently as he parsed the meaning of her statement. "He still loves her, but he's a mess, Maggie," he said cautiously.

"I know." The acknowledgement hung between them. "Well, I think she's going to try. At least, I hope she is. Tracy's kind of a mess too."

"Yeah."

She turned toward the empty pillow on what had become his side of her bed and twirled a lock of her hair around her finger. "Tom?"

"Hmm?"

"I told her I was seeing someone."

"You did?"

"I, uh, I guess I just needed to say something about it."

"Okay." He drew the word out. "Wow. Way to break your own rule, Mags. What did she say? Did she tell you you're crazy for getting involved with me?"

A laugh bubbled from her lips before she could catch it. "Oh! I didn't tell her it was you."

"You didn't?"

She blinked, sobering instantly when she caught the edge of hurt in his voice. "I mean, not by name. I just…I told her I was seeing someone. I said that we were having a good time together," she explained, the words sounding awkward and lame to her own ears. "I mean, I told her we were… That I'm having fun… That I'm enjoying… Crap."

"Crap?" he prompted with a harsh laugh. "You're enjoying crap?"

"I told her I'm seeing someone," she said with a little more force than was absolutely necessary.

"Okay. Well, thanks, I guess. Nice to be acknowledged… Kind of."

"I don't know what to say about us," she blurted.

"I thought we agreed that we were in a relationship—"

"We are, but this isn't your typical dating thing. You know? I mean, who says, 'I'm dating a guy who's going to father my baby for me'?"

"*The* guy," he corrected in a growl.

"Huh?"

"Not *a* guy, *the* guy."

"Seriously? Semantics?" She glanced at the clock. "It's two AM."

The tired rasp crept back into his voice. "Say whatever you like about us, Maggie, but get one thing straight. I'm not *some* guy or *a* guy. I'm *the* guy." His tone gentled. "I promised you I'd do better."

"You're doing just fine, no matter what my raging hormones might make you think."

"Yeah, well, we're going to do this, sweetheart, so you'd better get your story straight."

Maggie let the endearment slide without comment, but it brought a smile to her face. "We're going to do this," she affirmed.

Silence hummed over the line. Tom cleared his throat, but it didn't help. His voice came out in that husky growl. "Now tell me about the porn and vibrator."

She smiled and rolled onto his pillow. "Goodnight, Tom. I'll see you in a few hours."

His laugh rumbled through the line. "Call me as soon as the coast is clear."

****

His fingers slipped through her hair. Maggie stared at the tiny white lights dotting her miniscule Christmas tree, relishing the gentle caress. Tom drew a deep breath and she smiled. The past few weeks had taught her a lot. Now she knew his rhythms well enough to know another argument was coming.

"Are you sure you won't come with me to Sean and Tracy's?"

She stroked his denim-clad thigh and pressed the back of her head into his shoulder. "You want to drag me into a combat zone on Christmas Day?"

"They're okay. Besides, they'd never let on in front of company, or the kids."

Though she could practically feel his smile, the grim note in his tone wasn't lost on her. She gave his knee a gentle squeeze. "Sheila's expecting me. Besides, Tracy and Sean would have a stroke if we showed up together."

"Maybe not. You don't know."

"I'm willing to bet it would be a bit of a shock for them. Plus, your mother will be there, won't she?"

He shook his head. "She doesn't go to Sean's on Christmas Day. She says the noise gives her a migraine." He stroked her neck with his knuckles. "I'll go by her place after I leave Sean's."

She wrinkled her nose. "How can she not want to see her grandkids on Christmas?"

"It can get a little chaotic."

An indelicate snort propelled her from his embrace. “The kids aren’t little anymore. What are you going to do when our kid is born? Hide out at your Mommy’s house?”

He held his palms up in surrender. “Whoa! Whoa! I’m going to Sean and Tracy’s, remember? You’re the one who won’t come out of hiding.”

“I’m not hiding! I spend Christmas with Shelia every year.” A flash of humor lit his eyes and she lashed out, swatting his arm. “Stop laughing at me!”

“I love getting you riled up.” He launched himself from the end of the couch and tackled her against the opposite arm. “You’re so hot when you’re steamed, Maggie.”

“You should know. You manage to piss me off about once a day.”

He pinned her easily. The flirty dimple in his cheek winked at her when he flashed that boyish grin. “I was going for twice a day. I’ll have to work on my game.” He kissed her slow and soft, his lips lingering against hers. She caught his breath and hung onto it, clinging to his broad shoulders. “I don’t like the thought of you being alone on Christmas,” he whispered.

“I won’t be alone. I’ll be with Sheila,” she whispered back.

“I want to be with you.”

Maggie turned her head and squinted at the clock on the DVD player. “You will be with me on Christmas. It’ll be Christmas in just another thirty minutes. You weren’t planning on leaving, were you?”

“I’m not going anywhere,” he growled.

Stretching beneath him, she tangled her legs with his, watching as his eyes darkened with awareness. “Except to bed.”

“To bed.”

Her smile came slow and sure.

“You’re so damn easy.”

****

Sheila emerged from the kitchen of her elegant Lake Shore Drive condominium holding two generous glasses of white wine. She stopped short of Maggie and narrowed her dark eyes. "You're definitely not pregnant?"

Maggie blinked in surprise but quickly recovered, flashing a saucy grin. "Not that I know of."

Rolling her eyes, the older woman relinquished one of the glasses into Maggie's eager grasp. "I'd think at your age you would have learned how to avoid those little scares."

The wine was cool, crisp, and fruity, and slid down her throat like melted butter. Maggie gulped half the glass then lowered it with a gasp. "You don't need to worry about that, Sheila. I'm fine."

The older woman sank gracefully onto the plush cushions of the cream suede sofa, cradling her glass between her palms. "Well, you seem much better," she conceded. Still, her shrewd brown eyes focused on Maggie intently. "Thank you for helping today."

Employing far less grace and elegance, Maggie dropped down next to her friend. "I love Christmas morning at Haven House."

A smile lit the older woman's eyes. "It is wonderful, isn't it? For one day they forget the fear and the worry. One magical day when they all feel safe and happy." She sighed. "Makes you wish every day could be Christmas Day."

"They *are* safe and happy, and that's because of you." Maggie toasted her friend with her glass.

A pink flush rose in Sheila's cheeks. "Because of *us*," she corrected. "Everyone at Haven House."

Maggie let her head fall against the back of the couch and stared at the professionally decorated tree positioned in front of the panoramic windows. Closing her eyes, she conjured up the image of the little Charlie Brown tree perched on her end table. "You never told me, how was your Christmas party?"

Sheila snorted and toed off her glossy black pumps. "The usual… Cocktails and canapés. I picked a few pockets, of course," she added with a smug smile.

Maggie shot her a knowing glance. "I'm sure you did."

"I love holiday guilt. It carries us almost through to Independence Day."

"How appropriate."

Sheila smiled and tapped her glass with her fingernail. "I think so." Leveraging herself from the sofa, she padded toward the kitchen. "The usual? Moo shu with extra egg rolls?"

"Perfect," Maggie called after her.

"I'm ordering extra pancakes. I love ordering Chinese take-out on Christmas. Roasted turkey is for the birds."

Maggie sank deep into the couch and raised her glass. A smile curved her lips as the cool, crisp wine wet them. She let the barest sip linger on her tongue before setting the glass aside. The tight muscles in her neck sang out as she stretched. Her toes curled in her shoes. She sighed and kicked them off.

"There! Dinner is on its way," Sheila announced as she strolled back into the room. Maggie peeped at her through her lashes and grunted her approval. The plush cushions barely shifted when Sheila reclaimed her spot. "So, who's the guy?"

Her eyes popped open. The tension she'd released sprang back, pulling her muscles as taut as a bow. "Guy?" she squeaked.

"Whoever it is that's putting that glow in your cheeks," the older woman said, waving her hand impatiently. "You say you aren't pregnant…."

"Yet," Maggie muttered before she could stop herself.

Sheila's sharp gaze locked on her like a laser beam. "Yet?"

"I'm trying to have a baby." The admission came out in a whisper. Maggie braced herself, absorbing the shock and worry that flitted across her friend's face. "On purpose."

"I see." Sheila quickly schooled her features, lacing her fingers together on her lap. "Well, I guess I didn't need to stuff those condoms in your bag," she said at last.

"Condoms?"

"You know I keep a bowl of condoms in the office. While you were playing Santa, I shoved a handful of them into your purse."

Maggie sputtered a laugh. "You did?"

"Sue me." She shot Maggie a pointed glare. "I thought you were trying to *prevent* pregnancy."

A grin split Maggie's face. "I know! Crazy, huh?"

"Is it?"

"Wild." Maggie exhaled, letting her head fall back as the weight of her secret lifted from her shoulders. "So wild."

Turning her head, she eyed her friend and attempted to gauge her reaction. Sheila's face remained carefully impassive for a moment. Then a small smile twitched the corners of her lips.

"I thought you seemed happier," she said at last.

"I am." Maggie swallowed the lump in her throat and blinked back a scalding rush of tears, but emotion clogged her voice. "All I've ever wanted was a baby."

Sheila's brow puckered as she reached for Maggie's hand. "Just a baby?"

A searing jolt zinged through Maggie's body. Her fingers clenched her friend's reflexively. She forced a smile and tried to extract her hand. "That's all I need." Sheila squeezed, holding fast to her hand. The smooth silk of her skin cooled the heat pooling in Maggie's gut and calmed the nerves prickling her spine.

Weaving their fingers together, Sheila met Maggie's gaze directly. "I'm happy for you."

"Thank you." An uncertain smile quivered on Maggie's lips. "You never know what people are going to think."

"Do you care?" Sheila asked, arching one eyebrow.

"I know I shouldn't..."

"But it's hard not to," her friend concluded.

Another reassuring squeeze conveyed Sheila's tacit approval, but Maggie knew she wouldn't get off the hook so easily. She did her best not to squirm under intense scrutiny but failed. Wriggling into an upright position, she reached for her glass of wine. The tart flavor teased her tongue. The cool liquid slid down her parched throat. She closed her eyes, savoring the wine and waiting for the knockout blow.

"Who's the guy?"

Maggie swallowed hard then rasped, "Tom."

"Tom?"

Her head bobbed. "Tom. Tom Sullivan."

"Tom Sullivan," Sheila repeated in a bewildered tone. "Tom Sullivan?" Her voice rose. "My Tom Sullivan?"

The incredulous question struck Maggie like a blow. "*Your* Tom Sullivan?"

Sheila waved her concern away with a negligent sweep of her hand. "Not like that, you silly girl." She snorted indelicately. "Though an old woman can dream," she murmured, reaching for her wine glass. "I meant, the Tom Sullivan that I know and love."

"Do you love him?" Maggie asked, curious about the seemingly close relationship between her friend and her lover.

The question was answered with an exaggerated eye roll and the bleat of the telephone. Sheila pried herself from the cushions. "That'll be the doorman calling. Dinner is here."

"So fast?"

"I order from a place right around the corner. Plus, I assume Christmas is not their busiest day." Sheila answered the call. Satisfied that sustenance was on the way, she turned her full attention back to Maggie. "Please tell me Tom knows of your plan to conceive," she ordered with an imperious lift of her brows.

"Of course! It was his idea."

"Just checking." Sheila made her way back to the couch. "Tom Sullivan," she murmured. "You say it was his idea?"

Sheila's incredulous tone made Maggie snicker. "I know, wild, but it was. Well, his participation in my plan, that is."

"He's a good man." She offered her hand to Maggie.

Maggie nodded and slipped her hand into the older woman's firm clasp. "I think so."

The doorbell rang, and a brilliant smile lit Sheila's dark eyes as she pulled Maggie from the depths of the sofa cushions. "Good. I'm glad you see it too." Releasing Maggie's hand, she hurried to the door. "Thank God I ordered extra egg rolls," she called over her shoulder. "I'm going to want details. Lots and lots of juicy details!"

****

"And I told her she puts too much nutmeg in her coffeecake, but she never listens to me," Katie Sullivan said with a sniff.

Tom stifled the smirk that threatened. Instead, he focused on the crumbs dotting the saucer in front of his mother. As usual, his mother insisted on blaming Tracy for Sean's perceived baking failure. It was an old joke that Katie Sullivan never understood. His sister-in-law didn't bake. Hell, the woman could barely boil water. Sean was the culinary genius of the family. Sean was the one who put too much nutmeg in the Christmas morning coffeecake Tom had brought from his brother's house.

It was Sean who saved them from a lifetime of Hamburger Helper and tuna fish casserole, because even though Katie Angelini Sullivan was taught to cook like any good Italian girl, she didn't feel compelled to share the gift of her talents with her growing boys. His mother never could see the point in slaving over a hot stove when there were soap operas to watch and neighborhood gossip to fuel. She certainly didn't want to waste time fixing nutritious and delicious meals for her family when there was no man hanging around to compliment her superior parenting skills.

Tom sat back and crossed his arms over his chest as she pushed away from the stained and scarred formica table. He lowered his lashes to hide the laughter in his eyes as he shook his head. "That Tracy, she never learns."

"She's going to find herself without a husband if she doesn't wise up soon." She rinsed the saucer and fork she'd used and placed them in a plastic rack to dry. "Then what will she do?"

He rolled his eyes behind her back. "I imagine Tracy would be able to manage on her own."

Katie Sullivan whirled, fixing him with an incredulous stare. "With three children? There's no way. I could barely muddle through with the two of you after your father left. How could someone like Tracy possibly raise three children on her own? She doesn't even cook."

Tom bit the inside of his cheek to keep from snapping at her. "I don't think we have to worry about Tracy and the kids. Sean would never let it come to that."

"Sean." The derisive snort that accompanied her younger son's name had almost become another syllable over the years. "He's just like your father."

Wooden chair legs scraped the worn linoleum, causing her to jump. Tom ground his teeth as he pushed from the chair. "Shouldn't you be getting ready for mass?" he asked, nodding to her faded housecoat and slippers. "We'll be late."

His mother glanced at the clock on the stove. "It's already too late. We'll have to wait and go to the four o'clock service this afternoon."

"Ma—"

She held up one heavily veined hand to halt his protest. "You were the one who insisted on spending the morning at your brother's house. You know the last morning mass is ten o'clock on holy days."

The thought of spending the entire afternoon in the gloomy little bungalow where he grew up made his skin crawl. "I have to get back to the city."

"It's Christmas Day, Thomas. You're not married, you have no family of your own. Why would you need to rush back to the city?" She pinned him with a piercing glare. "Have you met someone?"

Tom inhaled through his nose and clenched his teeth, determined not to flinch. "What? No." He shook his head. "I have work to do, Ma. Big case. It's been in all the papers."

Katie Sullivan's face softened into a smile so angelic one could almost forget she was anything but a sweet old woman. "I know you do, but surely you can take one day off with your mother." She nodded to the seat he vacated. "Sit. I'll make you something better than that awful coffeecake. We'll have bacon and eggs, you can watch one of those football games they always show on Christmas Day, and then you can take me to mass." She pulled a heavy skillet from the cabinet beside the stove. "It is a holy day of obligation, after all."

He dropped into the seat, crossing his arms over his chest again and tucking his clenched fists into his armpits. "It sure is," he grumbled, casting a longing glance at the kitchen door.

"I told Cecilia Cogburn that Mary Therese Murphy was as senile as an old stump." Tom sat up a little straighter as she bustled from the stove to the fridge and back again. "Last week, at the golden jubilee luncheon she tried to tell us that she saw you cozied up with some redheaded hussy in a supermarket of all places!" She cracked an egg against the side of the skillet. "She tried to tell us it looked serious. How could it look serious? I said to her, 'Mary Therese Murphy, my Tom is not serious about any woman, much less some tramp who fools around in the market.' It made no sense."

Tom bit back the defense that sprang to the tip of his tongue. Instead, he forced a laugh. "She said it looked serious? How does something like that *look* serious?"

His mother crowed, "Exactly!" Shaking her head, she cracked two more eggs in quick succession. "I mean, I'm your mother. I would know if you were getting serious with a woman."

"Right."

"And what would you be doing up in the north suburbs anyway? You're a southside boy. And in a grocery store! It was too ridiculous." She waved the notion away with a package of bacon. "Anyway, I hope that Mairead is keeping a close eye on her. You know how those old people get when their minds start to go."

Tom fought the urge to point out that Katie Sullivan and Mary Therese Murphy were about the same age. Instead, he focused on a chip in the speckled formica in front of him. He dragged in a calming breath and rubbed the indentation with his thumbnail. "Right. Yeah, I hope Mari is taking good care of her," he managed to mumble.

Another snort was chased by the sizzle of bacon hitting a hot skillet, and the fine hairs on the back of his neck stood on end. "I told that old bat, 'My Tommy is too smart to get trapped by any woman. My Tommy is his own man. He'd never fall for some other woman…' You know that Mari is probably getting divorced, right?"

Tom blinked, stunned by the abrupt segue. "She is?"

Katie bobbed her head. "You watch yourself. She'll probably end up calling you to be her attorney, then she'll fall in love with you."

He forced a chuckle when she glanced back over her shoulder. "Not likely."

"Oh, I know they all do. You're just as handsome and successful as that fella who was the divorce lawyer on that show. But you're smarter than him. You won't get caught. You won't get trapped. Not my Tommy."

Chapter Fifteen

The lock's tumblers snicked and clunked. The hinges squeaked when he opened the apartment door. Tom turned sideways and slipped through the opening, making a face as hinges sang out again. The poker game had run later than usual. Actually, the game ended at the usual time. It was the minor inquisition he faced after shooting off his mouth that made him late. Still, he thought he acquitted himself fairly well. The Oak Park Mafia had nothing on Tom Sullivan when it came to the verbal thrust and parry.

He toed off his shoes and crept through the darkened apartment like a cat burglar. By the time he reached the bathroom, his shirt was balled in his hands. Fred squatted in the bedroom doorway, blinking lazily when Tom paused in the hall. The feline's silent reproach echoed off the darkened walls.

"Get in bed," he whispered, nodding toward the bedroom.

The tip of the watch cat's tail twitched and his purring motor cut out abruptly. He kept his piercing green gaze focused on Tom.

"She told Sheila!" His whispered justification sounded pathetic and he knew it. The fact that he was defending himself to a fat marmalade-colored cat didn't make him feel any better, either. "And Tracy," he added. Fred didn't seem impressed. "I don't care what you think. Sean's my brother. I get to tell someone."

He slipped into the bathroom and shut out the cat's low growl of disapproval. Within seconds, his clothes lay strewn across the chilly ceramic tiles and the shower hissed to life. Tom stood under the spray, lathering his body with Maggie's lemongrass soap and rehearsing his defense. Tipping his head back, he let the hot water trickle over his face. The weak spray barely raised a tingle on his scalp. He couldn't quite fool himself into thinking Maggie would be more apt to be swayed by his justifications than Fred, but keeping their relationship secret was killing him.

He would claim that he just needed to tell Sean. After all, how could she blame him for wanting to share something so important with his only brother? Tom glanced down at the water pooling in his palm then shook his head. He shifted and the tiny pool seeped through his fingers.

"Yeah, right. Doesn't hold water."

He snagged the bottle of mint shampoo from the ledge and popped open the cap. The problem was, he didn't just tell Sean. He told Sean and George and a small band of George's degenerate septuagenarians. And he didn't keep it light and vague. No, he couldn't just tell them he was seeing someone, like Maggie did with Tracy. He had to go and name names.

Damn Sean. It was his fault. The jerk-off sat there with that smug little smirk on his face. Hell, they hadn't even played out an entire hand before his little brother clocked no less than three cracks about Tom's staying power. He had to say something—anything—to shut the guy's trap. He found the magic words, though. The minute he said, 'Maggie McCann', his little brother clammed up. At least for a while. The minute the game was called Sean stretched back in his chair, crossed his arms over his chest, and waited. Just waited.

Tom twisted the knobs, cutting off the flow of water. He closed his eyes, standing stock still. The faucet dribbled to a stop. Cool air slithered its way around the plastic shower curtain. Droplets of water clung to his nose and eyelashes.

"Crap," he exhaled. "She's gonna kill me."

He yanked a handful of seafoam green terrycloth past the curtain. Goosebumps rose on his skin when he stepped from the safety of the tub. He knotted the damp towel at his waist and ran one hand through his wet hair before planting them both on his hips. Butterflies took flight in his stomach.

He hadn't told Sean about the baby—or possible baby. Biting the inside of his cheek, he met his gaze in the mirror. A shiver raced down his spine. He wanted to blame his spinning head on a bit too much scotch or the ever-present smog of cigar smoke, but Tom knew neither was to blame.

He didn't want Sean to think Maggie was a means to an end. He didn't want to boil their relationship down to her ticking biological clock and his fear of mortality. What he and Maggie had was so much more than that. At least, he hoped it was.

The telephone rang and he jumped, stubbing his toe on the foot of the vanity. "Fuhhh…"

He doubled over and gripped his toes, hopping on one foot and biting down on his tongue. The towel unfurled. The phone blared another half-ring, and Tom cursed under his breath when he heard Maggie's sleep-husky voice. He hobbled to the bathroom door and jerked the handle. Fred greeted him with a plaintive meow. Tom shooed him away and limped toward the bedroom. Maggie sat straight up in the bed. Her gaze locked on him, and Tom stopped dead in his tracks.

"What?" he whispered.

She shushed him with a wave of her hand, clutching the phone a little tighter. "I know, I know…but I can't help it. I like him, Trace." Her mouth thinned into a thin line. "Too late," she muttered into the phone. Tom approached the bed with extreme caution. She glanced at him then turned away, pulling his pillow into her lap.

He shivered, suddenly feeling more exposed than nudity warranted. Turning toward the ancient dresser, he ignored his reflection in the funhouse mirror as he pulled open 'his' drawer and snagged a pair of underwear. Maggie's bitter laugh made him freeze. A shiver chased up his spine.

"Wouldn't be the first time. Probably won't be the last."

A long pause hung heavy in the air. He dared a glance over his shoulder. The soft curves of Maggie's face were stretched into taut lines of tension.

"Your faith in me is touching," she said coolly. For the first time in almost two years, Tom felt a twinge of sympathy for his sister-in-law. Maggie wriggled around, sitting up a little straighter. "What, Tracy? You don't think I can hang onto a guy like Tom?" He cringed, thankful he couldn't hear Tracy's response. "You think I don't stand a chance," she continued. "You don't think there's even a remote possibility Tom might want me."

"Maggie!" he whispered, desperate to get her attention.

"No, Tracy, I don't." She barreled ahead and he stared, shocked there wasn't steam blowing out of her ears. "For years I've listened to you talk about him like he's freakin' Warren Beatty. Well, maybe I'm Annette Benning!"

Swallowing hard, he shook his head. "I'm not worth it," he hissed.

Maggie glared at him, her knuckles draining bone white as she clutched the phone. She tipped her chin up a notch. "You know what? I wanted him, I got him, and I'll take him for as long as I can. Besides, you're really not the person who should be offering people advice on their relationships, are you, Tracy?"

"Maggie!" He shook his head adamantly.

"At least I'm not too scared of my own shadow to take the chance! At least I'm not stupid enough to throw everything away for nothing!" Maggie drew in a deep breath. "You worry about your Sullivan, I'll worry about mine," she said flatly. "Goodbye."

She tossed the phone down on the bed, fixing the hapless instrument with a defiant glare. He gaped at her. His mouth worked, but no sound came out. Maggie tilted her head and blinked up at him, her face deceptively calm. She smoothed her palm over the rumpled pillowcase, placed it back on his side of the bed, and gave it an inviting little pat. "So, did you win?"

****

He got lucky. When he arrived early that morning his mother was still in bed. Tom moved from spot to spot, trying to be a quiet as possible, but it was hard to be hush-hush about planting a metal ladder in a foot of snow and leaning it against a steel gutter. A tiny part of him clung to the hope that he hadn't awakened her. He had to cut that tiny bit loose when he spotted steam billowing from the dryer vent. Resigned, he trudged his way to the door.

Tom shivered and stomped the snow from his boots, rubbing his gloved hands together then clapping them in hopes of restoring circulation. He scowled at chunks of snow melting into the rag rug that protected the foyer floor. Every year he spent the first Saturday of Advent stringing strands of ancient C-9 bulbs along his mother's gutters so he could chisel them free just after the Feast of the Epiphany in January. He yanked the unlined work gloves from his cold-stiffened fingers and blew into his cupped palms.

Next year it would be different. Next year—God and Maggie willing—he'd be prying ice-encased Christmas lights off his own gutters. Next Christmas, he'd be setting up a tree and putting together toys. Next year, he'd be able to wipe the smug smile off his brother's face. He could do this. He and Maggie could and would do this.

Katie Sullivan emerged from the steamy kitchen, wiping her hands on a Christmas-patterned dishtowel. "Were you able to get them down?"

"Yep." Tom unzipped his parka and drew a deep breath. "Got them down. Everything's all boxed up."

His mother twisted the towel clutched in her hands. Eying him closely, she tipped her chin up a notch. "Thank you for making time in your busy schedule to do that for me."

Alarm bells started clanging in his head. "I do it every year."

She sniffed and looked away, fixing her gaze on the framed school photos that lined the hallway leading to the bedrooms. "Yes, well, I'm sure you're anxious to get back to the city," she said stiffly.

Like a firefighter rushing into conflagration, he ignored the signs of imminent danger and took a step closer. The sole of his boot squeaked on the tile floor. "Ma—"

His mother cringed and darted a quick glance at his slush-covered boots. "You're tracking on my clean floor."

Tom froze, his eyes narrowing against the arctic blast of her tone. He was busted. Either George or Sean ratted him out. He just needed to know which one to go after. "Which one of them called you?"

Her composure cracked. She turned on him, fire flashing in her dark eyes and acid dripping from her tongue. "You mean who told me you were whoring around with that McCann girl?"

"Ma." The one word warning wasn't nearly enough to make her back down, but he still felt compelled to issue it. The woman was his mother, after all.

"I don't know why I'm surprised. You always have let your pecker out-think your brain."

"Hey!"

His fingers furled into his palms. He reigned in his temper, reminding himself that she was a bitter, ugly old woman. A hateful woman who never cared about her younger son, ignored her grandchildren, and lived only to make everyone around her as miserable as she had been for the past forty years.

"But Maggie McCann, Tom?" Her dismissive scoff set his teeth on edge. "She's so obvious." The dishtowel fluttered, a red flag daring him to charge. "It boggles the mind to think a man as intelligent as you can fall for that. All big boobs and no brains. The girl's a hairdresser, for heaven's sake!"

"Stop. Stop it right now before you say something you'll regret," he cautioned.

"Regret? Why would I regret the truth? You think you're the first man a woman like that McCann girl has made a fool of?" The scorn in his mother's eyes made his blood run cold. "You're just as bad as your father. A sucker for a pretty face. An idiot willing to throw everything he has aside for a woman who can't keep her legs together. You're just as bad as he was!"

Tom snapped. "Maybe I am. You should know, right, Ma?"

She recoiled as if he struck her. "What does that mean?"

"I may be an idiot who only thinks with my pecker, but Maggie isn't the only woman I know who spread her legs, is she?"

"I'm sure you know many women like that," she said coldly.

"I'm looking at one now. You may act all high and holy, but my dick and I did the math when I was about twelve and your numbers don't quite add up."

"Don't you use that kind of language with me, young man!"

"Hypocrite," he spat. Katie gasped, her gnarled hand flying to her lips. "You are the biggest hypocrite I've ever known. Maybe you're right. Maybe I am just like my father. I hope so, in at least one respect. Most 'premature' babies don't weigh eight and a half pounds, do they, Ma?"

He advanced on her, his chest heaving with anger. His mother's fingers trembled as they pressed against her mouth, and his heart broke. The flash of fear he saw in her dark eyes cut him to the quick. "You think I'd hurt you? My whole life, I've done nothing but take care of you. Not that you deserved it."

When she stared back at him defiantly, he shook his head in disgust. "I'm doing my best to get her pregnant. You should know that. I hope in that way, I'm just like my father." Afraid to say anything more, he turned and stalked toward the door. "You'll be a grandma again, not that you care."

"You'll pay," she said in a trembling voice. "You'll pay for your sins, Thomas Sullivan. Just like your father. Just like me."

Tom stopped, letting the icy January wind slice through him as he stood clutching the doorknob. Turning his head, he stared at the tiny woman who had been a giant pain in his ass for far too long. "Yeah, that might be true, but you can be damn sure I'll never make my kids pay for them, Ma."

He pulled the door closed, holding the knob until the latch clicked quietly into place. Staring up at the gunmetal sky, he exhaled and rolled the stiff muscles in his neck. "That's the difference between you and me," he whispered to the heavens above, hoping he wasn't lying to himself.

Chapter Sixteen

Fred purred pleasure sublime as he stretched his plump body, his rump sticking up in the air and his sharp claws sinking rhythmically into ring-spun cotton. The imprint of Tom's foot was stamped into the fibers of the bathmat. Her cat's girth spread over the impression of his heel and masked the arch, but Maggie could pick out each of the five toe-prints left behind. She bit her bottom lip, resisting the urge to shoo Fred from the rug. There was no need to preserve that footprint. Thousands of matching prints were already stamped all over her heart.

"Idiot," she whispered. She sank to the edge of the tub, but her gaze drifted back to the cluttered vanity. A thin plastic stick balanced precariously on the lip of the sink. Five more lay scattered amongst the jumble of cans, jars, and bottles. Tears pooled in her eyes, but she didn't bother trying to blink them back. It was too late.

Early that morning she squatted above the toilet waving one of those little wands and battling back the urge to give in to the first wave. Her heart rose into her throat, a valiant attempt to block the gush of tears to come, but they burst free, flowing thick down her cheeks like hot lava. Swirling tides of conflicted emotion crashed against her throughout the day, breaking her resolve into tiny grains of sand. Just when she thought she was holding it together the trembling would start, and soon she'd be swamped again. Maggie pressed her lips together and inhaled through her nose, ignoring the molten-hot droplets tickling her chin.

Idiot. Fool. How could I possibly think this could work?

But it had been working. For over a month things had been perfect. Day after day, night after night, her relationship with Tom worked perfectly. Beautifully. They could be the poster-children for...whatever their situation could be called. The prefect prototypes for how to make a relationship between a woman with a screeching biological clock and a man who wanted to have his cake and eat it too.

Tracy's well-intentioned-but-dire predictions weren't coming true. That was the rub. They'd been wrong about Tom. Terribly wrong. Maggie couldn't help but hold a bit of a grudge against her friend. As pissed off as she would have been if Tracy were right, somehow it was harder to accept they were both wrong. They both misjudged him. They both underestimated his power.

Instead of the relationship devolving into tears and recriminations, he filled her evenings with easy conversation, infectious laughter, and enough heat to leave scorch marks on her sheets. The bastard.

More than that, he'd settled into her life as if he'd belonged there all along. Not only did he know Fred's favorite brand of cat food, but the finicky feline's preferred flavors. He knew she liked extra cheese on her pizza and no cheese on her burgers. He knew where and how to kiss her to make her squirm, the exact spot to bite to make her scream, and just the right thing to say to dissolve her into a puddle of helpless laughter. The man even scrubbed the bathtub. What kind of guy does that? Worse yet, what kind of girl would let a guy like that go?

"One who never really had him in the first place." She groaned and let her head fall into her waiting palm. "Oh God."

Fred's motor kicked into overdrive. He rolled to his back and onto her foot, his emerald eyes conveying a clear demand. The breath whooshed from her lungs as she leaned down and gave his belly a negligent scratch. "You have to be careful what you wish for, handsome." The cat ignored her whispered warning. His eyes drifted shut as his paws reached for the heavens. Maggie shook her head. "I'm serious. Be grateful. This is a pretty good gig here. Was even before Mr. Perfect came along and swept you off your paws."

He lashed out, taking swipe at her hand. "You little shit!"

Cradling her knuckles in her palm, she stood and stepped over the prone feline, her eyes fixed on the stick teetering on the edge of the sink. The tiny window proclaimed the result clear as day. The faux-marble top was blessedly cool under her hands. She hung on for dear life, sucking in one steadying breath after another.

The moment she was sure her legs could hold her, Maggie dared at peek at the mirror. Loose tendrils of curling red hair escaped the knot at the nape of her neck. Spots of dried wax dotted the tunic top of her paisley scrubs. Her lips were dry and cracked, gnawed a bright red that matched the patches of color rising high in her cheeks. She peered at her reflection, forcing herself to stare straight into panicked green eyes.

Her hand slipped to her stomach, instinctively cradling the rounded curve. *What's done is done. I got what I wanted. That should be enough. Most of what I wanted….*

She blinked slowly then leaned a little closer, knocking the stick into the sink. Soon it wouldn't matter anymore. In a few short weeks she'd go from voluptuous vamp to baby beluga, and the point would be moot. There was no way he would want her once she began to expand.

Inhaling deeply, she rolled her shoulders back and stared at her reflection. Her hormones were just running rampant, that's all. Enjoy it while it lasts. Enjoy him while she could.

Resolved, she plucked the pregnancy test from the sink. Fred wound his pudgy body between her ankles, his tail coiling sinuously around her calf then drifting away. She stared at the glaring result and sighed. "You have to be careful what you wish for, buddy," she murmured to the marmalade cat. "Make sure it's not more than what you can get."

****

Tantalizing aromas greeted him at her door, tempting his taste buds with the promise of savory seasonings. He dropped his briefcase, shrugged out of his coat, and called out, "What smells so good?"

"Roast," Maggie sang out. "Pork roast."

He tossed his suit coat over the arm of the couch, flicked open his cufflinks, and palmed them, rolling his sleeve up as he wandered toward the dining area. The tiny table was set for two. Slim tapers in vividly painted ceramic holders cast a flickering glow over the scarred surface. He wandered over to admire her efforts. "Wow. Is it my birthday?"

"My last appointment cancelled, so I was done early. I thought I'd surprise you."

He glanced up then blinked rapidly as his jaw hit the floor. Maggie posed provocatively in the kitchen doorway wearing a little black dress that clung to her curves. Her feet were bare but for the pale pink polish on her toes, and her smile a little shy. An intense jolt of longing pinged his brain.

The husky timbre of her voice shot straight to his groin. "Surprise." Thick, glossy black lashes fluttered. "Are you hungry?"

She was the whole damn package cinched with a gauzy apron. He managed to scrape his jaw off the floor and swallowed hard, but that was as good as it got. When he tried to summon an actual word, it came out, "Wuh-huh-huh."

"I have mashed potatoes with garlic and herbs and green beans too." She waved the spoon clutched in her hand. "The beans are canned, but I doctored them up a bit…."

He saw something there. Just for a second. Those brilliant green eyes flashed with uncertainty. She fidgeted, shifting her weight from one foot to the other and his hand shot out to still her. Anxious to freeze this moment in time, his fingers curled into the soft curve of her waist. Drawing her to him, he bent his head to brush a kiss to her glossy lips. "You're perfect."

"You don't even know if I can cook," she whispered.

"I don't care."

He kissed her slow and unhurried, tasting, testing, and tempting her closer. Their breaths mingled, his lips lingered. The spoon clattered to the floor when he deepened the kiss. Her delicate hands smoothed his shirt over his chest. When they parted, he raised his hand to tuck her hair behind her ear. The wide French cuff flopped at his wrist, drawing his attention.

The shirt was just an indicator of how well she fit his life and all the things he didn't know he was missing. He bought it one rainy Sunday in the suburbs. They stumbled into a tumbledown old flea market and spent hours pawing through pile after pile of junk. In the midst of the chaos, Maggie unearthed a pair of cufflinks made of delicate strands of sterling woven into a Celtic knot. She pronounced them perfect and flashed a coy smile as he completed the purchase, murmuring something about loving a man in French cuffs. One quick swing through Nordstrom's, and he was the proud owner of five crisp, new shirts without buttons on the sleeves.

Tom sighed and closed his eyes, resting his forehead against hers. Women had tried to dress him before. He'd humored them to a certain extent—picking up a sweater one noticed on a display or choosing a blue shirt over white because his date thought it made his eyes look bluer. But the cufflinks were different. Maggie was different, and that difference terrified him.

Christ, I'm a goner.

"You don't want to eat?"

The question startled him. Shaking his head to clear it, he latched onto the distraction. "Yeah. Yeah, I do. I just…It smells great, Mags."

Her smile widened exponentially as she gestured to one of the place settings. "Then let's get to it before it gets cold."

Ten minutes later, she shot him a glance. "You're not eating." Spearing a bit of over-cooked pork, she offered the tines of her fork. "Do you want me to feed you?"

Tom yanked his gaze from his rolled-up shirtsleeve. He couldn't stop thinking about those cuff links, this shirt, and the woman sitting across from him. French cuffs were a declaration—a lifestyle change. French cuffs meant eschewing the convenience of tiny plastic buttons and espousing a world where effort had to be expended to hold things together. And he did it. For Maggie. He couldn't help but wonder how far she'd go for *him*.

Raising an eyebrow, he fixed her with a steady stare. "Would you?"

"Open wide."

He closed his eyes as he took the bite she offered. The fork was warm from her mouth and the meat savory. He wanted her. Not in the naked and bent over a table kind of way, but in the whole wrapped up in his life way. The thought had him practically vibrating in the seat.

"Maggie."

Her name came out too abrupt, too urgent. He opened his eyes to meet her wide green gaze and forced a shaky smile. He plucked the fork from her hand and dropped it to the plate, weaving his finger through hers as if she could anchor him. She blinked away the confusion clouding her eyes when he opened his mouth and no words came out.

A nervous smile twitched her lips. "What? What's the matter? Speak, boy. Is Timmy in the well?"

He managed a weak chuckle in appreciation of her lame joke and shook his head. "I just…" His finger tightened around hers. "I just…You're happy, right?" he managed in a rush. "With how things are going? I mean, obviously we're not pregnant yet, but other than that…Me and you? You're okay with how things are with us, aren't you?" When she reared back, he leaned in, desperate to keep her from slipping from his grasp. "I am, I mean…Really happy. I think things are going really well—"

Stubborn pride had him clamping his mouth shut the moment she wrested her hand from his. He looked away as she slipped from her chair and rushed into the kitchen. He stared at the wall, the muscle in his jaw ticking with tension. Somewhere, there on the cat-hair-dusted floor, his heart lay split open wide and bleeding. He didn't want to risk a peek.

"I have something for you."

His head jerked up. He clenched his teeth and sucked in a deep breath before turning to look at her. Maggie leaned against the doorway, waving a plastic stick as if it was a magic wand.

"I'm happy with all that and with how the getting pregnant thing is going, too," she said, a slow, sly smile creeping across her face.

"Huh?" His forehead creased into a frown when she waved the stick in front of his face again. He caught her wrist and leaned back, squinting to bring the scrap of plastic into focus. A blue line streaked across the tiny window. His head jerked up, their gazes met, and her smile unfurled like a flower in bloom. "You're pregnant?"

The quick, herky-jerky movements of her head could have gone either way, but his brain engaged at last, reminding him that she wouldn't be standing there brandishing a stick she'd peed on if the answer wasn't yes. Eyes locked on hers, he rose from his seat, winding his fingers around hers and trapping the magic wand in her closed fist.

"We're pregnant," he whispered, dipping his head to seal the declaration with a kiss.

Tom rested his forehead against hers and waited. Her fingertips trailed along his spine scattering sizzles of sensation to the tips of his toes, but the urge to bolt he expected was a no-show. He gave it another full minute, but the panic he'd almost banked on didn't come.

Her last hope for escape had evaporated. So had his. The stark realization made his heart skip a beat even as a chuckle rolled up from his stomach. He let it fly as he wrapped his arms tight around her. Relieved, he gulped a huge lungful of the fresh, lemony scent of her soap.

"Maggie," he whispered into her ear.

"Hmm?"

He grinned as she buried her face in the crook of his neck, swaying into his body. His hands slid down, tracing the line of the zipper that snaked down her spine. He sank into the chair again and pulled her into his lap, shaking his head in wonder.

"Nothing…Just Maggie."

Her smile tickled him. The lift of her cheekbones nudged his jaw. Her lips curved as she kissed his throat, branding him as hers. Sharp teeth scraped his pulse, nipping playfully. He knew damn well she could make it jitter like a jackhammer.

"Tom?" She pressed a soft kiss to his ear. He shivered and shied away when her warm breath washed over damp skin.

"Mmm?"

Soft, tender kisses trailed along his jaw before looping back to his ear. He gathered her closer. Burying his face in her hair, he took another hit of pure Maggie then released his breath on a chuckle. He tugged her hair until she lifted her head.

Her cheeks glowed pink, and her bright eyes sparkled with delight. She pressed the pregnancy test into his hand and sealed the deal with a giddy smack of a kiss. "You okay there, Daddy-O?"

Tom snorted but clutched the tiny wand tight. The pad of his thumb caressed the tiny window with the blue stripe. She settled against him once again and he hugged her a little tighter, resting his chin atop her head. "A-okay, little mama. A-okay."

****

Maggie blinked at the darkened ceiling. "Are you going to tell her?"

"Hmm?"

She turned her head, a smile curving her lips. "I know you're not asleep yet, and you know what I'm asking."

Tom dragged in a breath and rolled onto his back, resting his hands on his stomach as he exhaled in a gust. "No."

"No?" She propped herself up on her elbow. "You're not going to tell her?"

He cut her a look. "Asked and answered. Next question."

She cocked her head and stared at his impassive expression. His attitude boggled her. She was stunned by how callous and dismissive he was of the woman who gave birth to him. "How can you be like that?"

He turned his bland stare on her. "Really? You're asking me this about my mother?"

"I'm just…I'm not accusing you, or saying she doesn't deserve it. I'm just," she shrugged and held up a helpless palm. "I don't have any parents, so what do I know, right?"

"You know my mother. You've met her. She's cold and cruel. She uses people, and she doesn't care who she hurts." He covered her stomach with his hand, pressing his warm palm to the sweet curve that concealed their child. "I know it's horrible for me to say it, but I can't help thinking our baby will be better off without her around."

"Tom," she chided.

His hair rasped against the pillowcase. "Maggie, I hate to break this to you, but on the rare occasions you've been around my mom, she was using her company manners." She made a face, and at last he cracked a smile. "Scary, huh? I can't subject an innocent baby to that, now can I?"

She settled in, pillowing her cheek on his chest. "Maybe when we get closer to time."

Tom chuckled and gathered her hair, pulling it back from her face. "There's my cockeyed optimist."

Sliding her fingertips along his leg, she tickled the sensitive skin of his inner thigh. "See, I was thinking your cockeyed optimist was something entirely different."

He branded her with a searing kiss, but within moments his lips gentled. His breath mingled with hers. She tasted her name on his tongue. Smiling, she wrapped herself securely around him as he covered her. Her fingers slipped through the crisp waves of his hair.

"I think you should tell her," she whispered as he trailed hot kisses down her neck.

"Shh."

"Tom." Her breath snagged when he cupped her breasts and buried his lips deep in the valley of her cleavage.

He nuzzled the rounded curves then glanced up at her with a wicked smile. "Nobody here but us sinners, Maggie." He began to kiss his way down her belly, tugging at her nightshirt with his teeth. "No one matters but you and me. And our baby. No one at all."

Chapter Seventeen

Gloom cloaked the frigid February morning. Oblivious to the frost clinging to her windows, Maggie snuggled into the warm spot Tom left behind. She hummed softly when he kissed her goodbye but refused to open her eyes as he fumbled his way to the door. The muffled juggling act of curses, coat, keys, and cat wrangling was her morning lullaby. He liked to start his day early and she liked the snuggly spot he left behind. The arrangement worked for both of them.

She dozed until her phone jitterbugged across the nightstand. The ungodly-early calls didn't even annoy her anymore. That's how pathetic she'd become. She actually looked forward to these feeble excuses to talk. He couched them in the pretext of pre-natal vitamin reminders, solicitous inquiries on the state of her appetite, or a sheepish apology for some domestic disaster he'd left behind. Lame or not, she loved these calls. She loved Tom. God help her.

"Mags?"

His husky voice crumbled and trailed away and she shot straight up in bed. This wasn't the usual call. That wasn't his normal tone. As much as she hated to admit she looked forward to his morning calls, it didn't take a genius to know this one was different. Little pangs of fear tweaked her tummy. This could be the call. This could be the day he decides he's had enough. She pressed one hand to her belly and pushed the anxiety down. Nothing had changed from the moment he walked out her door. If he was done with them, there would be nothing she could do to change his mind.

Resolved, she indulged her pride by attributing the tweaks of apprehension to morning sickness and made a mental note to heap a few extra complaints on him. It wasn't hard to gather the ammunition—the guy was disgustingly chipper in the morning. More cheerful than any sane person should be. At least, he was usually chipper. Tom didn't sound very perky at the moment. He did any number of things to irk her in the early morning hours, but he definitely didn't croak her name like a heartbroken frog.

"Are you okay?" she asked, breathless.

He cleared the frog from his throat. "Maggie, my mom…."

The low, hoarse, unnaturally calm tone of his voice catapulted her from the bed. "What happened?"

"I'm not sure. I'm on my way to the…" His voice caught on a hitch.

"Is she okay?" Silence sizzled on the line. She lunged for the dresser and yanked open a drawer. "Tom?"

"No."

"Where are you?" She pawed through her underwear.

"I'm, uh…at the house."

Her heart leapt into her throat. "The house? Your mom's house?"

"She was at six o'clock mass."

The tremor in his voice shook her to her core. "Her house?" She snatched a pair of panties and a bra from the drawer when he grunted an affirmative. Tucking the phone against her shoulder, she danced her way into the underpants. "What happened?"

"I don't know. I guess she just collapsed. They're saying it's an aneurism."

She stumbled to the closet and yanked a clean top from a hanger. Confused by his location in the context of his mother's diagnosis, she paused for a second. "And they took her home?"

"She's at Little Company of Mary." His voice broke on the hospital's name. He cleared his throat again and made a valiant effort steady his voice. "George and Sean are on their way."

"And you're at the house? Are you waiting for them there?"

"I didn't make it to the office."

He sounded bewildered and more than a little lost. Maggie clenched her shirt and bra to her stomach. "Tom? Do you need me to come?"

"Oh, no… No. Sean and George… I think George was going to call Tracy." He sucked in a breath. "I just have to…the paperwork."

She sank to the edge of the bed, knotting the clothes in her fist. "Paperwork?"

"She didn't want any machines," he murmured. "I need to get the papers."

Tears prickled her eyes and her stomach sank to her toes. "Oh, Tom…."

"They already have her on the ventilator. She didn't want that, but I wasn't there, and my copies are at my office. I don't know why I kept that stuff at the office…."

Maggie started to wrestle her way into the bra. "I'm on my way."

"No, don't. I'm okay. I just have to get the papers. Medical power of attorney…."

"Tom, I'm coming."

"No. Don't come." The car chimed, and she heard the clatter of keys against the phone. "Don't…I'll just…I'll call you later," he promised before disconnecting.

In just over an hour, Maggie canceled her appointments, hopped a train to the south suburbs, and wrangled a cab ride to the hospital where she'd been born. Her heels clicked on worn tile. As she jabbed the call button for the elevator, she wondered if Tom was born in the same maternity wing. He probably was. More than likely Sean and Tracy too.

In so many ways, their little world within the great big Chicago metropolitan area was very small. The volunteer at the information desk once served in the Altar and Rosary Society with Maggie's grandmother. The nurse manning the station had a daughter who was a beauty school graduate who interned at The Glass Slipper. She flashed a wan smile as she directed Maggie to the empty chairs across the hall from Katie Sullivan's room.

The edges of the molded plastic chair bit into her butt. Maggie stared at the extra-wide door across the hall. A man wearing a white lab coat over teal scrubs hurried from the room. A moment later, a nurse wearing silent crepe-soled shoes followed. A full minute passed before the door opened again and Tom's uncle, George Angelini, appeared.

She stood and took a hesitant step toward the older man. "Hello, George. I'm Maggie McC—"

Tears brimmed in his dark eyes. His mouth trembled. "I remember you, Sweetheart," he murmured, clasping her hand between his.

She opened her mouth to speak and the door swung wide again. Her gaze was automatically pulled to Tom as he worked one finger into the Windsor knot at his throat and stepped into the corridor. He caught sight of her, his forehead puckering in confusion and his lips parting in shock. Before he could voice the question, she extricated her hand from George's grasp and rushed to fold Tom into her embrace.

"I'm sorry," she whispered, cupping the nape of his neck.

He held himself stiff for a moment then gave way. His shoulders shook as a torrent of hot, moist emotion rushed against her neck. He whispered her name in a ragged rasp. "You came…" he murmured into her hair. A sigh shuddered through him. "You came."

"Of course I came." She smoothed the stubborn cowlick at his crown and offered his uncle a weak smile before pressing a soft kiss to Tom's ear.

The door opened again, and Sean appeared. The taller brother stopped dead in his tracks when he spotted them. Maggie looked up to find Sean's vivid blue eyes filled with a pain so stark it stole the breath from her lungs. Tracy peered around his arm and gasped.

Wetting her lips, Maggie raised her head to meet their curious stares head-on. "I'm so sorry, Sean."

As if shaken from his trance, Sean gave a jerky nod. "Thanks." He stepped aside, letting Tracy slide out from behind him as he turned to George. "You okay to drive?"

"I got you here, didn't I?" his uncle grumbled. Tom chuckled as he straightened, surreptitiously wiping his eyes with the backs of his hands. Clapping a hand to his uncle's shoulder, Sean nodded. "You did." He turned to Tom. "What do you need me to do?"

Tom shook his head and pulled his shoulders back. He slid his hand into Maggie's. "I've got it."

George gave Sean's arm a squeeze and moved to Tom's side. "You two go on home and get the kids. I'll help Tommy take care of the other stuff."

"But I can—" Sean began.

Tom held up his hand to stop him. "We can take care of this. You've got the tougher job," he said with a wince. "Go home. Kiss the kids and hug them." His fingers tightened around hers. "I'll call you in a little while, and we'll sort the rest out."

"Okay." Sean's nod was stiff, each movement jerky. "Okay."

Without a word, he began to walk away. Maggie met Tracy's gaze for the first time, and her friend wet her lips. Tracy nodded to Tom. "You'll take good care of him," she said, a statement more than a question.

"I will," Maggie answered.

Tracy kissed George's cheek then Tom's, but Maggie caught the envy clearly etched into her friend's frown as her gaze lingered on Tom and Maggie's clasped hands. Tracy sucked in a sharp breath then trotted down the hall in search of her husband.

Tom's fingers wound around hers. He turned toward her, misery shimmering in his eyes. "I can't believe you came all the way down here," he murmured. "What about your appointments?"

"Don't worry about that," she shushed him, fussing with the already smooth lapels of his suit jacket.

George cleared his throat and their heads swiveled toward the older man. Offering a pale imitation of his usually roguish smile, he gave her arm a quick squeeze. "You're a good girl, Maggie. Keep an eye on him for a few minutes. I'm going to go talk to the administrator."

As George wandered down the hall, she nudged Tom toward the hard plastic chairs and they dropped into the seat. "What happened?"

He raked a hand over his face. "Just what I told you on the phone. She collapsed at six o'clock mass. They called an ambulance." He freed his hand from hers and leaned forward, resting his elbows on his knees. Tucking his chin to his chest, he wove his fingers together. "She was on a ventilator by the time I got here. I had to… I had the legal papers."

She leaned closer, wrapping her fingers around his clasped hands. "I'm so sorry."

He lifted his head, and Maggie could clearly see the pain and confusion clouding his midnight eyes. She held his gaze for a moment, hoping her sincerity shone through. He didn't reach for her. His fingers remained tightly laced together, his elbows propped on his knees. Without warning he lunged, capturing her lips in a kiss so sweet tears blurred her eyes. She batted her lashes, feverishly trying to blink them back.

"I was so ugly to her the last time I—"

Maggie grimaced and leapt into the fray, anxious to head off his wayward self-recriminations. "No, Tom. No. You were so good to her. Everyone saw how good you were with her. Better than she was to you." She covered his hands with one of hers and squeezed as hard as she could, hoping to instill that cold comfort through sheer force of will. "She loved you so much. She knew you loved her too."

Tom stared at her hand, unblinking. He swallowed hard, bobbed his head in a slight nod, then cleared his throat. "I love you, Maggie."

The declaration was made in the same low, steady voice that reminded her about her vitamins, prodded her into drinking her milk, and confessed to opening a second can of Seafood Selections. He didn't stare deep into her eyes or sweep her feet from the worn tile floor. He simply laid his feelings out for her in clear, uncomplicated terms without fanfare, argument or even a hint of artifice.

"Shh," she crooned and urged him into her embrace before he spotted the tears which filled her eyes.

****

He meant what he said. He loved Maggie McCann, and he told her so. So what if she simply shushed him and pulled him into her arms? It didn't matter that she didn't reciprocate. Actually, he preferred it that way. He didn't want to hear it if she wasn't feeling it.

He told himself it was enough that she held him tight until his uncle reappeared toting a plastic bag emblazoned with the hospital's logo and with his mother's purse and well-worn rosary inside. She went above and beyond, sitting quietly at his side holding his hand while he and George made arrangements, so she obviously had some feelings for him. Aside from whatever feelings she had about carrying his baby. At least, that's what he told himself.

After all, she stuck by him, quick with a hug, a kiss, or a funny remark just when he needed it. For two days, she blockaded his mother's front door, intercepting casseroles and putting her own unique spin on the messages the ladies from the Altar and Rosary Society left for him. And if she wasn't always the most reliable messenger, she more than made up for her shortcomings in other ways.

"She did not say that," he scoffed.

Maggie shrugged and smoothed the lapel of his jacket. "That's how I heard it."

"Mrs. Kaminsky, who was my third grade spelling teacher, by the way, did *not* say I have a fine ass."

She sniffed and gave the skirt of her dress a tug. "Maybe she said she'd see us at the Mass."

"Uh-huh." He ran his hand over his tie, eying the crowd of elderly people milling near the entrance to the viewing room. His sister-in-law shepherded his youngest nephew into the room and pointed sternly to a chair. "Have you talked to Tracy?"

"We said hello."

He grimaced. "I hate this."

She trailed her fingers down his tie, stroking the silk gently. "I do, too. I hate it for you."

He caught her hand. "All of it. Ma, the old ladies with their endless parade of cream of mushroom soup and potato chip casseroles….George looks so old…" He trailed off and her fingers tightened around his. He met her gaze directly. "You should talk to Tracy. She didn't mean to hurt your feelings."

"She's just good at that," Sean muttered as he passed by.

Tom shot his brother a quelling look as Sean handed a Styrofoam cup of coffee to their uncle. "Yeah, well, maybe between the three of us we can talk some sense into her." Turning his back on Sean, he glanced past Maggie's shoulder as he brushed a kiss to her knuckles. "Go talk to her. I have to flirt with Mrs. McMahon."

He released the gorgeous redhead he loved and took up with a tiny woman wearing a pale purple cardigan that matched the rinse on her stiff bouffant. The mingled scents of rosewater perfume and eau de funeral carnation made his eyes water. At least, he was blaming the flowers. He didn't want to admit that the sight of Maggie and Tracy huddled together at the back of the room made him misty. He'd already admitted far too much.

Tom caught his brother staring at the women in their lives. He opened his mouth to hurl a smart remark, but Sean stiffened and took a staggering step back as if he'd been struck by bullets. Instantly protective, Tom's head swiveled. That's when he spotted his uncle escorting Daniel Sullivan toward the casket.

He stepped back, his shoulder brushing Sean's arm in silent reminder of brotherly solidarity. Eyes glued to his father, he kept his mouth clamped shut. Daniel Sullivan was bent like a question mark, the hand gripping an ebony cane knobby and gnarled. It galled him to give the old man the satisfaction of his attention. After all, their father never bothered to give them his.

The sight of him hit Tom like a punch to the gut. Daniel was a portrait of Sean in another twenty-five years. Tom searched his father's face for signs of himself but barely scrounged a strong resemblance. It hurt to see the man he loathed wearing Sean's face. The son-of-a-bitch dared to have tears in his eyes when he peered into the gleaming coffin. A rush of protectiveness he hadn't felt in thirty years drowned him, but his feet felt as if they were encased in cement.

The old man nodded a brief acknowledgement then slowly knelt in front of the coffin. Tom planted his feet wide, guarding his mother's casket and protecting the little brother who towered over him from this frail stranger. George wedged himself between Sean and Tom and clamped their elbows in a vise-like grip.

"What's he doing here?" Sean hissed.

His uncle shot them a glance. "He came to say goodbye." When Tom opened his mouth to speak, George shook his head sternly. "Grow up, damn it. He came to say goodbye. Let him say goodbye, and be done with it."

He watched as his father crossed himself then pressed his hands into the back of the kneeler, trying to leverage his weight off arthritic knees. He couldn't stop himself. Years of training took hold, and he stepped forward to help the old man to his feet. It was a reflex. Hell, he'd done the same for a dozen others over the course of the evening.

Daniel straightened his suit coat. "Thank you."

Two words. His father spoke two words to him after over thirty years of silence, and Tom felt disturbingly grateful. Masking his confusion with cool distance, he nodded.

"You're welcome." Chagrined, he struggled to keep his expression neutral as he stepped back and reclaimed his spot between his uncle and brother. "It was good of you to come."

The old man nodded, his gaze flickering to Sean then traveling over the sea of floral arrangements flanking the casket before landing on Tom once again. "Of course. I'm, uh, I'm very sorry," Daniel Sullivan murmured before walking away. Again.

****

That night, Tom and Maggie lay spooned in the ancient single bed in his boyhood bedroom. His breath stirred her hair, setting tame red tresses free from the somber restraint she forced on them. "You should have let me take you home."

She stroked the hair on his arm. "I'm staying with you."

"This bed's too small. We'll never get any sleep here."

She shook her head and a few more curls frizzed to life. "No sense in going back into the city. The Mass is at ten."

He ran his hand over the curve of her hip, allowed his fingertips to graze the bare skin of her thigh, and then gathered the hem of her t-shirt in his palm as he worked his way higher. His hand slid to the curve of her belly and pressed a soft kiss to her ear, smiling when she shivered. "Thank you," he whispered, his voice thick and husky.

Maggie stretched like a cat, pressing every inch of her body against him. "For hogging your bed?"

"For being here with me."

She covered his hand with hers, holding him snug as she turned her head. "She was our baby's grandma."

He couldn't repress his sad smile. "Poor kid. Now he's got no one."

She shifted onto her back and gazed up at him solemnly. "*She'll* have George and Sean and Tracy."

He let the change of pronoun slide, happy to shift into the comforting routine of banter. "And *his* cousins," he added with a nod. "That's one of the costs of having kids late in life, huh? No grandparents left."

She fell silent for a moment. "Well…"

The way she drew the word out made the hairs on the back of his neck stand on end. He tightened his arm around her and shook his head slightly, hoping to divert, derail, or demolish the thought before she could articulate it. As usual, Maggie beat him to the punch.

"She *does* still have a grandfather."

He shook his head more adamantly. "No. He *doesn't*."

"Tom—"

"Maggie, no."

"But—"

"I have not laid eyes on that man since I was ten. No." She turned her head, and he wagged his harder. "No, no, no."

"But he came!"

"To her funeral," Tom growled. "He came to her *funeral*. Where the hell was he when she needed him? Where was he when *I* needed him? Or Sean?" He rolled onto his back and nearly tumbled from the bed. The edge of the mattress cut into his shoulder blade. He planted one foot on the floor to keep from falling. "No, Mags, don't make this more than it is—"

"He was so in love with her," she whispered into the darkness.

"He had a funny way of showing it."

Undeterred, she rushed on. "Oh, but he did. You should have seen his face when he walked through the door and saw her picture. It nearly broke my heart."

"You have a soft heart."

Maggie rolled onto her side and propped her head up on her hand, scooting to make more room for him. "He looks so much like Sean…When I looked into his eyes I saw Sean's eyes." Her voice caught, but she went on in a rush. "Sean still loves Tracy. Your dad still loved your mom. And my heart broke, Tom. My heart broke for all of them," she whispered. "He missed so much. Not just the life he could have had with your mom, but you, Sean, Tracy and the kids…"

He turned to look at her. "He chose to leave, Maggie. He chose to leave, and he chose not to see us, and he chose nothing. He *chose* to be nothing to us," he insisted. He exhaled, letting the air slither from his lungs on a hiss. "Now you know why Sean won't leave Tracy, no matter what happens between them. He will *never* leave his kids."

"No, of course not."

Rolling to face her, he snaked his hand under her shirt again, seeking the warmth of her belly. A mixture of pride and stubbornness welled inside him when his fingers molded to the shape of her instantly, curving protectively over his child. His mouth thinned into a firm line. "And you'll never get rid of me now. You know that, right?"

"I know."

She nuzzled his nose. Her warm breath whispered across his lips. The hairs on his arm rippled with awareness. He kept his eyes wide open as she coaxed him into a soft kiss. Heat pulsed against his palm. He pulled his hand from her stomach, curling his fingers in an attempt to hang onto the warmth. "Do you?"

Maggie nodded. A smile curved her lips as she lowered her lashes and leaned in to kiss him again. He met her halfway, catching her soft, "I love you too," and swallowing it whole.

Chapter Eighteen

How dare he sit there like that? How dare he look all…good? If she didn't love him so damn much, she'd hate him. Lucky for him, she found it difficult to work up the rage necessary to eject him. Maggie wasn't exactly sure how one went about dislodging a middle-aged man clad only in underwear and half glasses from her couch, but odds were she couldn't bounce him without spilling the box of Cookie Crisp cereal propped against his hip.

Tom tossed a section of the Sunday *Chicago Tribune* aside and reached for the glass of juice on the end table. She bit back a sigh as long, lean muscle danced beneath smooth skin. It was her own damn fault he looked so good. How was she to know he'd take things so personally?

To be perfectly truthful, she liked the burgeoning belly brought on by night after night of take-out dinners. The fact that he was expanding made her feel better about her own rapidly blobifying figure. Whatever shape she once had seemed to melt like marshmallow over hot flame. The waist was the first to go but the rest followed too damn quickly for her liking. The only taut part on her entire body was her belly, and what was once a soft, sexy curve now had the tensile consistency of an over-inflated volleyball.

So, yeah… The fact that Tom was sprouting a sympathy belly made her happy. So happy she felt compelled to poke him in the stomach to see if he'd giggle like Poppin Fresh.

He didn't.

Not only did he fail to chortle, he decided to start making use of the gym at his condo. The jerk-off dropped ten pounds in the blink of an eye. Okay, maybe it was more like six weeks, but in those same six weeks Maggie had outgrown even the fattest of her fat pants.

What was worse, the bastard looked to be working his way toward a six pack. She narrowed her eyes, glaring intently at his flat stomach. The muscles bunched and released and the faint shadows of regained definition winked at her.

"I hate you," she said in a loud, firm voice.

He flicked a glance over the tops of his readers. "You don't hate me. The dress you bought looks incredible on you, and I think we should look at this duplex." He folded the section of newspaper into fourths and tapped a picture as he handed it to her.

A puzzled frown tugged at her lips. "Why do you want to look at duplexes?"

He shrugged. "Need a bigger place."

"Your condo is huge," she murmured. "Ugly, but huge."

Okay, that wasn't the truth either. She'd only seen his place once—on a quick stop to pick up clothes and collect mail—and it wasn't ugly. Or huge. Actually, the place was pretty nice. Definitely less cluttered than her place, so that made it look bigger. She just couldn't imagine spending much time there. The apartment was too impersonal, and the Tom she knew was nothing if not up-close and personal. She had a hard time imagining him there. Not that she had to imagine him there. He seemed to be permanently camped out on her couch.

Tom smirked. "If it'll make you feel better, we can run by Pier One so you can pick out some useless crap to hang in the apartment I haven't slept at in nearly three months."

She snatched the newspaper from his hand. "I don't do Pier One. I'm a Bed, Bath & Beyond girl," she grumbled. She scanned the page. "You want to move to Evanston?"

"Well, we'll need more room when the baby comes...."

Her head jerked up. "You want me to live with you?"

He laughed. The jerk actually laughed. And when he laughed those now-tight abs of his rippled. Rippled! The man was sliding headfirst into fifty, and he dared to sit on her sofa and ripple. In his underwear. Eating her cereal. Laughing at the big, fat hippopotamus and staring at her as if she were…the only girl in the world.

The man was a total shit.

If she didn't love him so damn much, she'd hate him. She'd hate him for moving into her life and taking over her cereal cabinet. She wanted to resent him for sitting there looking so beautiful when she felt so utterly disgusting. Every day, she did her damnedest to work toward despising his twinkling blue eyes and rippling abs. She prayed for the power to resist that boyish cowlick. And each time a starburst of hope rose in her throat, she swallowed it whole, leaving her feeling raw but safe.

"Things are fine the way they are."

"For now." He tugged her hand, and she dropped to the cushion next to him. "I'd like…It would be nice if we had something a little more…" Tom searched her eyes as he grappled for the right word. *Permanent.* She squeezed his hand, trying to will the word into his brain. It only took a moment to click, then his face lit. "Spacious," he said with a brisk nod.

Her heart dropped to her toes. She bit the inside of her cheek, desperate to swallow the hot lump of emotion balling in her throat. "This is all I need."

The odd thing was, the moment she said the words out loud, she knew they were the absolute truth. She didn't need the band of gold and a matching mortgage. A piece of paper binding him to her until death—or divorce—they do part meant nothing. Maggie stared at him in puzzled wonder, trying to remember why she would ever think 'I do' could add up to more than 'I love you'.

Resolve renewed, she leaned in to kiss him. "This is all I need," she whispered.

He angled his head, capturing her mouth in a kiss so soul-achingly sweet she stopped breathing. "I want you to have what you want, too."

"I want you." She offered her mouth again and he took it, willing, hungry, and possessive. "I love you," she whispered as he pressed her into the cushions.

He wouldn't say it back. He hadn't repeated those words since the day his mother died. But she felt them. Oh, she felt them. They rang soft in his voice when he said her name. They tasted tangy on his tongue and reverberated in the beat of his heart against hers. He trailed hot, wet kisses down her throat and she sighed.

"I love you, Tom." Blinking at the speckled ceiling she smoothed his stubborn cowlick and arched against his body. "This is all I need."

****

She was lying, of course. He knew it was a lie. This crazy half-relationship/half-agreement they were living left too much gray area for both of them.

Tom jabbed the speaker button on his office phone and speed-dialed his brother. When Sean answered, he sat up, braced his elbows on the polished surface of his desk, and blurted, "I'm going to ask Maggie to marry me."

Sean barked a laugh. "How was the blow job?"

"What?"

"I have to live vicariously through you these days."

Scowling, Tom tried to make sense of his brother's bizarre segue into his sex life, but detoured around it in the end. "I said I'm going to propose to Maggie."

"I heard you. You told me once that a guy only gets the urge to propose when a girl has his dick in her mouth. Is your dick in Maggie's mouth?"

Tom cast a sheepish glance at his partially open door and snatched the receiver from the cradle, tucking it under his chin. "No, my dick is not in Maggie's mouth," he hissed.

"So, you're not being coerced?"

Spinning in his chair, he stared out the window. "We're having a baby."

"Which is gonna happen whether you give her a ring or not."

"I love her."

Sean blew out a long breath. "God help you."

"I know." Tom let his head fall back and ran a hand over his face. He blinked at the ceiling. "How are things going with Tracy?"

"Things are going."

Looking past the hesitation in Sean's answer, he latched onto the faint note of hope he heard lingering in the undertone. The hope that had been absent for too many months was now back with a vengeance. Tom felt compelled to push. "You said things were better. You guys are talking, right?"

"We are…co-existing," Sean conceded.

"And that's better?"

"Better than the months Tracy was sleeping on the rec room couch and we weren't speaking at all." Sean paused for a second. "So, uh, proposing to Maggie?"

The sigh leaked out of him and a note of panic crept into his voice. "Christ. What am I doing?"

"Sounds like you're signing for a lifetime vacation in Purgatory."

Tom snorted. "Purgatory?"

"Somewhere between Heaven and Hell."

He blew out a breath. "I remember the term. Can't you just lie to me and tell me it'll be okay, Sean?"

The silence stretched between them. "I think it will," his baby brother said at last, his voice deep and gruff. "I think everything's going to be okay for both of us."

"God, I hope so."

Sean chuckled. "Have you got a ring?"

"Not yet." Tom stood, and stared down at the teaming sidewalk below. "I was waiting for the lunch rush to pass before I hit a couple of jewelers. Maybe I'll find something that looks like Maggie."

"Big."

"You sayin' my girlfriend is fat?"

"No! Just make sure you get a big one. A baby is enough work. She'll need extra incentive to take you on full-time."

"You suck at this, by the way."

"I'm just giving you the same advice you gave me when I wanted to propose to Tracy." Sean chuckled again. "Don't forget, you have to do the romantic, grand gesture crap. Rent the Goodyear blimp or the scoreboard at Wrigley…."

Tom cringed, remembering the boatload of helpful hints he'd doled out so freely nearly seventeen years before. "Yeah, like I knew what the hell I was talking about. Why would you ever listen to me?"

"Because you're my big brother. When I was five, you told me I had to do what you say or you'd beat the crap out of me," Sean reminded him. Tom heard the rumble of voices in the background, then Sean said, "Look, I've gotta go. Good luck."

"Thanks." Tom stared at the phone for a moment before hanging up. "Huh. Who knew you actually listened?"

****

The heebie-jeebies started the moment he stepped foot in the jewelry store. Fear tickled the back of his throat when a woman with a gunmetal gray bouffant and rhinestone studded—he assumed they were rhinestones—half-glasses approached. Terror squeezed a tremor from his voice when he asked to see the latest and greatest in engagement rings. The woman's amused smile turned terror into trepidation. She fixed him with a challenging gaze, almost double dog daring him to bolt for the door. Being a man—and not entirely confident in the support of his knees—he stood his ground.

The woman, Eunice, seemed impressed with his display of intestinal fortitude. For his part, Tom was just glad he didn't yak in front of her. That would have been embarrassing.

Instead, he focused on the glimmering hunks of compressed carbon submitted for his approval. One by one, Eunice pulled each offering from its cushioned slot and extolled the virtues of each ring as she slid them onto her slender fingers. Tom tried to imagine Maggie's delicate but extremely capable hands weighted down with miniature headlights flanked by ruby trillions or encircled by pave sapphires and the fear-terror-trepidation cocktail that fueled him morphed into downright panic. Not one of the bevy of brilliant beauties looked like Maggie to him.

Shaking his head, he took a staggering step away from the case. "No, I'm sorry."

"Too big? Too small?" Eunice asked. He could do nothing but shake his head harder. "Sweetheart, you have to give me something to go on here," she persisted. "Tell me about your girl."

"We're having a baby," he blurted, and his mind began to reel.

A smirk twitched the woman's lips. "Mazel Tov."

He stared at Eunice in shock, waiting for her expression to match the stunning knot of reality settling in the pit of his stomach. Failure was not an option. He had to pick out a ring. Maggie was having his baby. Without benefit of clergy. Without that flimsy piece of paper binding her to him. Yes, he had the custody agreement they'd signed, but that was about the baby, not Maggie. The ticking muscle in his jaw told him maybe he'd left getting all old-fashioned a little late.

Eunice snatched the trays from the top of the case and quickly locked them in the case again. The bubble of panic in his gut popped him like a punch to the solar plexus. "Wait!"

She circled the end of the counter, reaching for his arm. "Sweetheart, I think you need to sit down."

He allowed himself to be led to an ancient armchair perched in the corner and fell into it like a sack of bricks. Looking up, he blinked at Eunice's concerned frown. "It's okay," he croaked. He cleared the frog from his throat and forced a wan smile. "I'm okay."

The older woman gave him a brisk nod. "You stay put while I get you a drink of water." Bustling toward the back of the store, she tossed another sardonic smirk over her shoulder. "See if you can think of something else about her, other than the baby thing, and we'll try again."

Eunice stood quietly and patiently, watching him sip tepid water as he stumbled over the first few words. Red hair seemed an entirely inadequate way to describe Maggie's crazy curls. Green eyes…He leapt from the chair and rushed back to the case, jabbing his finger at the glass. The emerald he pointed to wasn't an exact match, but it was pretty damn close.

Tom rambled on, babbling like a brook. He gushed about her hair, her figure, her skin, and the way she always smells faintly of lemon. He burbled about The Glass Slipper and the successful business she created from scratch. A rush of funny things Maggie says and quirky things she does tripped from his tongue, and the next thing he knew, a tiny black velvet box was thrust into the palm of his hand.

Steadfastly, he ignored the wisps of smoke trailing from the edges of his credit card as he strode from the store. He hit Wabash Avenue a few thousand dollars poorer, but even Tom recognized that he was infinitely happier than he'd been in…forever.

The ring was perfect. A simple, classic solitaire, the stone he'd chosen was as blindingly flawless as Maggie's smile and big enough to put someone's eye out. Eunice was a miracle-worker. And damn good at her job, too. The woman must be some kind of jewelry-pushing juju goddess. After all, good old Eunice almost made him forget that he was about to go chasing after the very piece-of-paper-type commitment he made a living undoing.

****

Unbearable. The entire day was unbearable. She was awakened by a spate of nauseatingly chipper whistling. As if that happy tune wasn't bad enough, moments later she actually *was* nauseated when the faint aroma of canned seafood medley wafted down the hall. The moment the apartment door closed behind Tom, she was worshipping the porcelain god.

Things didn't get any better as the day ticked on, either. She spilled paraffin down the front of her last clean set of scrubs. The moo goo she ate for dinner the night before must have been loaded with extra sodium and mega MSG, because her fingers were swollen to the size of kielbasa. Her skin creaked like too small shoes stretched taut across her breasts and belly and leaving barely enough to cover the rest of her. Even her scalp was tight, which just exacerbated the low, strumming headache she'd been harboring for two days.

Her feet dragged as she started up the steps to her apartment. The extra-small epidermis she wore itched. The rolling sick in her stomach was now her constant companion, intensifying each time she got a whiff of anything citrusy.

She switched out all the products she used in her treatment room, insisted they change the lime slices floating in the purified water they served their clients to cucumber, and threatened the massage therapist who dared to bring an orange in her lunch with instant termination if she broke the rind. Still, she couldn't escape the tangy tinge in the air or the wringing in her gut with each shallow breath she took.

It wasn't until her two o'clock Brazilian wax client scurried from the room muttering about labia-hating, lemon-scented, lipstick lesbians that Maggie realized she was the source of her own discomfort.

She stumbled into her apartment armed with unscented bar soap and a bottle of baby shampoo from the nearest drugstore. On her way in she also snagged a tube of hypo-allergenic body lotion from a display downstairs. Making a beeline for the bathroom, she ignored Fred's plaintive meows.

Using the shower curtain as a shield, she pinched the bottle of lemongrass body wash between her thumb and forefinger and averted her face, holding the hazardous toiletry at arm's length as she scurried to the kitchen. Fred purred and wound between her ankles as she pulled the liner from the trash can. The cat's trolling motor sounded vaguely like a threat.

"Just give me a minute, okay?" she huffed.

She tied the bag in two secure knots then set it outside the apartment door for Tom to haul down to the dumpster. Closing the door, she pushed a loose tendril of hair back with her forearm and caught another whiff of her skin. Fred's rumbling purr morphed into a growl, but she was too far gone to care.

"Ugh!"

She whirled and stalked back to the bathroom, oblivious to her companion's mounting protests. The wax-spattered scrubs fell to the floor in a heap. The ginormous granny bra she'd bought in a futile effort to restrain her bosom hit the deck. She yanked back the shower curtain then tore into the package of inoffensive soap as the water heated.

Maggie caught sight of her rapidly expanding figure in the mirror above the sink and grimaced. Covering her belly with one hand, she used the forearm to gently lift her boobs. A frown creased her brow as she studied her reflection critically. This was the awkward stage. Her waist had completely disappeared. Her breasts looked almost cartoonish. Her stomach was round but not obvious. Yet.

She sighed and turned away from the reflection. At this point in time, it was too depressing to even look. She was too small to look pregnant, and too fat to look small.

A grimace twisted her mouth. She scooped Tom's softening bar of Irish Spring from the soap dish and chucked it at the sink. The bar of unscented, un-pretty, un-sexy soap slid into the pale green pool of water left behind. She nudged his bottle of Head and Shoulders aside, making room on the shelf for the baby shampoo, doing her best not to think about the half-hideous dress she was forced to buy for the Haven House fundraiser they were scheduled to attend the following Saturday.

Maggie yanked shut the shower curtain, snatched the bar of soap from the dish, and inhaled deeply, drinking in nothingness and exhaling a relieved sigh. She set to work, scrubbing the last vestiges of her tangy tormentors from her skin. The bar slid over what seemed like acres of new real estate. She tried to picture herself in that dress, wearing shoes that weren't made of rubber, and clinging to Tom's arm as they sailed into a crowded ballroom.

She scowled at her body and muttered, "Might need a Coast Guard cutter."

Soapy hands caressed her burgeoning belly. The firm warmth chased the dark thoughts from her mind. The distaste in her mouth dissipated as her palms cupped the curve that cradled her baby.

"Hope he likes herding beef on the hoof, because Mommy's feeling like a cow." A small smile tugged at her lips. "Of course, Daddy is as stubborn as a mule, so we make a good couple."

The image of a pretty shuttered colonial house perfectly situated on a shaded lot popped into her head and her smile faded. Her hands stilled, fingers splayed wide over the comforting swell of her stomach as the water pummeled her back. A scowl pulled at the corners of her mouth, chasing off the last vestiges of that serene smile.

He pulled over during their weekend jaunt to the suburbs for groceries. Right smack dab in front of that house. Her house. The house of her little girl dreams. The bastard skipped right from duplexes to her dream house without blinking an eye and without asking.

"Maybe that's why he wants all that grass, Kitten," she whispered. "Mules want to graze."

Hell, the damn thing even had a picket fence. The 'For Sale' sign planted in the front lawn called to her like a siren's song. When Tom put the car in reverse to take a better look, she caught sight of the tented canvas of a wooden playset in the backyard, and her heart stutter-stepped.

"They're having an open house," he said, squinting through the windshield. "Wanna take a look?"

She stopped breathing altogether, her eyes locked on the striped awning that covered the redwood jungle gym. The car's engine purred. Her blood hummed in her veins, pulsing in her ears. Her eyes shifted back to her dream house. She shook her head, unable to force so much as a squeak past the lump in her throat.

His eyebrows rose. "No? You don't?"

She tore her gaze from the gleaming white façade and forced her lungs to expand. "No," she managed at last, darting a glance in his direction.

Disappointment flickered in his eyes and her heart seized. Tom eased back in the driver's seat and put the car in gear again. "You don't like traditional houses?" he asked as he pulled from the curb.

She fought the urge to turn in her seat, the unbearable need to catch one more glimpse of the dream she'd never have. She twisted her fingers together in her lap and kept her gaze locked on the road ahead. "No, I do…."

"Because I think maybe we should start looking for real. Your apartment is going to be way too small once you start cramming all the baby stuff in there. We'll need to figure out what we're looking at for a down payment—"

She bit her lip and closed her eyes, inhaling through her nose in a vain attempt to ease the ache in her chest. "We'll be fine where we are."

The truth was, she didn't want to look at houses. She already had a bedroom that wasn't quite his. She didn't want to test faucets he might not be around to fix or admire green lawns he wouldn't mow.

"Maggie…" Unwilling to be cajoled into setting foot in that too-perfect house, she forced her eyes open and gave her head a sharp shake. "Are you sure? We could go back." His foot eased from the accelerator and her heartbeat sped up. "It looked like a really nice house."

Managing a wan smile, she shook her head again. "I just…I'm tired."

He nodded, but disappointment etched its way into the lines bracketing his mouth. A smug tingle of satisfaction tickled the back of her throat when he turned the corner. She kept her gaze glued to the road ahead, resolutely leaving that dangerous dream house behind.

The bar of soap spurted from her fingers. The forgotten shower spray cooled enough to make her shiver. She stared down at the wrinkles puckering her fingers and shook her head to clear her muddled thoughts. Fumbling with the knobs, she shut off the water and snaked one prune-y hand from the curtain to grope for a towel.

Plush Egyptian cotton rasped like sandpaper against her waterlogged skin. Cool air seeped in around the curtain. Maggie wrapped the bath sheet around her expanding girth and brushed the curtain aside. The moment her toes sank into the bathmat, Fred's claws pierced her ankle, and their howls of displeasure rang out in perfect harmony.

****

Thirty minutes later, Maggie sat on the sofa in her biggest, softest pajamas, her hair drying in untamed ringlets around her face. A cake baking war raged on the small screen. She rubbed antibiotic ointment into the jagged scratches Fred gave her as a token of his undying love.

Right on cue, her stomach growled the moment Tom's key scraped into the lock. The hinges sang as the door opened. "If you're not carrying dinner you might as well go home to your place," she called without a backwards glance. She heard a sharp intake of breath then the soft hiss as he let it go.

"I thought I'd take you out tonight."

She groaned and slumped lower in the cushions. "Unh."

"Unh?" The door squeaked a little wider. "Is that a no?"

"That's a 'Hell no, I feel disgusting.'"

"Gotcha."

The leather soles of his shoes whispered against the hardwood floors. He crouched beside the couch, his hand gripping his thigh. His smile was wan and a bit distracted. Maggie wondered at the faint lines of disappointment that tugged at his mouth. "Maybe another night?"

He nodded. "What can I bring you?"

"Chicken," she mumbled, shooting him a baleful glance.

"Fried, grilled, baked, Szechwan, Kiev…"

"Grilled would be best, I think. And mashed potatoes." He moved to brush her hair back, but she flinched. "Don't. My skin's too tight."

"Okay." He drew the word out as he slowly lowered his hand. "Grilled chicken and mashed potatoes."

"And corn," she added as he straightened. "And cake."

"Corn and cake," he confirmed, shoving his hands into the pockets of his suit pants.

Tom fidgeted with something in his pocket, obviously nervous. She conjured a smile, her fingers closing around his wrist. "I'm sorry. Bad day today."

He nodded then dropped a soft kiss to the top of her head. "Chicken, mashed potatoes, corn, and cake."

She nodded, fluttering her eyelashes for effect. "Yes, and if you're successful in completing your mission you will be rewarded with the opportunity to rub my feet."

"Really? Can I?"

His mocking gasp evoked a chuckle. Her smile widened, taking on a wicked gleam. "If the cake is chocolate you might get to rub other things, too."

Tom did a quick about-face and strode to the door. "On it!"

Chapter Nineteen

The damn ring was burning a hole in his pocket. Not literally. At the moment he wasn't wearing pants. Well, he was wearing underpants, but those didn't have pockets. The ring was scorching him *figuratively*. He'd had the damn thing for over a week and still hadn't any clue what to do with it.

He couldn't carry it with him all the time because Maggie was all too familiar with the bulges in his pants. She'd spot it and be on him in a second—and not in a sexy way. He couldn't leave it at her place because there was no way of knowing when she'd go into one of those bizarre cleaning frenzies that always end with his belongings in a pile at the center of the bedroom rug. He blamed the pregnancy for those little whirlwinds of insanity. At least, he hoped they were hormonally induced. Otherwise, the woman he had chosen to carry his child was severely unbalanced.

As it was, he was having a hard time coming up with a decent chance at a proposal. Maggie spent most of the week with her head in the commode, and he spent most days and nights feeling wretched for putting her in this position. He shook his head, gathering more of her wild crimson curls in his palm. Only Maggie McCann could super-size morning sickness into morning, noon, and night sickness.

"Better?" he asked, stroking damp curls away from her face.

"This sucks," she rasped as she took the glass of water from his hand.

"I'm sorry." He wiped a tear trail from the corner of her eye. "Wanna stay home? Shelia will understand."

Her forehead puckered into a frown. Lines of misery bracketed her mouth as she shook her head. "No, I want to get out of here."

He nodded his understanding then leveraged himself from the hard tile floor. Offering her a hand, he smiled at her snarled red curls. "Want to hop back into the shower?"

She cast a disparaging glance at her naked body. "I don't think I'll be hopping anywhere for a while."

On impulse, he dropped to his knees again and buried his face in the curve of her belly, tipping his face up with a worshipful smile. "Good. It'll make it easier to keep up with you."

"I'm already waddling," she complained.

"You're incredible." He ran his hands over the marvel of her barely-rounded stomach. "A miracle."

She tugged at his arms, urging him up. "A miracle that happens every day," she said with a smirk.

Heaving a groan, he rose to his feet then gathered her into his arms. His heart strummed, strong and steady against her soft cheek. He pressed a soft kiss to her tangled mop of hair. "Not to us, Maggie." He gathered her closer still. "This hasn't happened to us before."

"No."

He pulled back, framing her face in his hands and stroking her jaw with his thumbs. When he leaned in to kiss her, she shook her head and he jerked back. "What?"

"I just relived my afternoon snack, remember?"

He shuddered. "Oh yeah."

"And I need to get back in the shower."

She wriggled out of his arms and he couldn't help but leer. She was round and ripe, her skin flushed and rosy, like a juicy peach. "Want company? I could scrub your back."

Maggie fixed him with a bland stare. "You've already showered, remember?"

He started to maneuver her back toward the tub. "I can shower again. The other night you told me I was a dirty, dirty boy—"

"Tom—"

The ragged impatience in her voice was all too familiar. Holding his hands high, he took a hasty step back and bumped into the sink. An aluminum can clattered to the floor, rolling to a stop beside his foot. The shower curtain rings slinked along the metal rod. Heaving a sigh, he stared down at the warming shave cream she kept just for him. He rubbed his clean-shaven jaw then let his hand trail down his chest.

"Are you sure you're up for this?"

"Bought a dress," she called over the spray.

"Yeah, but…" He glanced around the cluttered bathroom and tamped down on the cabin fever gnawing at his gut. This was why the ring stayed locked in his desk at work all week. "We don't have to go."

Maggie peered around the edge of the shower curtain. "I may come after you with my fancy can opener if I don't get out of this building for a while."

He nodded, smiling as Fred threaded his fat body through his legs. "I'll feed the cat."

The shower curtain twitched and his favorite redhead peeped around the edge again. "Tom?"

"Huh?"

"Thanks."

He scraped an entire can of tuna delight into Fred's dish, accepted the fat cat's head-butt of masculine solidarity, and straightened, his spine snapping to attention one vertebra at a time. Upon hearing his name, his companion paused long enough to cast a bland look in his direction. White whiskers twitched. The orange 'M' on the tabby's forehead changed to italics and he smacked his lips, his tail swishing dismissively as he turned his attention back to his meal.

Tom chuckled and hitched the waistband of his black boxer-briefs. "What? I'm wearing my formal underwear. Still not good enough for you?"

He turned to retreat to the bedroom for final preparations for a night trussed up in a monkey suit making small talk with people he didn't know and didn't want to know. He was the lucky guy who would spend an evening of squiring the crankiest pregnant woman north of the Eisenhower Expressway around an over-crowded, over-heated hotel ballroom. He could only think of one way to cheer her up.

Just down the hall, spray hissed against steamy tile walls. A bar of soap tumbled into the tub with a series of *thunks* only to be chased by a string of muttered expletives. Decision made, Tom shot a furtive glance at the bathroom door as he lunged for his bulging briefcase.

Grinning from ear to ear, he gave the black velvet box a little toss as he straightened. The water shut off and curtain rings screeched against the rod. Shooting the fat orange cat a glance, he asked, "This okay with you, bud?"

Fred didn't bother to look up. Settling down on his generous haunches, the cat ate with renewed vigor. Tom decided to take that as an affirmative.

"All-righty, then. Well, I'll treat her right and all that stuff." He gave the cat a brisk nod and started toward the bedroom. "Glad we had this talk."

****

Her ankles wobbled as she shimmied from side to side, cursing the fit of vanity that prompted her to squish her body into a set of pre-baby Spanx with each puff of breath. She worked the steel-reinforced spandex to the tops of her thighs then slumped against the side of the stall for a rest. She managed a quick inhalation before the ladies' room door swung open, allowing the jazzy strains of a twenty-piece swing band to waft into the tiled room. Unwilling to expire in that stall, Maggie allowed the rhythm to rouse her to action.

The click-click of toothpick heels bounced off the walls. "I'm not saying she's unattractive," a woman said with a lilting laugh. "I was only commenting on the fact that his tastes seem to have…expanded. That's all."

"Expanded," her friend repeated. The second punctuated her snotty snicker with a snort. "Nice."

"Oh, come on." The instigator's syrupy southern drawl dropped a full octave, growing broader and more effusive as she picked up steam. "We all know the man is a bit of a cowboy, but did you honestly ever think you'd see him wrangling a heifer like that?"

The mere mention of beef on the hoof had Maggie tugging on the girdle with renewed vigor. She gritted her teeth as she hiked the smothering synthetic over the rounded mound of her baby bump. "Sorry, Sweets," she whispered to her unborn child. She yanked at the wide elastic band, urging it higher. "Never again, I promise."

"I've seen him with all sorts of women over the years." A lipstick cap clattered to the marble counter. The water ran in the sink. "The man just likes women in general. That's part of his charm."

Something in the second woman's nasal drone tweaked Maggie's antennae. Leaning to her left, she peered through the crack in the stall door, but she couldn't get a clear peek at the mirror.

"I know, but you have to admit she's a little…healthier…than his usual type," Bettie-Southern-Belle insisted.

"Oh, I'll admit that," Nancy Nasal conceded. A compact snapped shut. "Actually, I've known Maggie for years. Never pictured her with a man like Tom, but I suppose it was just a matter of time in his case. Her little salon is cute."

The too-tight waistband slipped from her fingers and snapped into place. Maggie sucked in a breath, her ego reeling from the sting of her name, and what was left of her waistline smarting from the betrayal of her body shaper. They were talking about her. And Tom.

"Heifer?" she exhaled on a whisper.

An evening bag closed with a crisp snap. The shuffle of stilettos heralded their impending departure. "She's a hairdresser?" Bettie chortled. "That explains the dye job."

The heavy door swung open on the *shoosh* of well-oiled hinges. Nasal Nancy's sniggering laugh swirled through the room. "Well, you'd have to ask Tom to be sure, but I don't think that red hair is Miss Clairol's work."

Maggie stared at the tips of her black peep-toe pumps. The hem of her dress fell to her knees and her hands splayed over the gently rounded mound of her belly. She closed her eyes and drew a deep breath, trying to ignore the prickle of hot, angry tears. The door opened again, and she sucked in a sharp breath and ground her molars.

"Maggie? If you don't hurry up, I'm going to run away with this handsome scoundrel of yours."

The warmth in Sheila's voice rang clear and true, nearly dislodging the sob in the hollow of Maggie's throat. She swallowed hard, pressing her palms to her stomach, praying she could keep her canapés in check. To buy time, she indulged in an unnecessary flush then fidgeted with the seams of her dress.

"He'd like that, Sheila." To her relief, her voice came out with only the barest of tremors.

The older woman's snort ricocheted off the walls. "The man only has eyes for you, my dear." Maggie took a deep breath and opened the stall door. A cool wave of calm washed over her when Sheila turned and her warm, dark gaze swept her from head to toe. "Is it any wonder? My God, Maggie, you're a walking, talking fertility goddess. I thought Russell Tupperman was going to trip over his tongue when you walked in."

Arching her eyebrows, Maggie stared at her friend challengingly and smoothed her hand over her non-existent waistline before moving to the sink. "Oh? Because I heard the word 'heifer' bandied about, and I'm pretty sure those women weren't discussing livestock."

"Women." Sheila dismissed the incident with a sniff and a regal wave of her hand. "Jealous."

Maggie had a harder time shaking her doubts. She plucked a wad of paper towels from the dispenser and dried her trembling hands. Moving to the vanity, she rummaged through her tiny bag for a lipstick. She freed the tube but fumbled the cap.

Sheila recovered the wayward lid before it could roll away. Her hands were cool and steady when she pried the tube from her quivering fingers and snapped the lid onto the tube with a click. "You're not silly enough to bite into those sour grapes, are you?"

Maggie turned to face her friend, hot tears fueled by injured pride and abject humiliation pooling in her eyes. "I feel so stupid."

Setting the lipstick aside, Sheila pressed her cool palms to Maggie's flaming cheeks. "You are anything but stupid," she said firmly.

The tears broke free, spilling over to tangle in her lashes, sizzling their way down her cheeks. "I am…I am," she whispered brokenly. "I love him. I fell in love with him. How stupid was that?"

As fast as they fell, Sheila caught the tears with her thumbs, brushing them away as if she hadn't managed to screw up her entire life, as if somehow everything could and would be okay.

"Of course you love him," Sheila murmured without a trace of sympathy. "What sane woman wouldn't? Tom is a much better man than he gives himself credit for being, and you, my darling, you are magnificent."

"You don't understand—"

"I understand far more than you think I do." Sheila pressed her palms too firmly against Maggie's cheeks. "He loves you too. It's written all over his gorgeous face." She grinned. "If I wasn't so damn happy for you both, I'd call you a heifer too." Soft hands slid to Maggie's shoulders then gripped her upper arms. "All we have to do is convince our boy to make it official—"

"Oh! No!" The tears stopped and a tiny hiccup lodged in her throat. Her eyes widened in horror. She wagged her head, a fierce denial burning on her tongue. "It's not like that, Sheila. I told you Tom and I—"

"I know exactly what you and Tom are doing."

"We're not… Our relationship isn't like that."

"Grow up, Maggie," the older woman snapped. "You're not a teenager anymore. You know you didn't invent this dance."

Her friend's terse tone snapped Maggie to attention. "Dance?"

"The 'I'll pretend I don't want him, this is enough' dance." The derisive snort Sheila used as punctuation stung far more than the harsh words. "I mean, you don't have to do a damn thing, do you? You'll just sit back and take what he's willing to give and pretend it's what you want too."

"Sheila!"

"You don't have to make demands, and you don't have to meet them. The two of you can just go along pretending you don't need more from one another if that makes you feel safe, but don't try to sell me. It's not as easy as you thought, is it?"

Maggie stared in shock as Sheila snatched her evening bag from the vanity and spun for the door. Her dark eyes blazed as she fired her final shot. "I wasn't born yesterday, Maggie, and, remember, neither were you."

The door *shooshed* shut. Her fingers bit into the granite countertop. She gaped at her shell-shocked reflection, taking a moment to be sure she could hold steady. Snapping her mouth shut, she swiped at her cheeks with her fingertips. Groping for the abandoned tube of lipstick, she uncapped it with trembling fingers.

"This is a horrible bathroom." Maggie applied a fresh coat of courage, pulled her shoulders back and tipped her chin up to meet her reflected gaze. "Come on, baby. Let's find Daddy and get the hell out of here."

Chapter Twenty

The swing band was certainly swinging when she stumbled from the powder room. Tom smiled, pushing away from the wall he'd propped himself against nearly an eon ago. He smoothed his tie as she approached, trying not to ogle his date and failing miserably.

Her dress was red. Screaming red. Look-at-me red. Or—as he rechristened it the moment she stepped out of the bedroom—please-please-please-let-this-girl-want-to-fuck-me red.

What made his head spin was the fact that the dress itself wasn't even all that sexy on its own merit. The neckline didn't plunge to her belly button. The pearly skin of her back wasn't exposed. The sleeves gathered gently at her wrists. But on Maggie? That slinky fabric molded to her shoulders and arms, clung desperately to her generous breasts, then fell like a waterfall, the hem swirling around her beautiful knees.

Tom ran a hand over his face, trying to wipe the self-effacing smirk that sprang to his lips the moment his befuddled brain paired the world beautiful with Maggie's knees. If that didn't prove he was a complete goner, nothing would. She came to a stop in front of him and he automatically reached for her, settling his hand in the small of her back and pulling her just a tad closer. "So worth the wait…."

"I want to go home," she said at the same time.

He blinked in surprise. "Home? We haven't even made it to the bar yet."

She waved her hand toward her stomach. "I'm not much in the mood for a drink."

"You threatened me with a can opener," he reminded her. "I got you out of the apartment. What's wrong? Are you sick again?"

She shook her head. “No. I just…I forgot how much I hate these things.”

Somehow she managed to encompass the entire elegant extravaganza with a limp wave of her hand, and he grinned. “Me too.” Tom pulled her closer, wrapping her up in a strong, one-armed embrace. He ducked his head, grazing her cheek with his nose and tickling her ear with his lips. “One drink, one dance, then we’ll get out of here.”

He felt her soften, and suddenly he was transported to that night months before. The heady anticipation of seduction. One night laden with promises of pleasure without pain. The night that changed their lives.

“Yeah?” The question came out in a breathy whisper.

He nuzzled her hair, her cheek, her neck, uncertain how he’d manage to hold off, but determined to give it his best shot. “I’ll let you take me back to your place and seduce me again.”

“I seduced you?”

She shivered when his breath stirred her hair. “Yes, Maggie.” He kept his voice steady, speaking to her just how he wanted her—soft, slow, and deep. “Don’t you know I haven’t stopped thinking about you since that night?”

“Let’s go now,” she blurted.

He chuckled and pulled back, still holding her close but putting just enough space between them. Her emerald eyes glistened. He picked up the familiar glints of amusement and arousal, but something darker shadowed them. He clenched his teeth, prepared to do battle with whatever it was that made her unhappy even for one moment.

“Maggie? What do you say?” His body pressed against hers, cushioned by her curves but prodded by the barely-there baby bump. The music changed, shifting the mood in the ballroom from joyfully frenetic to soulfully sexy in just three bars. He kissed her softly, his lips lingering against hers as he continued negotiations. “Forget the drink, but I want the dance, Mags.”

She wet her lips and the tip of her tongue grazed his bottom lip. He jolted as if she'd shot a thousand volts through him. He closed his eyes and tried to absorb the shock. The way she affected him was ridiculous. As if they hadn't kissed a thousand times.

His fingers clamped around her wrist, and her pulse leapt beneath his thumb. She felt it too. She felt it just the way he did. He met her slumberous gaze and nearly collapsed in on himself. She wanted this. She wanted him.

Maggie swayed against him, using her bountiful breasts for all they were worth. "You sure you want to dance?" His gaze slid down to the hint of cleavage displayed by the dress. His fingers tightened on her wrist. "Take me home, Tom," she whispered.

He almost gave in. There was nothing he wanted more than to give her exactly what she asked for, exactly what they both needed. Oh, he would take her home. To her home. For now. But no matter what she said about things being fine the way they are, sometime soon he would take her home to *their* home. Not his. Not hers. Theirs.

Tom glanced down at the delicate fingers curled into a loose fist. He drew her hand to his mouth and brushed the barest of kisses across her knuckles. Her breath hitched, just as he knew it would. Their eyes met, and he knew Maggie McCann was meant to be the girl for him. He pressed her hand to his chest and knew without a doubt there would be no better time, no more perfect place. The words tumbled from his lips on the frantic beat of his heart.

"Marry me, Maggie."

****

Maggie reared back, blinking as the facets from the chandelier above their heads scattered the light. She tried closing her eyes, but pinpoints sparkled behind her lids making her even dizzier. "What?"

Tom snapped from his trance and shoved his hand into his pants pocket. "Hang on…" He grunted in frustration as he struggled to free his hand. Maggie took a stumbling step back, desperate to find her bearings again.

"There!" He prized a glittering circlet from his pocket and held it up with a triumphant smile. "Marry me, Maggie."

His voice carried through the foyer. The milling crowd stilled. A cluster of silk and satin-clad women unknotted nearby, their attention riveted on the two of them. Her jaw dropped as her gaze fixed on the sparkling diamond pinched between his fingers. A rainbow of promises shot from the facets, dimming the glow of the chandelier. Her head wagged, trying to deny the reality of the scene unfolding in front of her. She tried to pull away, but he held firm, his fingers biting into the tender skin of her wrist.

"Oh! Sorry." His smile faltered as he sank to one knee. "I should do this right, right?"

A woman nearby gasped and another squealed. A wave of murmurs rose around them, but she couldn't care less about what anyone else had to say about them. She knew who and what they were, and for that reason, she had to stop him.

"No, don't! That's okay," she blurted.

He chuckled and pulled her hand to his mouth. Soft, firm lips brushed her knuckles. Bold, confident blue eyes gazed up at her. "No, I'm going to do this right…" He released her wrist and his hand grazed her stomach. A smile of delight lit his face as he lowered his gaze, smoothing the silky fabric. To her horror, he leaned forward and pressed a kiss to the gently rounded mound. His voice came in a hoarse rasp. "I want us to be a family. I want to do this right." He tipped his chin up, gazing at her with his jaw set in determination. "Maggie McCann, will you marry me?"

Maggie bit her bottom lip so hard the metallic tang of blood curled her tongue. She glanced around at the hopeful, expectant faces of the strangers surrounding them, unable to bear to look into the eyes of the man she loved. A group of people to her left parted, and Sheila appeared. The two women locked eyes for a moment. Maggie shook her head slowly.

Turning her attention to Tom she drew a deep breath then exhaled slowly. "No."

A flicker of confusion crossed his handsome face, but his natural confidence chased it away. The corners of his mouth twitched as if he was anticipating a joke he wasn't privy to yet. A nervous chuckle burbled from his chest. "No?"

She continued to shake her head as she backed away, her voice thick and hoarse with unshed tears. "No, Tom. No, I won't marry you."

Clamping her hand over her mouth, she turned and fled for the grand staircase leading to the bustling hotel lobby. The polished mahogany banister slid under her damp palm. Halfway down, she dared a glance over her shoulder. Certain he hadn't followed her, she paused to pull the too-high pumps from her feet.

Maggie hit the brass-framed revolving door with her purse and shoes clutched in her hands. One pump clattered to the marble floor unheeded. She stumbled out onto the sidewalk, flushed and breathless. The startled doorman scrambled for the door handle on the nearest cab. She settled on the cracked vinyl seat, her brow puckering as she stared at the clouded plexi-glass partition.

The driver set the meter and turned in his seat. "Where?"

His heavily accented English didn't register. The impatient wave of his hand failed to snap her from the haze.

"Where?"

The guttural demand jolted her from her stupor. She pressed her palm to the safety glass and gaped at the heavy-set stranger. Where could she go?

The man's expression softened. "You okay, ladee?"

Maggie shook her head, blinking back the tears that scorched the back of her throat. He proposed. Where could she possibly go? Home to the apartment where his shoes were parked under the coffee table and the cat that preferred his company to hers? Of course she wasn't okay. The man she loved just offered her everything in the world she ever wanted. How was she supposed to sleep in a bed that would forever be his? Tom Sullivan just asked her to marry him, and she told him no. She told him no, and now she had nowhere to go—all because there was no way in hell she could possibly have said yes.

****

A woman with alligator skin and perma-frosted hair clutched the arm of the man next to her as she turned away. His eyes narrowed to slits as he wondered what could possibly make that woman feel so awkward. He was the one kneeling on the fleur-de-lis patterned carpet holding a diamond the size of a robin's egg.

Tom scowled at the ring pinched between his fingers. The diamond sparkled in the light from the chandelier. Perhaps it was a joke. Maybe once the blood stopped roaring in his ears, he'd look up and find Maggie grinning at him, poised to grab the ring. He sneaked a peek from under his lashes. No go.

His vision fuzzed, black encroaching around the edges as the white noise in his ears receded. A hand closed around his elbow. He blinked back the gloom, forcing himself to focus on the golden gleam of hope in Sheila's brown eyes.

"Stand up, Sweetheart," she murmured into his ear.

Tom did as he was told, struggling to his feet with a grimace. He tugged the bottom of his suit jacket and fumbled the ring. It fell to the floor near the toe of his shoe. As if sensing his urge to kick it, Sheila swooped in to snatch it from the rug. A wan smile curved her lips as she unfurled her fingers to offer it to him nestled in her creased palm. He grunted as if she kicked him in the nuts.

"You can keep that."

Her amused chortle would have delighted him if he'd coaxed it out of her while she was hunched over her desk at Haven House or fretting over the canapés at a cocktail party, but he hadn't. He turned on his heel and his gaze locked on the staircase Maggie used as an escape route. He took off, his jaw set and his step steady.

Sheila hurried after him. "Don't be stupid," she huffed, making a futile grab for his arm. He shook her off, but she kept pace with surprising agility. "Thomas Sullivan, do not do this. Do not let your wounded pride get the better of you."

"Wounded pride!" The words echoed through the suddenly hushed corridor as he whirled to glare at her. "You think this is about pride?"

The diminutive woman drew herself up to an imposing height, leveling him with a dark glare. "Of course it's your pride," she said, unperturbed by his ire.

She reached for his hand and he let her take it, too wrung out to struggle. Tom cringed when the warm metal of the ring pressed into his palm. Her soft fingers closed around his, trapping his rejection in a tight fist.

"She's in love with you," Sheila said, a fond smile lighting her eyes.

"Got a funny way of showing it."

"Not funny at all." With her free hand, she patted his cheek. "She wants you to *want* to marry her."

"I *do* want to marry her." The heat of his words melted whatever cool he had left. "Dammit, Sheila, I do want to marry her. She's the only woman I've ever even thought about marrying. I bought a ring. I got down on one fucking knee!"

"Hush," she hissed. Gripping his arm, she steered him to a corner and backed him in. "Of course she is." She framed his face with her hands, but the cool strength of her palms only steamed him more. Her tone was soothing, but it did nothing to calm him. "She is. She is the only woman for you, Tom."

The quiet confidence in the confirmation broke him. Turning away, the muscles in his throat worked on the brick lodged there. The damn thing wouldn't budge. "Shit."

"Maybe you shouldn't have mentioned the baby."

His head swiveled. "What?"

"Oh, Tom." She sighed. "A woman like Maggie wants to be loved. Wholly. Completely. Passionately."

"I do." He said the words, but they came in a weak whisper.

"Do you? Do you love Maggie, or do you love that baby she's carrying?"

"What?" He shook his head, instinctively denying the unspoken implication. "I love *her.*"

"Are you sure?"

"I proposed. If that doesn't say I'm sure, I have no fucking idea what will," he sneered.

"Don't you swear at me, young man."

"I'm out of here." The platinum band seared his palm as he started down the steps.

"She's in love with you, Tom," Sheila called after him. Grasping the glossy rail, his feet barely skimmed the plush carpet as he picked up speed. "She loves you so much she said no to the fairytale ending she's always wanted."

The slick sole of his shiny Italian loafer slipped off the bottom step. Gripping the newel post, he grappled for balance. He stared up at Sheila, transfixed. A serene smile tipped her lips as she floated down a few steps. "What?"

"Cinderella turned her Prince Charming down. Or would Maggie be Sleeping Beauty?" she mused.

"Sheila—"

The older woman cut him off with a brisk shake of her head. She continued down the steps until they stood eye to eye. She cupped his cheek gently then gestured beyond his shoulder. He turned to find the doorman standing just inside the revolving door holding a shiny black high-heeled shoe.

"Cinderella it is." Sheila brushed a kiss to his cheek then gave him a not-so-gentle shove. "If the glass slipper fits, Sweetheart…."

Chapter Twenty-One

Maggie leaned from side to side, trying to stir some sensation in her tush. She stretched her legs, grimacing at the faint musty scent of industrial cleaner wafting from the carpet. Orange. Or lemon. Oddly enough, it didn't make her want to hurl. At least, the stray citrus scent wasn't at the *top* of her list of things that made her want to toss her cookies. At the moment, it wasn't even close.

An intricate berber pattern pressed into the puffy skin of her ankles, but she didn't have the energy or the inclination to rub it away. Her clutch purse disgorged its contents at her side. An ancient roll of Certs she unearthed from its depths lay in tatters in her lap. One shiny black shoe laid cast aside in the empty spot where a welcome mat should be. Maggie sighed, let her head fall back, and gazed listlessly at the ceiling.

She probably, most certainly, definitely wouldn't be welcome here, but she wouldn't go home. Couldn't. And she had to go somewhere. After twenty minutes cruising Lake Shore Drive, the driver eyed his meter and started casting wary glances at the basket case in the back seat. She had to give him an address, so she blurted the first one that came to mind.

Not that this was any kind of refuge for her. She only knew the actual address from the mail that spilled from his briefcase or piled up on her coffee table. She probably would have been better off to go to Sheila's. Then again, she didn't want to have to loiter in the lobby making small talk with the doorman on duty. There was also a slim chance her friend would toss her out on her fat ass after the scene she and Tom created at her elegant fundraiser. Maggie didn't think she would, but certainty wasn't her strong suit at the moment. Hell, she wasn't even sure what happened to her other shoe.

The entry door slammed shut, rattling the walls of the old row house. Heavy footfalls stamped the treads of the steps. She held her breath. Maggie didn't need to see to know it was Tom. She knew his footsteps all too well.

They drew to a halt. His raspy breaths rattled in the empty hall. The familiar prickling sensation that danced over her skin whenever he drew near made her stomach twist. She knotted her fingers together in her lap.

"I'm sorry." The apology tumbled from her lips before she could stop it. Opening her eyes, she fixed her gaze on the opposite wall. She needed to be calm and rational. She needed to set her girlish dreams and broken heart aside for the moment and focus on the reality of her situation. She needed to stop wishing on stars and keep her feet planted firm on the ground. Maggie figured it should be easy, now that she only had one shoe.

His knees creaked as he squatted beside her. "What are you doing here?"

The gentle rumble of his deep voice nearly broke her. Try as she might, Maggie couldn't detect a single note of anger in his tone. Her stomach went into freefall. The treacherous thing reached up and snatched the hammering heart from her ribcage and sank to her toes. Of course he wasn't angry. That would let her off the hook too easily.

Maggie wriggled her toes, a vain attempt to set her aching heart free. It didn't work. She chanced a quick glance at him and nearly tumbled into the depths of those deep blue eyes. Her bitter laugh bounced off the pockmarked wall. She squinted at the discrete numbers attached to the door of his condo and shook her head. "I couldn't go home, Tom."

His heavy sigh pressed on her, squeezing the tears that clogged her chest into her throat. "I waited for you there." He rocked back, falling onto his ass with a grunt. "Then I thought maybe you weren't coming home because you knew I was waiting for you, and I—" He squinted at the paneled door. "I should have given you a key. I never thought to give you a key…."

"We never hung out here," she said with a shrug.

"Still, you should've had a key." He pressed the heel of his hand to the furrow between his brows. "Maggie, I—"

"I'm sorry—"

"Don't—"

She shook her head, desperate to stop the apologies, needing to move past those two words, eager to explain. "I can't marry you, Tom. It's not that I don't want to… I can't."

He propped himself against the opposite wall then fixed his gaze on her. That's when she saw the shoe clutched in his hand. Every muscle in her body tensed. Determined not to squirm under cross-examination, she prayed she wouldn't melt at the sight of her Prince Charming holding her lost shoe.

"You don't believe me," he concluded. "You don't believe I want this, that I'm committed to you. To us."

The flat resignation in his tone made her skin ripple. "It's not that I—"

"I don't blame you," he continued conversationally.

He dropped the shoe and bent his knees, letting his head fall back against the wall but keeping his eyes locked on her. Maggie found it safer to focus on the long fingers skimming his shins. She didn't want to think about the swirling pool of disappointment that threatened to swallow her whole the moment he set her black patent-leather slipper aside as if it didn't matter.

"A year ago…hell, even six months ago I would have told you I'm not a very good bet."

His chuckle was low and warm, wrapping around her like a hug. She glanced up. His soft, supple lips were twisted into a wry smile. The stubborn cowlick she'd fallen in love with sprang free.

"But I'm much more domesticated now," he said, setting that cowlick to bobbing. The lock of dark hair fanned the scarred plaster and a rush of heat prickled her face. "I grocery shop, share my Cocoa Puffs and entertain your sadistic cat. I also give excellent foot massages. You said so yourself."

"Tom, it isn't that I—"

"And you're forgetting the most important part of this whole crazy thing—"

She shook her head, plowing forward before he could run over her objections again. "I can't, no matter how much I—"

"I love you, Maggie." His voice crackled with sincerity, effectively slaying all opposition. She clamped her mouth shut, and he took full advantage. "I'm in love with you."

Tears welled in her eyes, clinging to her lashes and scattering the light. Sparkles of fairy dust blurred her world. She tried to wish them away, blink them into oblivion, banish them with a hard shake of her head, but they refused to budge. She pressed her trembling fingers to his lips, a weak attempt to stem the flow of words made even weaker by the tender kisses he pressed to her fingertips.

"I want this, Maggie. I want all of it. You, our baby, even Fred. But more than that, I need it. I need you."

His whispered confession tickled the kiss-dampened pads of her fingers. Buoyed by hope, her heart rose from her toes with astonishing speed. Her stomach followed, borne on the fluttering of bluebird wings. Maggie figured there were probably a few bat wings in there too, because the man was definitely making her batty.

Averting her gaze, she stared at the unadorned carpet at his doorstep. When it swam into focus once more, she sighed in relief. "You *need* a welcome mat."

He wrapped his hand around her fingers, hold her snug in the palm of his hand. "No, I need you. No sense in dressing this place up since I listed it for sale last month."

That got her attention. "You did?"

"Got an offer yesterday. Not bad. I countered, so we'll see where we end up." He kissed the tips of her fingers again. "I told you, I'm committed. I was hoping you'd take me in, or I'll be homeless, Maggie."

"You could rent," she whispered.

He shook his head. "I want something more…permanent."

"For now." The words popped out before she could think them through, but his head snapped back as if she'd slapped him full-force.

He dropped her hand. Lounging against the wall once more, he fixed her with a challenging glare. "You think I don't know what permanent means?"

"I think you think you know, but permanent has never been your thing."

"And I can't change," he challenged.

"I'm only saying that permanent hasn't even been in your vocabulary up 'til now." He sat up a little straighter, and she huffed in frustration. "I know you, Tom. You have a pretty extensive vocabulary." When he opened his mouth to argue, she stopped him with the palm of her hand. "No. Let me finish for once, okay?" His jaw snapped shut with the satisfying click of teeth. Maggie smiled at the mulish set of his mouth. "I love you too, Tom. Honest, I do."

"I know you do. What I don't get is why you won't say 'I do'," he grumbled. "I thought you were the happily ever after girl, Maggie."

"Happily ever after." She tipped her head back, blinking up at the ceiling. She pinched the silky fabric of her skirt and let it glide gently back and forth between her thumb and forefinger. "You know, I used to tease Tracy about hooking up with you all the time. Me hooking up with you, not her," she was quick to clarify. "I mean, what a joke, huh? Mr. Onenightstand and Ms. Happilyeverafter—"

"I was never Mr. Onesnightstand," he interjected.

Maggie raised an eyebrow. "Never?"

"Not as much as people thought I was."

Heaving a sigh, she waved away his objection. "Doesn't matter. What I'm saying is that maybe we should never have taken this," she wagged a finger between the two of them, "seriously."

"Seems to me you're the one not taking it seriously."

"How can I, Tom? How can I when I know it has to end? What happens when you decide permanent isn't your thing after all? What do I do with my ever after then?"

"I won't! That's what I'm telling you. I *want* this, Maggie."

"Want." Anger spiked his volume and her impatience rose to match it. "Of course you wanted this. It's been nothing but sex, sex and more sex. But will you still want this when I'm too huge to have sex? Will you still want me a year from now when I'm still trying to shed the baby weight? Will you want me in ten, when I'm fifty?" she demanded.

"And I'll be staring at sixty," he reminded her.

"It's not the same for guys."

"Maybe for some guys it isn't, but all I've been thinking about for the past few months is how much time we've wasted, Maggie." He pried her hand from her lap, dislodging the fabric she'd worried into a nubbin. "Jesus, Mags, all I can think about is how I spent the last decade and a half running away from you when I should have been running away *with* you."

She fixed him with a level stare. "Easy for you to say now."

"No. No, it's not easy. Saying these things scares the shit out of me. Asking you to marry me…" Tom took a deep breath and snapped the taut line of tension strung between them. "I make a living asking questions, but tonight I popped the one I thought I never would, and you shot me down."

"I had to."

"Why? Why do you think you had to?"

When she didn't answer, he slid closer, pulling her hand to his chest and holding it captive until she met his gaze. His palms warmed her chilled fingers. His heartbeat strummed slow and steady against her knuckles.

"You're sad, Tom. I get that. Your mom is gone and now you're feeling guilty—"

"You think this is a guilt proposal? You think I'm asking you to marry me to make up with my mother somehow?"

"I think you want to try to make things right."

"I never said things were wrong," he argued.

"You know what I mean."

"I think I do, but I'm a little freaked out that you think I'm that Oedipal." He shook his head and squeezed her fingers. "Maggie, this proposal had nothing to do with my mother."

"Tom, your whole outlook on marriage and family is colored by your mother."

"Aren't everyone's ideas on marriage shaped by their parents? Doesn't mean I don't see things clearly."

Maggie bobbed her head. "A little too clearly sometimes."

He blew out a huff of exasperation. "When did this become about them? This is about us. I love you, Maggie. I want to marry you. I want us to be a family. You, me, our baby, our cat."

"I'm scared," she whispered.

"I am too."

"I need—" Maggie dropped her gaze to the gentle swell of her belly. "I couldn't stand it if you decided you couldn't handle…."

"I couldn't either." The catch in his voice captured her attention. She looked up and found his eyes glistening with unshed tears. "I won't leave you, Maggie. Don't you know I couldn't?"

She knew. He would never leave her. He'd never leave their child. There would never be another little Sullivan wondering why his father didn't love him or want him enough. She knew that as sure as she knew her own name. She just didn't know if she could give up that name in the hopes that he'd be as committed to her as he would be to their baby.

"A year," she whispered.

"What?"

Rubbing her damp palms over her belly, Maggie tipped her chin up to meet his gaze. "Give me a year," she said, her voice growing stronger with each word.

"A year to what?"

Maggie bobbed her head in a decisive nod. "One year from the day the baby is born. If you still want me, ask me again on her first birthday."

"First birthday? A year *after* he's born? Don't you want to get married before?"

She cocked an eyebrow and chose to ignore his blatant pronoun misuse. "You're not getting all old-fashioned on me now, are you, Sully?"

His mouth opened and closed like a fish. She grinned, basking in the pleasure of his flummoxed expression. "A year," he repeated, his lips thinning into a line of dissatisfaction.

"If you still want me after a year," she confirmed.

Tom looked up, a self-deprecating smile flirting with the corners of his mouth. "You say that like I have a choice, Maggie." Raising her hand to his lips, he brushed a kiss across her knuckles and closed his eyes. "Don't you get it?"

"Get what?"

He pressed the back of her hand to his close-shaven cheek. His lashes fluttered as he nuzzled her fingers. "I need you so much more than I want you," he said, his voice softly compelling. "And Maggie, I'm going to want you forever."

Her sharp intake of breath spawned a glimmer of a smile. "Tom…."

He kissed her ring finger then rubbed the spot with the pad of his thumb. "Do you at least want to wear the ring?"

Maggie shook her head. "No."

"No?"

"No."

The skeptical lift of his eyebrows collapsed into a furrow of confusion. "You didn't like it?"

"I loved it. It was perfect."

"Then why don't you want to wear it?"

"And give you a head start on wearing *me* down? No, thank you. I know how you work, Counselor."

His boyish grin lit his eyes. "You'll never last another fifteen months, Mags."

She narrowed her eyes. "Try me, Sully." The deep, rumbling laugh that gathered in his chest and erupted into the empty hall made her toes curl in anticipation. A shiver raced down her spine when his warm hand closed over her cool toes.

"I intend to, Ms. McCann. I intend to be a trial to you every day until you cave." He pressed his thumb into the arch of her foot then rubbed gently, working toward her toes. Maggie let her head fall back, surrendering to his touch with a grateful purr.

She didn't bother opening her eyes. She couldn't stop the smile that curved her lips. "Mmm."

"Ready to go home?" he asked softly.

Maggie snorted. Somehow she'd just acquired another roommate without her consent, but at least this one didn't tear her ankles to shreds. This one worked the achiness from the balls of her swollen feet. "Mm hmm." She groaned her disappointment when he let go. Mustering super-human effort, she peeped at him through cracked eyelids. "Carry me?"

Tom chuckled. "I could try."

Something cool and unyielding nudged her foot. Forcing her eyes open, Maggie gasped when she spotted the shiny black pump cradled in the palm of his hand. Warm fingers closed around her puffy ankle. He caught his bottom lip between white teeth as he guided her foot into the stiff leather. His eyebrows knit in concentration. The cowlick stood straight up on his crown.

"Or, we could see if these still fit and catch a cab. What do you say?"

Maggie nodded and wriggled her toes into the high-heeled slipper. Just like Tom, they were a perfect fit. Her Prince Charming helped her to her feet, enfolding her in his warm embrace in one smooth move. She smiled as together they found their balance. That's when she realized it didn't matter whether she wore his ring or not or if they put the baby carriage before the marriage, she was already living the happily ever after she'd dreamed about for so long.

Epilogue

Maggie brushed soft kisses to the tuft of downy hair atop Finbar Angelini McCann-Sullivan's head. "See, this is what happens, Finn," she murmured into the feathery cockscomb that stood on end at his crown. "First, the eyesight goes, then they start ranting about capital gains taxes and voting Republican."

Tom shot a glare out of the corner of his eye but kept his mouth clamped shut. He nodded, bobbing his head as if the caller on the other end could see his enthusiastic agreement. "Yes, yes. That should work perfectly," he assured the other party. "We'll see you at four-thirty this afternoon. Thank you, Your Honor. Thank you so much."

She raised an eyebrow as he ended the call to Judge Moseby and immediately started dialing again. "I still haven't agreed to this."

The reminder had little effect on the man standing in front of her. As a matter of fact, he ignored it entirely. Flattening his son's cowlick with one finger, he simply smiled when she batted his hand away.

"The hearing is the next thing to fail," she whispered to the baby sotto-voice. "Then they start having trouble in other areas, if you know what I mean."

"He doesn't, and I obviously don't either," he countered, pressing the phone to his ear. "Hey, it's me. Can you shake free this afternoon? Actually, we'll need both you and Tracy. The kids and George can come too, if they want."

Shaking her head, Maggie stretched her arms, raising Finn above her head so she could beam up at him. "Then even the wildest of wild men start turning all traditional and conservative. That's what's happening to your Pop."

She glanced up to see Tom waving a dismissive hand. "I know, I know, it's last minute." He locked gazes with Maggie, a smug smile twitching his lips. "Can you make it to the courthouse?" He bent at the waist, holding her steady gaze as he smooched Finn's chubby cheek. "I need a Best Man and Mags could use a Matron of Honor."

Angling for the phone she called out, "I didn't agree to this plan, Sean."

"She's pregnant," Tom added, raising an imperious eyebrow as he upped the ante.

She leaned in closer. "But I've figured out what causes that now, and it won't be happening again."

"We're not having another hyphenated kid."

Maggie tsked for the benefit of their audience. "Your brother is a sex maniac. Molesting a sweet, innocent new mother like me…."

Tom waved her away, pressing the phone to his ear. "Yeah, yeah, whatever. Lecture me later. Just be there at four-thirty." Tom held the key to disconnect, huffed, and tossed the phone onto the couch cushion.

Catching her chin in his hand, he dropped to one knee in front of her. "We're getting married today, Maggie." Fred took the opportunity to insinuate himself into the family portrait, wedging his portly body into the space between the couch and his mistresses' calves. Tom's one-time ally fixed him with an unwavering glare. "This afternoon, at four-thirty, in Judge Moseby's chambers, we're going to make this official. Got me? You, me, Finn, Fred, and whoever else we've cooked up in there."

He pressed his lips to hers in brisk, efficient kiss that sizzled with restrained passion. Instinctively, she leaned into him, aching for more even though her lust for more was what got her into this predicament in the first place. His blue eyes danced with pleasure. His sunny smile was edged with triumph and his deep voice rumbled rough with emotion. That was the only thing that kept her from slapping him down.

"Make whatever calls you want to make. Buy yourself a new dress if you want. Your fate was sealed the minute the strip turned blue."

"He's only four months old. We were supposed to wait a year."

"Says who?"

"Says, uh, me."

"I say I love you, Maggie. I love you, I love our baby, I love our cramped apartment, and our fat cat, but I'm done waiting." He plucked the burbling infant from her arms and held Finn to his shoulder facing her, unabashedly using his progeny as a means to an end. "We love you, Mommy Maggie, but now it's time for you to make honest men out of us."

Maggie blinked back a rush of tears. "You think?"

Tom snatched the plastic stick from his shirt pocket and waved the positive pregnancy test in front of her eyes. "I know. It's time to make us official, Mags. There's no getting away from me now. Not when I know how good we are at this."

She grinned at the baby gleefully drooling on his daddy's shirt. "We are good at it, aren't we?"

His stare was stern, his tone no-nonsense, and his smile irrepressible. "I want a girl this time."

"Hey, that's your gig, not mine."

"I want her to have red hair and green eyes and exactly seventeen freckles on the bridge of her nose."

"I'll see what I can do," she conceded, suddenly breathless. "You really want to do this?"

"Want to. Need to." He tucked a stray lock of hair behind her ear. "Need you. I want you forever, Maggie McCann. You, our kids, Fred, and whoever else we can throw into this crazy mix of us." He kissed her sweetly then captured the tiny fist that flailed at her jaw. After pressing another kiss to Finn's dimpled knuckles, he hit her between the eyes with that naughty boy grin. "Say yes, Maggie. Everything else…we'll work things out. Just say yes."

Helpless to resist, she whispered, "Yes."

Tom let out a whoop that startled his son. He laughed when Finn's chin quivered and ignored his newly betrothed in favor of smothering their baby in contrite kisses. At last, he planted one on her, pulling away with an exuberant grin. "Come on, we only have a few hours. Wanna squeeze in one last round of pre-marital relations?"

Maggie snorted and gave him a playful shove, knocking him onto his ass. "Are you kidding? I'm getting married this afternoon. I have a zillion things to do."

Clutching the baby to his chest, he scrambled to his feet as she rose. "Do me first."

"Yeah, right." She sashayed toward the bedroom, calling over her shoulder, "Where did you put my ring?" Her smile widened when she heard his put-upon sigh and heel-scuffing steps.

"See, this is what happens, Finn. First, you have to practically beg to get them to commit, then the minute they do, they start demanding jewelry."

The End

ABOUT THE AUTHOR

Margaret Ethridge lives in Arkansas with a sweet-talking Southern gentleman who claims to be her lawfully wedded husband. She is the (not-so-wicked-but-she-has-her-moments) stepmother to their two children, the adoring mistress of three spoiled dogs, the food purveyor to eleven hungry goldfish, and the comic foil for one rather impertinent house rabbit who thinks he rules the roost.

Stories in the *Long Distance Love* series:

'Concourse Christmas' in *Believe: Christmas 2010 Short Story Anthology*

New Year, New Expectations—A TMP Free Read by Margaret Ethridge!

I've Got You to Talk with Me—A TMP Free Read by Margaret Ethridge!

'Be Mine' in *Be Mine, Valentine Short Story Anthology*

Kiss Me, I'm Full of Blarney—A TMP Free Read by Margaret Ethridge!

'Going the Distance' in *All Bets are On! Derby Day Anthology*

The Feeling is Pari-Mutuel—A Sapphire Nights Books single short story release.

Books by Margaret Ethridge

Paramour

Contentment—After Happily Ever - Book One

Coming 2012

Inamorata

Visit Margaret at www.margaretethridge.com

If you enjoyed Margaret Ethridge's *Commitment*,
you might also enjoy these authors
published by Turquoise Morning Press:

Keri Ford, author of *On the Fence*
Maddie James, author of *Crazy for You*
Jennifer Johnson, author of *Double Dog Dare*

Thank you!

For purchasing this book from
Turquoise Morning Press.

We invite you to visit our Web site to learn more about
our
quality Trade Paperback and eBook selections.

As a gift to you for purchasing this book, please use
COUPON CODE Ebook15 during your visit to
receive **15% off** any digital title in our Turquoise Morning Press Bookstore.

http://www.turquoisemorningpressbookstore.com

Turquoise Morning Press
Because every good beach deserves a book.
www.turquoisemorningpress.com
~~~~
Sapphire Nights Books
*Because sometimes the beach isn't hot enough.*
www.sapphirenightsbooks.com
~~~~